HE HEARD THE VOICES FROM SOMEWHERE DEEP WITHIN HIS SKULL.

It was pure instinct. In an instant, the flick of a diaphragm snapping open, everything he had known and knew how to do snapped back into his mind and his hands and his body. He was moving without conscious thought.

In a fluid sweeping motion Ron jerked a beer bottle from the bar, smashed it below the neck, and hurled himself at someone he hadn't known for years.

The enemy.

The jagged glass ripped across Drexel's eyes. The thin scream Ron hadn't heard in seven years sliced into his brain like a needle. Ron jerked Drexel's head back by one thick ear, and the bottle plunged into his throat. Blood bubbled and foamed, and before the men around them could move, even before Charlie hurled himself across the bar to slam into Ron, Ron had managed four perfectly aimed kicks against the side of Drexel's skull.

Words blinked into existence in his mind: *SHUT THIS BASTARD UP. SHUT HIM UP FAST AND GOOD. HE CAN DESTROY IT ALL.*

DEATHMATE

Martin Caidin

BANTAM BOOKS
TORONTO · NEW YORK · LONDON · SYDNEY

DEATHMATE

A Bantam Book / October 1982

ISBN 0-553-20355-X

Published simultaneously in the United States and Canada

Bantam Books are published by Bantam Books, Inc. Its trademark,
consisting of the words ''Bantam Books'' and the portrayal of a
rooster, is Registered in U.S. Patent and Trademark Office and in
other countries. Marca Registrada. Bantam Books, Inc., 666 Fifth
Avenue, New York, New York 10103.

PRINTED IN THE UNITED STATES OF AMERICA

H   0 9 8 7 6 5 4 3 2 1

This book is for
RON PREVIN
for whom obscurity is indeed a blessing

The world is not a safe place. If we are to protect our country, we must select, train, and constantly replenish a supply of human weapons: we must sow the dragon's teeth. We need—always in reserve—a squad of executioners to execute the executioners.

Ron Previn's story is true. His is one of many similar stories, and all of them are true. They just aren't told very often. Names, places, and events have been carefully disguised to prevent recognition and to protect the people whose lives make up the story. Many of them—including Ron Previn—are still alive and well.

—M.C.

1

She rocked gently, basking in the warmth of the cooking fire, a lovely child-woman with smooth brown skin and long dark hair. She sat cross-legged, comfortable on the mat she herself had woven, her fingers as dexterous as they were slender and supple. Kim Chan. His friend. She was everything he had ever heard about or seen or known of loveliness in a woman of the Orient. Here, in this remote Vietnamese village, she was the living personification of all his romantic dreams. Her husband, Nyugen, sat across from her, the glow of the fire reflecting from his body and highlighting his friendly expression. His skin glistened from the fire's warmth and from the rice wine the couple shared. Both had intensely dark eyes, deep somber pools that were both warm and mysterious. Kim held her infant son in one arm, the child sucking greedily at the nipple of a round and full breast. Michael Slater regarded the young family with appreciation; he had known the Chans for two years, and now they were his friends.

Slater sipped at his drink and sighed contentedly. He had lived here, in this village sprawled along the gentle slope of a hill; he had taught these people new methods of farming; he had brought modern medical knowledge to them and explained mechanical systems that would improve their lives. He had made friends of them all, especially this woman and her husband.

Kim removed the infant from her breast, covered her

body, and leaned to one side, offering her child for Slater to hold. Quickly he put aside his cup, for there could be no greater honor than this offer for him to hold their son in his own strong arms. Slater took the child, careful to hold him properly, looked over at Nyugen Chan, and was distracted as the child clapped his small brown hands with delight.

Which is why Slater never saw Kim move from his side with fluid grace to plunge a long dagger between his ribs. It sliced through his shirt and his skin with no resistance, cutting through fat and gristle, glancing off a rib and penetrating his heart. Kim performed her duty without a show of emotion and with not so much as a deep intake of breath. The decision to snip away the life of Michael Slater had been made by the village council for reasons Kim did not grasp, and for which she cared not at all. Enough that the council had honored her husband and herself to end the presence of the devil with round eyes. Michael Slater died, his eyes bulging and his brain stunned and trying futilely to comprehend the ghastly pain and the loss of cohesive thought. Blood burbled from the deep wound, staining his shirt and running down his side, but before his body could begin its rag-doll collapse, Nyugen's hands had taken the infant safely from the dying American.

The only distaste the Chans evinced came when Slater's body crumpled into the cooking coals; his final spasmodic twitch tossed glowing sparks in a soft shower over his head, causing smoke to curl about his hair. Nyugen and Kim waited patiently for the young men to enter the hut and remove the cadaver. They rearranged their fire. The body, now outside the hut, was stripped of clothing and possessions and dragged off to a swamp, there to be dismembered and fed to the dogs.

The young couple returned to their meal and the infant to its mother's breast even as the dogs, kept starving in their compound, gorged on the warm blood and flesh they craved so wildly.

Michael Slater was only the first. Friend of the people of Vietnam, devoted to their well-being, he was to achieve the dubious honor of being the first victim of the bloodlettings that soon formed a pattern. The morning after Slater's hacked and bloody remains were thrown to the starving dogs, a tent on a white beach of Vietnam's coastline was approached by natives who had waited with stoic patience through the night.

Harry Dobson and Tim White came awake as sunlight brightened their canvas-covered domicile. They enjoyed their tent, enjoyed the subdued whisper of breaking waves on the beach, enjoyed teaching their Vietnamese friends and charges how to use welding equipment, how to work sheet metal—how to use the tools and equipment their government wished them to use with proficiency. Dobson and White had lived in this tent for a year. They cooked their own food, enjoyed their friends, felt pleasure in the knowledge that they were imparting information to the people. Every morning at sunrise, except for Sundays and holidays, ten men came to the beach and waited for them to emerge from their tent. They would spend the first half hour of the day seated about their Sterno fire, drinking hot tea, discussing what they had done the day before, the work they would do on this new day.

Dobson and White weren't at all surprised at the sight of the group of men awaiting them when they came out to meet the crisp morning along the water. Dobson smiled and White had his hand high in a greeting when the poisoned arrows needled into their bodies. Each man took at least three direct hits. White knew only a brief spasm of brain-tearing insanity as an arrow squashed through his eyeball, entered the hollow socket beyond the pulpy material, and fed venom to his brain. He was dead before his twitching form struck the beach, hurled violently backward by the intensity of the poison in his system.

Not so Dobson, who took two arrows in his stomach, one in his left thigh, and the fourth in his groin. Impassivity on the part of the attackers turned to grins as they divined the horror suffered by the shrieking man who tossed wildly and ate sand and screamed as the poison squeezed and spasmed his prostate and genital system. They surrounded the maddened Dobson, pointed and hooted and danced with pleasure at their power, so evident in the naked agony. Dobson's teeth tore at his tongue and lips, and the bloody foam that sprayed the air and tinted the sand was soon matched in his groin, as his hands tore furiously at his clothes, ripping away his trousers and undershorts, and his nails tore the flesh of his penis and testicles in an attempt to extinguish the savage flames in his belly. He died, fortunately, sooner than the men anticipated. Annoyed, they dragged his body to the water, heaved it onto a wide canoe, and rode through the gentle surf into

calmer water. The game was still to be played as they dragged
the corpse in the water, the dark reddish stain sending out
calling cards to lurking predators. Dobson's upper torso ended
in a shark's stomach before his torturers released the rest of
the body, its entrails bobbing briefly along the water, to the
next mauling by a swiftly striking killer.

Stanley Hanover had spent his life as a missionary in the
Orient. There had been China and Malaya, a terrible four
years in a Japanese prison camp, and finally, after the great
clouds had risen high over Hiroshima and Nagasaki, the land
of South Vietnam. Here, his luck had turned, and he had
married into a Vietnamese family that was graced with beauty
and intelligence. His wife bore him three sons and two daughters, and the family lived in peace in a beautiful small mountain city. Their church had been built stone by stone, one
timber atop another, by his family and friends; now Hanover
was as much a part of local history as the hills and the valleys.

On the night of the same day that White and Dobson
died, Stanley Hanover fell asleep after dinner, a habit to
which his family was accustomed, for the years had lain
heavily on him and such naps were good for his constitution.
But on this night Hanover's nap was a drugged sleep, from
which he was jolted with a smashing kick against his ribs. He
awoke, startled, to stare at black clothing—trousers and loose-
hanging shirts worn by two dozen men who looked at his
astonished face with undisguised . . .

Hanover couldn't place it immediately, but in the limited time remaining to him, he would have a fleeting memory
of what he had seen at that moment. It was *anticipation*.

Here was no turning of friendship as had struck the others.
"My God, what are you doing?" Hanover cried out, for the
pain that slammed through his rib cage brought with it the
shocking realization that he could not see his family anywhere
in the long, high hut. These faces were faces of strangers. He
knew enough of human nature to recognize cruelty. In the
prison camp he had seen enough Japanese soldiers never to
forget that look, and now he saw it again. He knew they had
come from the hills, from the North, from where disquieting
stories had drifted down along the jungle trails. He had paid
little heed to such tales, for he had lived here a long time,
these were his friends, and . . .

Not these faces. They had come to teach the people of the city and its environs a lesson. They had drugged Hanover's food to teach him, as well as all the villagers and cityfolk who had been herded and prodded and beaten into the main square, a lesson that must not be forgotten. They dragged Hanover outside to see his wife and his children, and he shrieked to God in his mind that he could not see, that he might instantly be struck blind and those he loved so dearly granted the mercy of death. But not yet; not yet. God is busy and always occupied elsewhere at these terrible moments.

Hanover's three sons sat in a semicircle on the ground, their arms knotted behind their backs, tied to stakes, their legs spread painfully wide and straight and pinned by smaller stakes to the ground. Between the legs of each son burned a fire of blazing coals, and Hanover knew the stink, that sweetly putrid stench of burning soft flesh. He hurled himself forward with insane strength, only to be jerked to a choking halt by the leather thong held tightly about his neck. His arms were pinned behind his back and his feet hobbled, a pole was thrust between his back and his arms, and fists held his head straight by his hair. A man danced before him, and with tiny slivers of wood pinned open his eyes so he must see.

He implored God, and God, in His absence was toweringly conspicuous, especially when Frances was dragged before the multitude, her fourteen years displayed to one and all when her clothes were ripped from her body. A small cart was dragged to the center of the square, Frances was tied facedown, buttocks high, her thighs pulled painfully apart, and three dozen men used her body until the blood ran in rivulets and pooled by her ankles and clogged the dust near her feet. She was raped vaginally and anally and orally until she bled from head to foot. The last few men were not even aware that they were raping a corpse.

Corinne died much more quickly, although by now Stanley Hanover had forsaken his God and cursed every deity from the origin of man to this moment. The men stripped Corinne and tied her in the same fashion as her dead sister; Corinne was sixteen, and for her they had brought large trained monkeys. One mounted her from behind in a gibbering sexual frenzy, biting chunks from her back as he thrust madly again and again into any orifice his maddened member could reach. Not so the other creature from the front: starved and beaten and crazed, he was held on a leash just long enough for him to reach the already insane child, where claws and teeth tore, and he ate the girl alive even as she was assaulted from behind. She would have screamed except that her lips were chewed from her face and her tongue ripped by sharp teeth; and thus she died.

They saved the best for last. They let him almost save the frail, beautiful Mai who had borne him these five children. They tied her to a stake and spread her legs, but they did not molest her sexually. While Stanley Hanover ripped his lips with his teeth, frothing like a maddened animal, bleeding from his eyes as the wooden slivers held them open, they disemboweled Mai, and very carefully they laid out her entrails on the dusty ground, being certain that she was alive and that she would live for many hours. Then they released Stanley Hanover, who crawled forward, groveling and twisting like a huge worm to reach this beloved woman, his wrists tied together, his fingers tied together, so that clumsily he tried to carry her intestines back to her belly, where they had slit her open, and to stuff her back into herself. He was clumsy and her organs slippery with blood and mucus; the tubes fell from his tied hands and he cried like a child and begged her forgiveness. Her eyes told him she blamed him not, and she died with his hands plunged hard against her open belly above the matted pubic hair.

His anguish went quickly. A Vietnamese friend reached his own state of madness and, rushing between the guards, hurled himself against Stanley Hanover, plunging a knife deep into his side to reach his heart so that this man might die a few moments sooner than had been planned for him.

It was not a wise move. Far better that Stanley should have twisted and writhed within his final madness than known this act of loving mercy. For his love for this man, the young Vietnamese was himself raped by a hundred men, his anus a terrible gaping wound from which blood and feces and bile poured down his legs to the ground until he died.

As an act of attrition before the night ended, the young women in the rows of onlookers, held grimly in place by weapons and a clear knowledge of what would be the consequences if they did not obey these fellow Vietnamese, were forced to clean the genitals of the attackers with their tongues and lips.

A man who had watched stolidly through the night of horror blew a whistle. Moments later, the men in the dark baggy clothes were gone. The lesson would never be forgotten.

The round-eyes were to be shunned, murdered.

2

The sun went down quickly. A man didn't expect that after spending most of his life among the friendly hills and rounded peaks of the Appalachians. But that was home, and home was half a world away. Here in Vietnam, nothing was the same; even the sun was different—how it looked and what it did. The midday hours wound down slowly to late afternoon, and then the process accelerated like a speeded-up film. Hugging its shape, the great flaming orb sucked in the jungle haze and seemed to swell. As it fell into the shimmering layers of the tree line, it turned a touch of green fire and dropped away on the other side of the upward heaving planet. What little daylight was left faded swiftly, and night descended like a huge blanket released by invisible hands. Almost at once the insects appeared. By eight o'clock it was dark, and it was time for the nocturnal explosion.

They rose in hordes as if expelled from a jam-packed Pandora's box: creatures with wings and rubbing feet and biting pincers and shell-like bodies that whirred and clicked and sang and shrilled, some of them soft and velvety, others with the rasping screech of a buzz saw. It wasn't so bad for someone raised on a farm; a man could reach back into memory, touch it up with imagination, and bring to mind crickets and katydids and beetles, owls hooting and frogs garrumping like an anvil chorus from lakes and streams, and tree frogs adding their own din to the night uproar. Now take all that a man remembered, expand the number and the

variety by a thousandfold and ten times that for the ghastly
sounds, and increase the size of the creatures several times.
Only then could a man begin to imagine the Vietnamese
jungle and the undergrowth in that bedlam of darkness. A
racket hellish in every way, beggaring the imagination, crawling and rustling beneath a man's feet (and damned likely to
come up his trouser leg with biting, cutting, stinging pincers
and jaws and mandibles and poison and venom and God
knew what else), whirring noisily through the trees and the
brush, sailing through the air in a fluttering coruscation of
sound. There were hateful things with bug eyes, impossibly
thick bodies, curling antennae, and powdery wings; they
chewed and bit and stung and were everywhere some of
them as big as birds, and there were enormous insects with
fangs that fought and conquered and *devoured* birds. Those
that could not fly crawled and ran and dashed and slithered:
spiders larger than a man's hand, centipedes as long as his
foot.

Every night they emerged in the darkness beyond and
over and under and around and—much too often—within the
three huts where the three men lived. Ron had one hut,
Gary another, and George, huge and black and of great
rippling strength wrapped in gentleness, occupied the third.
Each hut was just big enough for one man, with a bunk and a
footlocker for personal belongings and, if it hadn't run out,
bottled water, some beer, and rations to keep away hunger.
No lights shone inside an open hut at night, for lights were a
signal beacon, a bright beckoning to the nightly swarm and
invasion. Yet the huts were strong, and when they were kept
tightly closed, a man could have a small light, and the walls
and the clamped door would stand as a bastion against the
devil hordes.

At this moment the huts were anchored to the ground.
But the solidity was a facade, for these were mobile homes
despite the absence of wheels or any visible means of transport. You had to look atop each hut for that, where a great
metal ring was implanted in the hut's structure, a ring large
enough to accept a snap hook or cable clamp from a helicopter that would hover overhead on its blasting cushion of air,
lowering the sling and the hook, and then swing up and away
with the hut to transport it from one jungle clearing to
another. These three huts had been in this place for many

days now, close by the great pipeline forming along the jungle path, near the heavy welding gear and the steel plates and the tubes and electrical cables and bulldozer and fuel storage and the rest of it.

But no weapons.

At this moment, the three men, each in his own abode, listened. Already knowledgeable in this act of acoustical sensitivity, their ears touched the night air with the wrinkling search of noses. They confirmed to themselves what each determined: no animal sounds. They expected that. It didn't mean animals weren't there. Big cats, maybe. They still had tigers here, for Christ's sake. Or wild boar in the thicker underbrush. Anything. But whatever was there, remained obscure beneath the blanket of insect frenzy and sound. Only one other sound penetrated the cacophony that owned the night jungle. Fifteen hundred feet away from the three huts, erect in its own clearing, chattered the two-cycle gasoline engine; but even its roaring clatter was muted and sometimes drowned out by the local insect hordes.

The generator was their friend in this strange land, their Spartan in the high mountain pass, their sentinel. It drank liquid fuel, and its contained internal combustion turned and spun and dragged belts about wheels and gears; it chattered and hummed and farted blue exhaust, and most important of all, it fed electrical juice through cables to each hut where, after the night was sealed and locked away, a man could turn on a light by which to read or eat or just look at his own tired feet. That was better than being engulfed in darkness when something forced its way into a hut, only to grow monstrously in size, fed by fear and imagination. A spider the size of a hand or a beetle with a savage bite can at least be walloped with a section of steel pipe if you can see the bugger.

One other light shone, fed by the energy of the chattering engine: it was a single great floodlight thirty feet high on a steel pole. It was the siren call for insects that defied description, insects that these men would not even attempt to describe to anyone who had not been in this country, for it is tough to believe that there are insects large and powerful and savage enough to strike after birds and fight viciously against great bats that come to seize them, drawn by invisible strands of biological sonar.

Six miles away, down a path gouged out of the intertwin-

ing growth by clanking bulldozers, was the base camp along
the Vietnamese coastline, to which this clearing and its three
men were one of many tendrils reaching inland. The base
camp had no name known to Ron, Gary, or George. Like
many others, they were in this jungle to weld huge pipeline
sections into a single artery that ran from many points deep
within the jungle to that base camp. It was a large-scale effort
to bring Vietnamese oil in great forced turgid motions through
those pipelines to holding tanks and waiting tankers that
settled slowly into the water as they took on their viscous
loads.

The enormity of the effort had not really touched the
comprehension of these three men, or thousands of others
like them, for the drive to wrest the black oil from the ground
of Vietnam had not reached the proportions common to many
oil strikes and wildcatting operations. No giant collection of
equipment was in evidence here. These men, brought here
as part of an aerial and ocean pipeline, knew virtually nothing
about the country they were in; their only familiarity was
with a small cluster of lanes and clearings chewed through
the jungle. Almost anywhere they pierced the surface and
extended their probes, they found oil. It was here, there,
everywhere along the coast. But they knew only their own
immediate area and their own job: to weld pipelines and to
teach the Vietnamese men sent to them how to weld. When
they completed their job here, two things would have been
accomplished: oil would be flowing in steady tributaries to
the swiftly growing fleet of tankers, and the Vietnamese
would be doing most of the work and running the field
operations on their own, save for the American overseers.

Ron, Gary, and George were semi-isolated. They saw
and knew only the edges of a world that was limited to direct
or peripheral vision, and they heard of other events only
through the human pipeline of remarks, rumors, scuttlebutt,
and infrequent conversations with crews from the base camp.
They remained within their own small sphere of activity; all
else had to filter through a network of distance and time. This
isolation imposed no hardship on them, for none of the three
cared about the mechanics of government or the interplay of
politics. They had not a shred of association with any federal
agency except the group that had hired them to do exactly
what they did every day, one day after the other. Oil was the

name of the game; their contract called for them to be here for one year, and that was that. Whatever the outside world knew, believed, or was told to believe didn't matter to them. Their job was to string together with welding rods the steel pipelines through which the oil would flow, and to teach the Vietnamese to do the same. It was just that simple.

Every day the Vietnamese came through the jungle and worked with them. The Americans didn't speak the local language and the Vietnamese knew little or nothing of English, but they communicated with signs and gestures. Both sides learned a few key words and phrases, and they learned to understand each other. When darkness approached, everyone put aside their tools and waved good-bye, and the Vietnamese went home, leaving Ron, Gary, and George alone with a radio that had died—jungle humidity and rot had eaten away its stored power and left it an oozing sticky mess.

At night they needed, above all else, that light thirty feet up on its steel pole, the light that flashed its siren call to the nightmare creatures emerging from the jungle. The word *insect* seemed inadequate to describe those monsters who perceived the strange radiance atop the pole: moths the size of bats that came rushing out of the night, so damned big you could hear their wings swishing as they shot into view and mindlessly bombed the light, banging like kamikazes into the steel pole. Sometimes they hit so hard they fell to the ground, stunned, whirring and vibrating madly. Often *something* rushed from the undergrowth to assault the fallen creature; there would be a swift and furious struggle and then only the fusillade of sound and whirring above.

The men needed that light during the night to reach their latrine. It had been set up just behind George's hut. It wasn't really a latrine at all, just a tree trunk they'd carved and cut as neatly as their power saws and tools would permit, but it gave them some semblance of a seat, so they could at least assume a respectable posture for relieving themselves. Whatever passed from their bodies fell to the ground. No collection buckets or anything of the sort here. There was no need for it; no waste remained more than a few hours before being consumed by the monstrous creatures flying, buzzing, and crawling along the jungle floor. The men needed the light because it distracted those voracious creatures and kept them away long enough for a man when he just *had* to go, no matter how thickly the air might be sown with bat-sized insects.

But tonight there wasn't any light. And for the last several days their Vietnamese friends had behaved more like strangers. The smiles had faded. The Vietnamese had looked at them with blank faces.

During the evening meal, Ron queried his two friends about it. "What the hell's gotten into these people? You guys have a fight or something?"

Gary shook his head; George shrugged, his brow furrowed as he sought an answer. "I dunno," he remarked finally. "Something's wrong with those cats, that's for sure. It's like we caught them stealing cookies from the jar. You know what I mean? Like when a man owes you money and he won't look you in the eye."

"It isn't cookies they're stealing," said Ron. "They're stealing everything. My welding gloves were stolen last night. Four hard hats are gone, and a bunch of tools."

"Why didn't you say something?" Gary demanded.

"Because I didn't want to program your answers," said Ron. "If I said something, you'd have both been looking for trouble."

Gary shook his head again. "I didn't see a damn thing."

"Except," George said, "they're acting like we all have bad body odor."

"We do," Gary said, laughing, "but no worse than theirs in this stinking jungle." He turned to Ron. "You see anyone grabbing the stuff?"

"Uh uh. That's not their way. They do it at night, after we're asleep."

George hunched up his powerful shoulders. "You think we should stand guard? Catch 'em at it?"

"No way," Ron said quickly. "This is their turf, man, and they know how to get around at night, and we don't. If they're caught, it means a confrontation. They got weapons, maybe. We don't have even a slingshot. No, we'll wait, see what happens."

They were restless that night, and they slept lightly, but the chugging of the generator and the screeching and whirring of all manner of creatures covered any noise they might have heard. In the morning, some tools were missing. Still they said nothing, didn't push it. Tension and fatigue made them irritable.

The morning after that, they were mad enough to spit. They went outside to face a real and terrible loss. "The generator!" Gary exploded. "They stole the fucking generator, for Chrissakes!"

"That's only half of it," George mused. "Take a look here." They joined him at their equipment shed. "Know what else they took? All our batteries; and they drained the fuel from our gas engine and stole the fuel tanks along with that."

"And half the goddamned tools we had left," snarled Gary.

"One thing's for sure," said Ron, surprised at his own calm, his stoic acceptance, as if he had been able to predict just this moment. It almost seemed like part of a pattern.

"And what the hell's that?" Gary demanded, still confused and fuming.

"Better take a crap *before* you close off your hut tonight," Ron told him airily, "and take a bottle to piss in when you go to bed."

"Yeah, that's for sure." George grunted. He poked Gary good-naturedly in the shoulder. "You take that thing out in the dark and God knows what's gonna jump up and bite it."

"And you can't afford to lose any of what you got," Ron added.

Later that day, well after sunset, Ron stood outside his hut studying the sliver of a moon that glowed through the jungle mist; it was painted a surrealistic silver by the tree-hugging haze. He knew how to look for things in this country and he could even make out the tree line against the starry backdrop. He sighed. He'd be damned glad when the planet turned far enough around to let the sun begin its climb from the other side of the world.

In the darkness he heard a sound he could never mistake. *Sffftt!* That was Gary spitting away a mouthful of chewing tobacco. Red Apple. The sound was welcome enough in this din of horrid clamoring. Too bad about that light. Gary used to amuse himself at night by holding the burning tobacco ready and then letting fly at a big moth as it fluttered past; he'd gotten some pretty good hits. But not tonight. It was like spitting into a well of darkness.

"Hey!" Ron called. "G'night, you guys!"

"Night!"

"Adios, mother!"

He listened to their disembodied voices and went inside, impatient to fall asleep. He didn't bother to remove his clothes or his boots. He stank of sweat and dust and particles of leaves and brush and whatever insects had made a home of his own physical mess, so it didn't much matter. There was a stream nearby, and when the sun daggered the sky and started steaming the jungle and all those mini-Draculas were gone, they'd wash their clothes as they did every morning and grab a fast bath. For now, to hell with the bugs. He was dog tired, and he turned over and fell into a deep, dreamless sleep.

Growing up in a small town in farm country had unexpected compensations now that he was out here in the jungle. Ron always awoke at daybreak, well before the sun glared at the world. It was as natural for him as for a barnyard animal. He stretched and yawned and scratched himself and pushed away some of the leeches that always came in at night to answer the summons of any warm body that was reasonably unmoving; then he went outside to the back of his hut to relieve himself.

Ron followed another habit, one he'd picked up since leaving the farm country, and that was eating breakfast without a crowd around him. Right now, that meant eating what came out of whatever tin can he happened to grab. He heard Gary and George moving about, talking; they knew Ron's habits and respected them. Morning was his time for solitude, his time to reflect. He sat on the edge of his bunk eating from the can with a hunting knife. The food was surprisingly tasty and he thought about that for a while, about his habit of picking a can in the blind to surprise himself. Then he wondered again, with a faint misgiving, about what the three of them were doing laying oil pipelines just off a jungle coastline. During these quiet morning sessions he had come to realize that they didn't really know who they worked for. Some things were like a pie in the face. This whole thing was government all the way, and the shams and facades were as subtle as a kick in the nuts. But there was a lot of high-powered civilian muscle in this, too. A gang of oil companies pooling their resources and manpower, moving men into remote areas and paying them triple time for their work. They painted over the oil company logos and signs, but that only seemed to make them more obvious. He'd spotted the same signs he'd always seen on gas stations plus a bunch more he'd never heard of.

It didn't much matter. One distraction was as good as another. He'd needed to get away from everything after the horror of Cynthia's death and the knowledge—hard to accept— that his scholarship at the agricultural college wasn't going to come through. All his dreams had been shattered, and the anonymity of this job had offered him a kind of numbing satisfaction, a chance to put one foot in front of the other, day after day, without thinking about anyone else or anyplace else. It was only for a year, the pay was fabulous, and maybe after a time of healing he'd have the courage to go back and start all over again. Besides, it was good work, and the locals couldn't have been friendlier when they first met. He frowned, jolted back into the present. Something was going to hell in a handbasket. It sure wasn't like this when they got here, and they still had never had a cross word with these people. Trying to make some sense out of this mess, Ron thought back to how the three of them had jumped at the chance for a job. In the early sixties good work was scarce enough, and when they saw this advertisement for qualified welders, with higher pay for men who could double in other jobs, it looked too good to be true. Ron had run tractors and bulldozers and pipe equipment, he was an expert mechanic, and he'd run explosives for tree stumps and blasting for roads; this was right up his alley. They'd get thirty thousand a year tax free, plus another thousand for personal bills and stuff like that, and the company—whoever it was or they were—would handle their expenses and clothing and medical bills and transportation. It was freaking fabulous, that's what it was. You signed up, guaranteed your year, and you'd come home with thirty big ones in the bank; that put you on the best street you'd ever walk in your whole life. You did it with your buddies, and sure, living in this frigging jungle was pisspoor, but so what? Ron had shoveled enough manure as a kid, so how bad could it be for a year? You did what you were good at doing and you taught the gooks to do the same thing. And you had the time to heal up inside.

Ron scraped the inside of his ration tin and nodded to

himself. He knew the heat and humidity and the bugs would get to them after a while, but to clear thirty grand for one year, each, they'd fight tigers with bamboo sticks. It was good, clean money and even if they had to sign sworn statements not to let anyone know where they were, what about it? They couldn't even pronounce the names of where they were, let alone try to make anyone else understand it. Who cared?

They'd already planned their homecoming. They'd pool a hundred thousand smackers, start their own welding business, and expand into machine shop work. Somewhere in Ohio, maybe—or maybe back home, in his beloved mountains. It was a good thought. Ron went outside and tossed his ration tin into the edge of the jungle. Littering, old man. He laughed at the thought. The rot and humidity and acids in this soil would chew up and erode thin metal almost as fast as fire consumes paper. Talk about instant garbage disposal.

Ron went around to the front of his hut and looked out across the hills through a clearing in the nearby trees. The sun was just breaking the horizon, and the world took on a mystical quality. The hazy air was tinged a sharp blue and seemed to contain billions of glowing motes. It wasn't like smog or the mists that swirled through the Smokies in the eastern United States; it was an Asian blue curtain that hung in suspension until the harsh sunlight burned it away.

Ron joined the other two men. Gary stood looking into the sky. "It's going to be another bitch," he said, and they knew he meant hot, humid, and sticky.

"And we can't talk to the camp," George said. They read his meaning clearly: no radio communications with the base camp—six miles through the jungle to the coastline, where the big holding tanks were, and where the great ships rode at anchor in the harbor waiting for the thick black substance to come rumbling and gurgling through the pipelines.

George looked about him slowly, his eyes narrowing when he turned toward the sun. "Nobody's here," he said. "Not one son of a bitch showed up for work. How the hell are we supposed to teach these gooks to weld when they don't even show up?"

Gary grinned. "Efficient and courteous self-help, man. We do it. The camp don't care how, just so long as it gets done."

Ron was grateful for the simplicity of Gary's response. That was the best thing about Gary. He might not be the most fascinating guy in the world, or the smartest, or the most fun, but you could count on him—as long as he had a leader.

"Three men can't handle it," George rebuked Gary.

"Sure as hell we'll get a lot more done by trying than by bitching," Ron said. To him, work was work. You had a short crew, you did what you could with what you had. He was surprised to feel himself taking charge—he'd had trouble in the past, not being assertive enough, letting other people do his thinking for him. Something about this place, this unreal situation, seemed to make him feel on top of things, capable. He noted a surge of confidence. "Let's get going," he said.

George nodded. "I'll signal the camp." That was a neat trick without the radio, but these men were ingenious in their knowledge of their equipment. George went to the pipeline on the ground, picked up a welding stinger, and grounded it to a section of pipe. The stinger in turn superheated the welding machine. Back in the base camp, this generated a signal that something was wrong out in the field, at this particular site. By grounding the stinger, George was creating a direct short which began to melt the welding rod. It was an instant makeshift electrical signal. As long as this direct, constant short was allowed to continue, it would trigger the main power source in the base camp. The men knew that a welding machine runs on a sixty-percent duty cycle. If you run it longer than six minutes for every ten minutes of operation, then it shorts out the system and throws a breaker. Keep it up long enough and it becomes obvious in the base camp that something's really wrong out there in the boonies, and it's time to get people out there to find out just what.

It didn't work this time.

During that dark night, when the small generator remained silent and the lights were out and the insects swirled and boiled through the air, the small field camp had visitors. Not one of the three men, each sealed within his hut, had seen or heard them. They came in the night like phantoms and left like jungle wraiths.

Ron and Gary were standing together five hundred feet from the pipeline when George connected the stinger to the big section of pipe. It was the last deliberate move George ever made. The instant the electric current flowed to steel, it triggered the igniter the gooks had set up during the night. The men with whom they had worked and joked, the men they had taught how to weld and run machinery, had left them a ghastly gift. The explosive charge they had concealed within the pipeline went off with a terrifying roar. The dazzling orange flash erupted like a visible sheet, rolled the ground beneath their feet, and smashed into them with a great invisible hand of concussion.

Ron and Gary couldn't move. Their senses froze. Fear and stupefaction, a total disbelief in what was happening rooted them to the ground as the blast struck their bodies, followed by a slow-motion eruption of flame and smoke and debris, within which they saw George, tumbling slowly and crazily and unbelievably, a rag doll floating through the air. They saw the body crumple to the ground, and strangely, impossibly, they saw it bounce. The earth rejected the body only once; it fell again, and the earth accepted the unmoving form.

3

They stood rooted to the ground for what seemed an eternity, but in truth it was only seconds. The stink of explosives and the wash of roiling dust stung their nostrils and smarted their eyes. Neither man could remember who shouted, "Oh, my God!" and then they ran, hearts pounding madly, to reach George. The big black man lay tossed on the ground like a stained rag, mottled and chewed upon, bleeding copiously from his ears and his nose and his mouth, bleeding from his ribs and throat and chest and arms and legs where pieces of torn steel had punched into his skin. He lay unconscious, his breathing shallow, his body twitching. Frantically, they ripped their own clothing and his to bind his open wounds and apply tourniquets, and what they couldn't stop that way they tried to stop by shoving wadded cloth into the gaping body tears. The blood seeped through and stained the grass and wept onto their own hands and clothes.

Ron cradled George's head in his lap. He looked up with eyes of torment to Gary. "He's dying. He's dying, goddamn it! We've got to get him to a doctor!"

Gary sucked in air, trying desperately to think. He knew George was dying and he knew the base camp was six miles down a jungle trail. They had no way of letting the base know what had happened or that their friend was bleeding to death. "The bulldozer!" he said suddenly. "The one with the pipe picker. I'll bring it here."

"Right," Ron snapped. "We'll put him on top of the

cage. I'll drive and you hold him there." He looked around. "The huts. Get pillows, blankets; anything that will help." He laid George's head to the ground, hating to release him, knowing he had to. They ran to the huts and only then did they realize how terrible the blast had been. The explosion had smashed two of the three huts. Ron's was still erect but with gaping holes everywhere from the shrapnel of the steel pipeline. He dashed inside, grabbed sheets and a towel, ran back to George. Strange, he thought as his feet smacked hard against the ground, he still hadn't felt any fear. Now his only concern was to keep George alive long enough for a doctor to save his life.

To make a soft headrest for George they bunched the sheets and the towel atop the roll cage of the bulldozer, then Ron started up the big cat and clanked carefully alongside where their friend still lay unconscious. "Help me get him up there!" Gary shouted.

George was a terrible and clumsy weight. They grabbed him under his arms and held his legs together, but he slipped in their hands from his blood. They couldn't lift him up because his body kept shifting, twisting, folding, and slipping. Bit by bit they dragged him onto the bulldozer, struggling for footholds and handgrips and dragging George like a great sack of slimy meal, little by little higher and higher.

"Goddamn blood!" Gary screamed in frustration. "It's like grease. Jesus Christ, we'll never—"

"Shut up," Ron snarled. "Just stop your fucking whining." The harshness of his own tone startled him.

Gary stared, taken aback, but he confined his remarks to a low steady cursing. Every jolt and shove sent new blood spurting from George's wounds and making a mockery of their tourniquets. They tore dark skin loose to get George up on the roll cage, but finally it was done. Gasping for air, Gary gestured for Ron's attention. "Look, you're smaller. Don't take up too much room. You hold him and I'll drive."

Ron nodded. "Right. Do it."

Gary climbed into the driver's seat, got the big engine snorting. He moved the control levers several times, staring white-faced as his blood-slippery hands kept falling away from the controls. His body twitched as blood dripped down from above.

"Get this goddamned thing moving!" Ron shouted. "You dumb son of a bitch, he's bleeding to death!"

Gary shifted into gear and started the bulldozer rumbling slowly over the rough jungle trail. Ron felt his body snap from the jolting, and he bit his tongue as he started to curse Gary. Jesus, a man couldn't drive anything over this stinking trail without violent movement. Tree stumps, hollows and hummocks, rocks—shit. He braced himself, hanging on for dear life to protect George. Gary maneuvered the big treaded cat as gently as he could, dodging the most visible obstacles, but his caution was doing more harm than good, for George was bleeding too rapidly again.

"We can't afford the time!" Ron shouted above the blatting roar of the diesel exhaust. "Screw the goddamn bumps— pour the coal to it. At this speed he'll die before we get there!"

Gary nodded, wincing as a trickle of blood smacked wetly on his shoulder, splashing on the stained yellow metal. He gritted his teeth, kicked into road gear, and went full blast on the power. On a flat surface the big dozer could ram ahead at ten miles an hour. On this surface they could barely manage eight, and it was brutal punishment every foot of the way, the dozer screaming and roaring and the high exhaust stack bellowing its own steampipe roar. Ron hung on, crossing a leg over George, frantic to keep him secured and protect him against the punishing ride. A pale crimson spray often floated into the air as each slamming jolt of the dozer's motion whipped more blood from his body. Ron stared dumbly, eyes round and unblinking, until a particularly vicious blow brought him cursing back to reality.

Something caught his eye, and he squinted at the edge of the jungle clearing to his right; they had an audience. Shadowy forms were moving in the thick underbrush just beyond the edge of the cleared lane. He looked to the left and saw more of them. Their goddamned rotten fucking gook friends were moving back toward the camp. The dozer started down an incline toward a creek they had to cross, and Ron twisted in his seat, curses exploding from him, unheard by the unconscious George or even by Gary, whose whole world of sound was the blatting thunder of the dozer. Ron raged helplessly as he looked back toward the campsite, now swarming with men scurrying like ants, grabbing everything that could be carried, and running off, cavorting and laughing. Then the bulldozer reeled wildly down a sudden slope, sliding along a muddy embankment as it plunged through a creek, caromed up the other side, spun through a bend in the jungle lane, and charged toward the beach.

Gary flatfooted the dozer and yelled at the machine to go faster, faster; above him on the roll cage, clinging to his unconscious friend, Ron prayed to some unknown deity and besieged the unconscious George not to die, to stop that god-awful bleeding. "Hang in there," he prayed. It didn't matter that George couldn't hear him. He had to do something, say something; anything beyond this helpless clutching of a man whose life was oozing from his body through a dozen mortal wounds. Ron's mind spun with horror and a strange new sense of shock and detachment. He almost seemed to be floating above and to one side of the bulldozer, watching himself, studying the bloody tableau of the big machine clanking and roaring in its ponderous turtle race against time. He saw himself holding George, he understood what was happening, and he knew for an instant that he was two people: the one involved in the stinking mess, distraught and agonized and holding back tears as his friend lay dying in his hands; and that other mind, studying, watching, interested in what was happening, poised, controlling, unflinching, as different from the gentle and tentative Ron Previn of the mountain farm as a saber-toothed tiger was from a little tame rabbit. It was as if he were half man, half robot, neither half understanding the other.

The double-visioned moment of clarity passed, and Ron cursed steadily, more quietly now, a harsh condemnation of God and man and those stinking goddamned gooks. George's beautifully muscled black body was dying; his gentle soul was being consumed by the shaking world, by the bulldozer rattling his guts like broken dice in a ceramic cup. The world stank from one end to the other. Ron clutched George more tightly, accepting the spray of blood from each terrible jolt, lost in a funk, ignoring the dozer's thunder and the exhaust fumes and the death cloud of insects in a macabre aerial dance to the heady scent of fresh blood and torn flesh.

The camp showed finally, far down that terrible narrow lane. Just beyond the camp they saw the bright reflections of the ocean. Then they made out individual holding tanks and buildings and cars and trucks. Gary pounded the bulldozer with all its power straight to the radio shack. Several startled people jumped aside and looked wide-eyed at the blood-streaked machine and the two men on the top cage. Gary stopped, threw her into idle, and jumped from the dozer to the radio shack. The only man they knew by name, and even that was a nickname, was here: Sparks, the radio operator. What was his real name? Nobody knew a goddamned thing. Here, you called the radioman Sparks, and that was all you'd ever know about him. But even with his limited identity, Sparks was in authority.

Ron heard Gary shouting. "Sparks! You son of a bitch, come outta there! We got a man dying out here!" Ron watched, a helpless spectator as long as he was holding George, and he saw Gary come back into the blinding sunlight, a beefy man in a T-shirt right behind him. Sparks looked up at the roll cage, then spun about and took off at a dead run for a nearby building. He didn't bother to say anything; he just ran. Moments later he was on his way back, urging another man to hurry. The second man was big, in his fifties, his thick arms long and hairy. He wore a stained white undershirt and a pilot's bill cap. His expression was serious, all business.

Ron murmured "Thank God" under his breath as the big man clambered atop the dozer with surprising agility. Ron did his best to get out of the way, but he had to hang on to George. Jesus, he wasn't bleeding anymore! That was great. Ron looked around and saw people running from different buildings, then standing around and staring at the big machine and its strange bloodstained crew.

It didn't take the big man long. He looked up from George to Ron and he didn't say anything. He climbed to the ground, spoke to Sparks. "He's dead." Those were the only words he spoke; then he walked away and didn't turn back.

That was all. Shock washed over Ron like ice water. The onlookers drifted away until the only ones left were Ron and Gary and Sparks and a dead black man and buzzing flies. The dozer coughed a few times and died. No one spoke in the sudden, appalling silence.

Sparks finally shrugged. "You heard the man. He's dead." Sparks pointed in the distance. "See that hill? Take him over there and bury him."

Gary looked up at Ron and Ron looked down at Gary and

then they both looked at Sparks, but the radioman was already walking back to his shack. Like a madman, Ron scrambled down from the roll cage. He stood in the sandy ground, his neck muscles as taut as bowstrings. Behind and above him, in the steaming sun, lay George, already starting to bloat, a feast for large blue flies. Ron's hand balled into a fist and he raised it high, unthinking, unknowing.

"You rotten goddamned son of a bitch!" he screamed.

Sparks paused long enough to turn around. There was nothing for him to say. He shrugged, turned, and walked on.

Ron looked at Gary, who was watching it all in stupefaction. His face was stone, his eyes tiny pinpoints. They turned together to look up at George. Ron wanted to say something to Gary, but he couldn't. His mind wouldn't focus; he couldn't seem to take hold. George couldn't be dead. They'd gotten him here right away, as fast as they could travel. Jesus, they played cards and drank and ate and laughed with this man, and they planned for the future they were going to build with a hundred thousand bucks between them, and now they were supposed to take him over to some goddamned hill and just bury him? Just like that? Like a dead cow or something?

They slumped to the ground, their backs against the dozer, numb. For nearly an hour they stared at nothing, struggling for words that refused to come. Finally, like a zombie, Gary got up and climbed into the cab and started the roaring engine. Still in his own silence, Ron went back up on the roll cage. He ignored the flies and the other biting, stinging things, and he held George while Gary kicked on the power. The big dozer threw out sand as they started toward the hill where Sparks had pointed.

When they got there, they didn't know what the hell to do. Bury him? How? They looked stupidly at one another. "How do we do it?" Ron broke the silence, gesturing. "There's no goddamned blade on this goddamned dozer. We got a shovel or something?"

"Shit, no," Gary said.

Ron growled and jumped down to the soft sand. He looked around. "Jesus fucking Christ," he said. "Let's at least get him down off that cage." They dragged and hauled the slippery body from the roll cage and lowered it onto the sand. Sand clung everywhere to the blood. George looked as if he had died of some kind of sand leprosy. It only made a stupid, heartbreaking moment all the more rotten. Ron noticed that the flies had followed George in a snarling swarm. They crawled into his nostrils and his ears.

"Do it," Ron told Gary, and he watched Gary climb back into the dozer cab and start her up again. He spun the dozer about on its treads until it ground and clawed and mangled out some sort of depression in the sand. Gary drove off a dozen feet, shut her down, and came back. Wordlessly, they got down on their hands and knees to scoop away sand and dirt until their nails bled. Gary wept silently as he worked, tears staining his face. Finally, they knew without saying that it was deep enough for this kind of remorseless ceremony, and they dragged George into the hole. They stood, panting in the heat, looking down at him, and then they threw and kicked sand and dirt on him, again and again until there was only a shapeless mound where there had been a man and a friend.

Ron and Gary and George, three nice ordinary guys from nice, ordinary homes—what had they come to? One lay dead, half buried in a stinking jungle grave. One stood, confused and angry, dumbfounded with horror, tears of rage on his face. And the other—gentle Ron Previn, who had only wanted to get away for a year, make some money, and try to forget his dead girl friend and his busted plans—what kind of new Ron Previn stood at this grave, barely aware of the rush of killer rage deep within him that mingled with his grief and his horror?

4

They left the stinking bulldozer where it was and walked back to the camp, not saying a word. Shock still clamped tightly, and from within this numbness Ron felt a deep agony intertwining with the first faint hiss of something else: he couldn't identify the feeling, but it seemed to flow through his bloodstream like the first swallow of a strong drink on an empty stomach. Not stopping to analyze it, he pushed his way into a supply building. Other men stopped what they were doing to stare. Gary followed, looking as if he wanted to back out the door, but Ron's fingers dug into his shoulder.

"Stand fast," Ron growled, and he stood his ground, meeting the eyes of every man in the place until eyes dropped or flicked away.

Ron walked on to the lockers, Gary hurrying after him. They kept their silence as they stripped away their clothes and hurled them into a large wheeled basket. Then into separate shower stalls for the next hour, scrubbing hard with disinfectant soap, standing under scalding water, again scrubbing and scraping away the grime and blood and dust and sand and all the stink that had burrowed into their bodies. They dried off and went to the supply window. A potbellied man in a dirty T-shirt and dark glasses chewed on a cigar stub as he eyed them through a lidded gaze. "Whadd'ya need, pal?"

Naked, Ron stared down the clothed orangutan before

him. He turned suddenly and shoved open the door to the supply room, earning an instant "Hey! You can't come in here! You gotta get your things the other side of . . ." The voice trailed away as cold eyes drilled into him.

"Fuck off," Ron said. With Gary following he went down the rows of clothing; and when he was through they both wore jungle fatigues, heavy boots, and heavy-duty chino shirts. They left the building in silence, but this time Ron had a goal. The knots were still twisting inside him, but his mind was working now, and the adrenaline had faded enough for him to feel as well as see and hear and think. He led Gary to the grubhouse. He still didn't want to eat, not with his stomach a shriveled acorn, but they grabbed a bunch of cold six-packs and sat on the step outside the building. The shock and the heat of the day soaked up the beer; soon they had only empties.

Ron nodded to Gary. "Get some more," he ordered.

It was just that. Not a request or a comment but a demand. Gary looked at Ron with surprise and Ron returned the gaze, unblinking and expressionless. Whatever passed between them was enough to establish clearly that equality had been replaced with a system; in that system, Gary got the beer. He came back with one already open and handed it to Ron, and the smaller man drained the can without pausing. He belched, opened another, sipped at it, and stared off into the jungle.

Sometime later, the area littered with empty cans, Ron noticed that the sun was going down. Wonderful. Things still worked, a voice inside his head told him; some things anyway; the sun, for instance. Sparks came over from the radio shack. He didn't bother with preliminaries.

"Your buddy—how'd he get it?"

It was the first question anyone had asked them. Ron felt his eyes widening as he looked up at Sparks. "You just remember to ask?"

Sparks took no offense. "He was the fourth last night, okay? We managed to save one of the others."

The data began filtering through Ron's brain. Small pieces turned and rotated and tumbled, and new pictures began to assemble between his ears. "It wasn't last night. This morning."

"It was god-awful," Gary blurted. "You should have—"

"Shut up," Ron said, not bothering to look at him. He kept his gaze leveled on Sparks. By his side he heard Gary sucking more beer. "They booby-trapped the pipeline," Ron explained to the radioman. "We had no radio. George set up the stinger to short-circuit the system so we could alert you we needed contact. Pow. It blew up."

Sparks nodded slowly, but his expression might have reflected an idle conversation about the weather. Ron was becoming convinced that Sparks had been through this a bunch of times before today. "A big charge?" Sparks queried.

"Big enough to flatten the camp."

Gary pushed away the beer can. "It killed George, man. That big enough for you?"

Sparks ignored the needle. "What about the equipment, the machinery? You know, tools, stuff like that."

"They'd already stolen most of it."

"Had any trouble with the gooks?" He asked the question as if he knew the answer.

Ron shook his head. "None. In fact, just the other way around. Happy, laughing, good workers."

"The smiling natives," Sparks said with a touch of light acid. He sighed. "Well, they've done it before, and they're doing it more and more."

Ron's eyes narrowed. "Why didn't anyone tell us?"

"We needed to see the pattern."

"The pattern?"

"Uh huh. It could have been individual tribes or groups, or a village. If that was the case, we wanted to find the troublemakers and then we could waste 'em. But it's not the case." He looked unhappy. "It's a campaign."

"What the hell are you talking about?" said Gary, his gorge rising.

"Dead people," Sparks said quietly.

Ron climbed to his feet. "You bastards could have told us."

"No. Then you would have run. We need the oil."

"So why the hell didn't we get some protection? Or some weapons?"

Sparks smiled. "Protection? This is a civilian operation."

"You can go suck with that one, friend."

"And if you had weapons they'd have killed all of you."

"So you gave us the least of all evils? Is that it?"

"That's it."

"It stinks."

"*You* didn't wake up dead, friend," Sparks told him.

"But George did," Ron spat. "And we could have, if—"

"If my aunt had balls, she'd be my uncle. Stay cool." Sparks turned and walked away. They stared after him, not moving. Several minutes later they stirred again.

"Let's get some more beer," Gary said.

"You get it. I gotta piss."

"The head's over there," Gary said, pointing.

"No. It's over there," Ron corrected him. He went to the radio shack and, in full view of anyone who might be watching, relieved himself against the side of the door. Sparks watched him, not saying a word or changing his expression from a blank stare. Ron smiled at the radioman, and their exchange was as clear a signal as a red light in traffic or a gun in a bank robbery. Ron went back to Gary for a cold beer. They walked slowly toward a cluster of tents, found one with four bunks and no personal belongings, and went inside to the cooler air. Ron sprawled on a bunk while Gary sat on the edge of another, starting to voice his inner turmoil.

"Why the hell did they do it, man?"

"You heard Sparks. A campaign."

"That's a crock."

"I know."

"Jesus, Ron, we were friends with those bastards. I mean, if we'd have had any trouble with them, maybe I could understand. But—nothing! We got along great. We were teaching them. They came to us. We worked together—"

"Knock it off," said Ron. "We've already been there."

"Goddamn it!" Gary roared. "They didn't have to kill him! If they didn't want us here, why the hell didn't they just tell us to get out?"

Ron stared at him. He lifted his feet and swung to a sitting position. "That's just what they did, didn't they?" Ron was getting tired of Gary's talk, his groping for reasons, his bewilderment. A ripple of impatience passed through him.

Gary stared back. "Yeah. I guess that's just what they did." His outburst seemed to have calmed him.

Ron hoped Gary would shut up for a while; he wanted to think. He felt a new kind of awareness, a new sense of what was in that jungle and beyond it, up in the hills and around the corners. It was like mist swirling around them and diffusing into their bodies and their minds. It had always been there; they were just learning to see it. Maybe Sparks was right. Maybe they should be grateful for not waking up dead. But Ron didn't feel like being grateful. He kept seeing George's body and remembering how the blast had tumbled him raggedy-ass through the air and how they'd buried him under bloody sand like a dead cow. He could see George's dark face creasing in a smile and hear him talking about how they'd build the best welding shop there ever was and . . .

"Hey, you listening to me?" Gary was nervous in the silence.

Ron turned to him, cool. "Tell me again."

Gary gave him a strange look, shrugged, and went on. "I was saying, Ron, we got the option to get the hell outta here." Ron couldn't miss the note of finality in Gary's voice. "We don't have to stay, you know. You want to stick it out here?" He gestured in a wide sweep with his arm. "With all that's happened and nobody gives a shit and all that?"

"No, I don't want to stay."

"We'll lose the pay, but—"

"Screw the pay," Ron snarled. "They could at least have told us."

"Yeah."

Ron crushed a beer can in his hands. "First plane comes in we get on it. That's the contract. Like it says, we can leave any time."

"Shit, I feel better already."

So do I, Ron thought—*almost*. Still, there was something flickering inside him that felt like excitement—like not wanting to leave before the end. The end of what?

With the settling of darkness, other men drifted into the camp. Ron studied them, interested. He saw, as if for the first time, what should have been obvious from the first day he'd hit this place: they were in Vietnam and there weren't any Vietnamese.

What the hell was this? Ron had Vietnamese friends. *No, that's wrong*, he corrected himself. *I knew those gooks and they knew me, and we were never friends. I wonder if any of these people here have Vietnamese friends.* Somehow he knew they didn't.

Ron got up, Gary scrambling close behind. They returned to the grubhouse, entered the supply room, and came out with two bottles of Jack Daniels. Back in the tent they drank slowly and steadily. No talking, just a cocoon of silence and the hard alcohol to warm their bellies. Ron stood up in the darkness; the pain was back inside him. He went outside and looked at the stars. They seemed to wobble. "Let's find Sparks," he said suddenly to Gary. "Tell him where the hell we are. He can come get us when that plane comes in."

Sparks heard them out and nodded. "Okay. Can't blame you for wanting out. Not after what happened to your friend."

Ron looked at Sparks for a long time without speaking.

"Something wrong?" asked the radioman. He looked uncomfortable.

"You know something, Sparks? I been trying to figure out what the hell is wrong about you. All day long," Ron said slowly, "I been working on it, and finally I got it down. I been waiting for you to ask just one question you or nobody else asked."

"What's that?"

"You never asked once, not once, what his fucking name was, so maybe you could tell his family that George Somebody-or-other was dead. That's what. You're an asshole."

Sparks pointed wearily to their tent. "Go back and get some shut-eye. The plane comes in tonight I'll come get you." He turned back to his radio gear.

Ron considered walking around his desk and smashing him in the face with the whiskey bottle, but it wasn't worth the effort. He and Gary went back to the tent and for the next couple of hours they did a fine job of staring into darkness.

Ron's mind was in turmoil. He couldn't wait to get out, get home, and yet there was something else—that sense of excitement, of being in the midst of something wild and cruel and bloody and, somehow, satisfying. He pushed the thought away and concentrated on the advent of his hangover.

Suddenly he stiffened. Against the starry night at the tent entrance he made out two shadowy forms. A flashlight beam stabbed his eyes. "Turn that fucking thing off!" he shouted.

The light went out. From the darkness a voice rumbled at him. "We're going to close the tent flap. We want to talk to you."

5

They closed the flaps securely and turned on a battery-powered fluorescent lamp that lighted the tent with a soft pink glow. Ron sat on the edge of his bunk, strangely alert. He rubbed his eyes and studied the two strangers. Just for starters, their clothing struck him as odd. Here they were, in a godforsaken toehold on a Vietnamese beach, in an unnamed oil base camp, with people getting murdered in the woods, and these two maniacs were wearing double-knit slacks and shiny shoes. They even had on white shirts. No ties or jackets; that might have been too much, mused Ron. He judged them to be in their forties. They both wore glasses, and one had a moustache and thick curly hair. They were both tall, and they looked like a couple of businessmen on their way to lunch. But no matter what they looked like they sure as hell didn't belong here. Then Ron picked up something else. These men were like big cats—comfortable, sure of themselves. It was almost an aura.

Only one of them spoke. The one with the moustache. "We heard what happened. We're sorry about your friend."

Ron's stare was blank. "Who?"

"George Jackson."

"Holy shit. Somebody knows his name."

"Sparks is all dried out. He hasn't felt anything for years. That's why he is where he is."

"Sure," Ron said.

"We're serious about Jackson. You lost a friend, and we lost the kind of man we need over here."

Ron didn't think that one called for a reply.

"We understand you've decided to quit. To go home."

"You're right," Ron said. "It's bailout time."

"Any reason for leaving?"

Ron glanced at Gary, who shrugged. He turned back to the two men. "One of you talks. The other just sits there. Maybe one of you is a ventriloquist. But you're both dummies to ask a question like that. We just buried our reason. In a stinking sandspit—because nobody else would help bury him or even talk about sending the body home. Maybe there's a kind old black woman who'd like to grieve over her dead son's body. They do that sometimes, you know."

"We can understand your being bitter."

"Get the fuck lost. Both of you."

"Bugging out won't help George."

"Nothing will help George," Ron snarled.

"But you can help us," said the big man.

"Us? Who the hell is *us*?" Gary demanded.

"Us. Your government. Even yourself."

"You've been in the jungle too long," Ron said in disgust. "Who are you? Where are you from?"

"We're your friends. Let's just say we can always produce what we promise. That's our identification."

Ron and Gary stared at them. It would not occur to Ron for a long time that neither then, nor any time later, would these men go any further to reveal themselves. They would produce no identification, and no one would ever question their authority to do what they did. It was to become, over the years, one of the most penetrating exercises in control Ron ever experienced, for by no more than innuendo and nuance these men determined life and death on an awesome scale. Now, at this first meeting, their power was far beyond Ron's wildest imagining.

"You're losing me," Ron said, weary from recent events. "*We're* supposed to help *you*. And the government. And ourselves. What's next? Magic powders sprinkled over us, or maybe just a wand?"

The man who talked for both men smiled. "That's good. The ironic touch in your voice. You're breaking out of your shock."

Ron shrugged. Sugarcoating, he knew. But there was more, something he sensed.

"How would you guys like to get even?"

That pulled the trigger, hit them like a bucket of ice water in the face. It was the one element they had not considered all through this insanity. But all Ron could do at this moment was stare. The other man showed a thin smile. He seemed to be settling in, absolutely sure of himself.

"I'll lay it out simply," the big man went on. "You know what we're doing here. We know every detail of what you've been doing with the locals. We're here to take out oil and we're here at their invitation. I want that understood beyond all question. By invitation of this government. Vietnam and Cambodia are literally floating on enormous lakes of oil, maybe more here than they'll ever find in the Arab countries. We're paying top dollar for what we take, and you people know we're trying to turn over field operations to the locals. We're not trying to take over anyone's country."

There was the first slip. "Nobody said you were," Ron told him.

"Somebody has. The local opposition. It's backed by the people from up North, as well as by the Chinese *and* the Russians. They don't want us getting this oil because it will begin to swing all sorts of strength to our side: petroleum, military, economic, trade—the works. They don't like that. They're paying local dissidents top money to rock our boat. Even tip it over. The South Vietnamese have asked for our help to stop those forces who are killing our people. Understand something: it's not their losses. They'll take care of their own. We're talking about American lives. Because if we lose too many people the oil program falls apart and the locals get hurt just as much as we do. So the partnership is tight."

Ron was getting tired of the bullshit. "Forget the speech. I know when I see people with the big badge." Eyebrows went up with that remark, but Ron slipped right by. "You said something about our getting even."

"Right."

"How?"

"It involves the same people who killed your friend. Let me give you some background first. Those people trying to force us out of the country consist of two groups. There's the

North Vietnamese from across the dividing line between the two countries—"

"I don't know anything about that," Ron said quietly. "Politics isn't my bag."

"Their involvement is to arm the locals. They're known as the Cong. Not too many people have heard that name."

"I know I haven't," Ron said. He was getting bored with the details, his mind tightly focused on the idea of revenge.

"Their entire program is based on killing and terrorism, and the second group practices brutal torture every chance they get. They're absolutely merciless. They're after even more than people like your friend, George. They're butchering missionaries, people who have devoted their lives to helping these people out of the mud; they're fair game and so are their families. We intend to help the South Vietnamese stop it."

Ron rubbed burning eyes. "Get back to why you came here."

"We need men like you."

Ron's eyebrows went up. Gary shot him a questioning look, but Ron stayed poker-faced. "I think," Ron said slowly, "you better spell that out. I never even wore a uniform in my life and neither has Gary. And I know you've got military all through here. I don't need to see a uniform to know that much."

The stranger nodded. "That's precisely what we're talking about. You see more than the surface. Both of you have lived here for a while, under the roughest field conditions. You know what it's all about. You've worked on a one-on-one basis with the natives, and now you know their friendliness is a sham. You know what to expect. The people or the country won't catch you off-balance, and—"

Ron held up a hand. "Fish or cut bait, mister."

"You never wore a uniform, but you can handle just about any kind of weapon there is. You were a dead shot with a .22 when you grew up on the farm. You've got a box filled with sharpshooter medals. You worked on construction crews with explosives. Everything from dynamite to TNT to primer cord and beyond. You're an expert, and you're the best."

He paused, and Ron waited in silence. Jesus, the guy knew a lot. He had done his homework, or gotten some minion to do it for him.

"We asked if you'd like to get even. About your friend. But it's more than that. We've identified the people who killed him. We know who they are and where they live. I'm not going to tell you any fairy tales. We're interested in more than a vendetta. Much more."

"How?" Ron wasn't saying any more than he had to.

"A few hours ago they kidnapped an American girl. A child, really, about eleven years old. They kidnapped her from a town where the local people work with us. We're very much afraid for this child. What they might do to her. They haven't hit us for ransom, and that's not good."

"You said the locals were working with you. Can't they help?"

The stranger shook his head. "Not the kind of help we need. They help us with information. They're not fighters. So we need you. Like I said, this kid is only eleven years old. You already know what the people are like. Those who took her. They did the number on George."

Ron and Gary exchanged a long look. Shock was gone. Ron felt a mixture of emotions stirring within him—pain, hate, an urge to strike back. His whole chemistry seemed to scream for revenge, and for a fleeting instant he sensed the irony in that: he, Ron Previn, the kid who never wanted to fight back, who used to sicken at the thought of killing a squirrel, was now positively bloodthirsty.

He looked away from Gary to the two men. "You got it. Count me in."

Gary's voice was an echo, as usual. "I'm with him."

The stranger nodded. "Thank you. Get a good night's sleep. It's late and you're both exhausted. We'll fill you in after sunup."

The light snapped off, and they were gone. Ron was surprised at the feeling of warmth, the glow he felt. What had happened to change him so? He didn't ponder long; sleep came almost instantly.

6

Ron was learning fast. Always expect the unexpected, the side move, the opposite. In the morning they had company, but it wasn't either of the two slick characters who had shown up the night before. This visitor was very different—an old-timer, his face grizzled and his skin brown from years of exposure to sun and wind. He wore faded military fatigues and a crew cut, and when he grinned he revealed a dark gap in his front teeth. Ron knew the type. This was a fighter, a grappler, a man who liked to mix it up whenever the occasion demanded. Ron studied him carefully. He'd have bet a year's pay that this new character—Dominic, he called himself—was an old-line sergeant, but he wasn't wearing any dog tags. That jarred Ron; the pieces didn't fit. Dominic wore a GI-issue Colt .45 in a faded leather holster-with-flap, and he wore it slung low, not up-to-snuff military style, but the way an old dog-eared veteran would wear it. But veteran of *what*?

"You guys eat yet?" That was his greeting as he stepped into the tent entrance.

"Who the hell are you?"

The gap in the smile showed. "Dom. That's me. Dominic. I'm supposed to be sure you guys got a good breakfast before we go."

"Go where?" Ron prodded. Things were happening awfully fast.

"Shit, wouldn't mean nothing if I told you boys. Jungle trails ain't got names, anyway. You eat?" he repeated.

39

Gary shook his head. "Okay," Dom said airily. "Grab some chow at the grubhouse. I'll be there with a jeep exactly thirty minutes from now." He turned and was gone.

Dom was true to his word. The jeep drove up just as Ron and Gary came through the grubhouse door. Dom grinned and motioned for them to climb in. "Hang on," he said, and that was all he said. They went off with double-clutching on the gears, turned into a dirt road through heavy brush, and emerged on a beach. The jeep pounded along a combination of beach and dirt road for at least forty minutes, moving always toward the North. Whenever they had a clear view of the water there was some sort of ship in sight. Ron would have expected the tankers and the merchant ships, but he wasn't ready for the small fleet of torpedo boats scattered along the coast or the gray ghostlike destroyers hugging the shoreline.

They came around a sharp turn in the trail, and without warning they were in another camp. Ron's eyes moved constantly as he made photo-memories of everything he saw. They were moving through a tent city. Not another kind of structure anywhere, or at least not in sight. There were people walking around and the usual jeeps and trucks. At his first glimpse of olive drab tents, Ron judged the area to be military; then he found himself confused, for in the middle of this thick jungle, in a clearing, loomed enormous circus-sized tents as well. He spotted the dye jobs that covered over the old brighter colors with jungle camouflage and olive drab. Interesting. He spotted more jeeps and several trucks, and beyond the tents, a lone helicopter without any marking on it—just drab olive green. Dom stopped in front of one of the big tents and motioned for the two men to go on in.

Surprise—the same guys they'd had their little conversation with the night before. The talkative one and the dummy with the zippered lip. They gave Ron and Gary each a cup of coffee and then leaned back in their straight chairs. "How are you two this morning?" asked the spokesman.

"The only thing missing here is tea and crumpets," Ron said. There was a moment's hesitation and then two smiles met his words. Ron struggled to adjust his thinking, to try to visualize this meeting from their side of the table. These guys were trying to psych him out: punch this button and press that nerve and see if he or Gary had changed attitudes, in any way, from the night before.

"Very good," said the leader. "You still, ah, feeling strong about helping us?"

"Strong?" Ron echoed the word. Careful, he warned himself. These are very sharp people. They had to have legal backgrounds. Almost everything they said was a box. It was the big badge, all the way. How could he have missed it for an instant?

"I never said a word about feeling *strong* about helping you," Ron answered. "The way I remember it, you asked us if we wanted to get even about George, and you needed some help getting back a kid snatched by the locals. The enthusiasm is all your bag." Ron scratched his chin. "By the way, what the hell are your names, anyway?"

"Harry. Call me Harry," said the spokesman.

"Does the sphinx have a name?"

Ron earned a sharp glare for that one. Harry fielded it. "He's Al."

"I think you got your names from a vaudeville billing."

"You're playing guardhouse lawyer, Previn."

Ron laughed. "What do you expect from a jack-in-the-box? It *is* a box you're word-painting, isn't it?"

Harry showed a thin smile, and Al sat like granite. "Okay, okay," Harry said soothingly.

"Let's keep it clean," Ron said. "Clean and low key. You laid it out. We said we'd help. You're pushing now, trying to get more than we bargained. That's bullshit."

Harry leaned back and sipped his coffee. He lit a cigarette and went through his own house brand of mental calisthenics. You could practically hear the wheels turn. Obviously he reached a favorable decision. He pushed aside his coffee cup and stood up. "All right. Come with me," he announced. Ron felt the difference—something had changed, shifted. Harry led them across the compound and into another tent. Here, protected from the staggering glare of the sun, sat a huge man behind a makeshift desk of crates and boards. It was the first time Ron had ever seen another human being who *loomed* while he was sitting down. Jesus, Ron thought. This animal is a Buddha with muscles.

He was the biggest man Ron had ever seen. Not just tall, or heavy, but enormous *all over*. A scaled-down King Kong with muscles rippling like liquid steel. Between massive shoulders and a bull head there was a thick column of corded tendons and muscle. No neck. He wore a thick handlebar moustache and his skull was shaved and freckle-darkened from long sun exposure. He literally exuded strength. Seeing a man with wrists as big as your own arm is disconcerting. Ron felt as if his body were made of cardboard. Yet when this monster moved there was nothing ponderous in his motion. He flowed like a three-hundred-pound ferret, and you knew that without even pausing he could with one mighty hand crush the life out of a man. When he stood, Ron noticed that he wore a bandolier from which grenades hung like swinging grapes. He had another bandolier in his hand, loaded with .45-caliber rounds and more grenades. Upright, he was even more overwhelming.

He pointed a thick finger at them and his voice rumbled as from deep inside a well. "You're Ron. You're Gary." A bandolier swung like a key chain. "I'm Mike. We don't need no more names. My job is to teach you to use certain tools. Your job is to learn. Come with me."

Ron tried for a moment to gauge his reactions to this hulk, to this whole incredible adventure. He got as far as recognizing curiosity, excitement, a kind of hunger—then he gave up. He just wasn't reacting as the old Ron Previn—something was new.

7

Gore factory.

That was Ron's immediate impression when they went into a tent that was surrounded by three separate barricades of barbed wire. Mike took them across the compound and approached the big tent that had a red stripe down the front and all those barbed-wire fences and wooden crossbars in front of it. He stopped before the first barricade. "Don't go any closer. In fact, *don't move*." He looked at them and his face showed there wasn't any joke here. "You're standing on a whole platter of land mines. Everything we do is being monitored by other people. The mines are detonated by pressure or radio signal. The barbed wire is hot. Its got enough juice to fry you in an instant. So you stay right where you are until I tell you to move. Got it?"

"Shit, yes," Gary said.

They waited, feet planted solidly on the hard-packed dirt. Ron heard a high tone signal and he knew this giant carried a radio receiver in a pocket. "It's clean now," Mike said, walking forward and pushing aside a section of barbed wire that swung easily on invisible hinges. They went through the next two barriers and stopped in front of the tent. Another tone signal. "You don't try to get out of here unless I'm with you or someone sets you up with the right equipment," Mike warned. "What stops you on the way in also stops you on the way out. Okay, let's go."

He lifted the tent flap and led them inside. That's when

Ron stopped dead in his tracks and the words *gore factory* flashed in his mind. He didn't know why. The valley of death would have been just as appropriate. A warehouse for killing. The tent was cavernous and brightly lighted by glaring bulbs on each side and overhead lights that were suspended from thick wooden rafters.

A world of weapons: machine guns, rifles, handguns, riot guns, shotguns, grenade throwers, flamethrowers, knives, bayonets, crossbows, and God knew what else. Everywhere Ron looked he saw cases upon cases of equipment with which to kill, maim, burn, and destroy. Ron couldn't take it all in; he closed his eyes and felt as if he'd been dealt a physical blow. He knew explosives. He'd used dynamite and primer cord in construction work. But this was something else—this was demolitions stuff, intended for tearing things apart, for destroying. He walked ahead slowly, ignoring Mike and Gary. He had to see for himself.

Good God. Incendiaries, shaped charges, antitank charges. Plastic explosives, mortar shells, flash grenades, killing grenades. His eyes darted from one case to another, read the stenciled lettering. Knives, darts, rockets, poisons and—he went back to a row of cases and forced himself to read the labels: Tear gas. Vomiting gas. Choking gas. And some other names he didn't recognize.

Mike loomed behind; Ron felt his presence. "Forget what you're reading."

Ron turned and his eyes met and held those of the human giant. "Let's get something straight. We're here for you to teach us about weapons. Not to tell me how to think or what to remember or to forget."

The man radiated power. That was all to Ron's advantage. Mike was so goddamned overwhelming that a mere mortal had nothing to lose by standing straight and being counted. The exchange went on silently and Mike nodded slowly. "You got it, little man," he said, and the words came with respect. Ron had the feeling that the giant Kodiak bear might have been nodding approval of a much smaller but worthy opponent—maybe a wolverine. Strange; it was just how Ron had come to feel since he'd entered this charnel house—like the kind of crafty small animal that survives by going for the groin; definitely not like a gentle young man who had grown up religious and peace-loving.

He tried to make one mind work on two tracks. The first was the impact of everything within his sight and his exchange with this professional killing machine called Mike. But what began to slow his swirling thoughts was that he had gotten into this entire affair for one reason above all else—to help get that young girl back. He didn't much give a damn for revenge—or did he? This crap of "getting even" was sixth-grade quality, but saving the girl was worth the coin. If they hammered the same people who killed George, so much the better. So it boiled down to one element above all others—that kid.

Even this attempt at simplification produced its own complications; it was like opening a large box and looking inside to find another, barely smaller box, and then you had to open that one to see what was inside, and there was another damn box, and—Well, what it added up to was that they weren't simply going to rush out into that bloody hilly jungle and get the girl. There was much, much more to it. They were going to get weapons and learn how to use them, as well as whatever else they needed, and *then* they'd go after the girl.

Who might be dead for several days by then. Jesus. It was like a web they were wrapping around him. Ron kept trying to make sense out of it as he walked past row after row of killing power that could level a small city. All right here in this one tent. Kill-power. He was aware that he was being drawn into the web. On another mind level, his very awareness was interesting to him. Interesting? He asked himself if that was what he really meant, and then he nodded to himself. He was way over his head, and the only way to get back on top of the water was to stay very, very cool and assimilate all this. And quit trying to figure out what it all meant, or how he would have reacted to it five years ago.

"You ever work with clothesline?" Mike's voice jarred his thoughts, and he wrenched his mind back to the job at hand. Mike held a coil of ordinary clothesline.

Gary looked at the big man as if he'd gone crazy. "What the hell would I do with clothesline?" he asked.

Mike didn't answer. But he smiled at Ron. "Tree stumps, huh?"

Ron nodded slowly. "Yeah," he said after a pause, during which he'd decided not to play coy. "Tree stumps, old buildings, even taking down houses. Once we used it for a Fourth of July celebration." He saw Mike's eyebrows go up. "We carried a thousand feet of it up in a helium balloon. Tethered. When it was a good safe distance, we ignited it. Instant lightning bolt."

Gary was getting pissed at being left out. Ron turned to him. Good old Gary—always there, always reliable and predictable, but somehow blank. In a way Ron envied that blankness; his own mental turmoil was beginning to wear him down. "It isn't clothesline, Gary. Just looks like it. It's primer cord. Explosive, and a lot more bang than dynamite. Needs an electrical charge to detonate it. Until then, you can cut it, bang on it, even burn it, and it won't go off. But you wrap that stuff around a tree, and you'll bring down a giant redwood in one shot."

Gary nodded, satisfied.

Mike demonstrated a few more items Ron was familiar with, such as dynamite and nitro and fuzes. But he'd known only a fraction of the kinds of fuzes Mike displayed to them. Once they got past the stuff Ron knew about, it was heady going, a whole new world of weapons he never knew existed. Direct fuzes and impact fuzes and acid fuzes and detonator and time and radio signal and ultrasonic-triggered fuzes, as well as cordite and a dozen different kinds of plastics explosives. They had a bewildering variety of stuff in a caulking gun, the same kind you use to seal windows and waterproof doorways, only this caulking gun had eight times the explosive yield of dynamite. You could stick it anywhere and detonate it in a dozen different ways. That was just for starters.

At the back of the tent a thick wooden wall had been erected, supported by bracing and cables. Lights shone onto the wall. Ron stared in awe and stark disbelief. The whole wall was covered with guns on racks.

Sure, he had seen guns before. Gun shops were home to him. He'd grown up with guns, starting with .22 rifles, as most kids do in the country. And shotguns and 30 calibers and high-powered rifles for deer hunting, and he'd handled revolvers from .22 right on up to .45. Even automatics—from little .22s through .32 and .380 and .38s and .44 magnums—but only for target shooting. Most of them faded into memory as toys as he stood contemplating the bewildering arsenal that had only one purpose: killing on a wide, efficient, overwhelming scale.

Mike's voice rumbled behind him. "It tells its own story, doesn't it." No question there. "Take a good look, fella. There's over a hundred different types there. Russian, Chinese, German, Israeli, Italian, Czechoslovakian, British, American—you just think of it and it's in front of you. You want 19 caliber, you got it. You want 13 millimeter—that's 60 caliber—you got that, too, but you got to be a big bastard like me to handle the recoil. You want rocket shells in a handgun—right over there, lower left. But you can't get much out of them in a fire fight, and they take too long to reload. They're special mission jobs."

Gary stopped by some strange clustered tubing, each tube no bigger than a straw, but with fifty or sixty tubes arranged together. He couldn't identify the apparatus, and he held it up. "This looks like something out of a boiler. Like a steam condenser," he said to Mike.

Mike hefted it in a powerful hand. "You won't believe it," he said, smiling, "but each of these tubes contains a minirocket, and each minirocket is dead on for three hundred yards. It carries any kind of warhead you want. Armor-piercing, incendiary, cyanide or some other poison, or even a small explosive charge."

Gary stared, unblinking. "*Each* tube?"

"You got it, friend. You can line up clusters like these in a row—as many as you want. We use them for field saturation. Set them up and ignite them by wire or radio control. They'll take out an entire line of a hundred men on an advance. Then you throw away the clusters. Hell, they're only plastic, like you got in kid's toys."

Kid's toys. Ron studied the automatic weapons and Mike studied Ron. "That's right," said the big man. "What counts is not the one-shot deal, but something with staying power. One shot is like a kiss in the ass. They can wait you out. See anything you like?"

Ron let his eyes move slowly across the staggering display of weaponry. He was astounded by the ingenuity of these things. After all, how many ways were there to build a weapon to perform the basic job of killing as many people in the shortest possible time from the greatest distance? Well, there were more ways than he'd ever figured, and all of them were right here in front of him.

Again Mike's voice intruded on his thoughts. "Think about what you like best. It's gonna be yours."

Ron couldn't judge them all. He astounded himself by deciding to choose what he felt was the most amusing weapon. He was amazed just to realize that he was using *amusing* as his criterion. He realized that the snaking out of this one quality among all others was partly the new and perplexing coolness he felt, but also partly because guns had been part of his life as far back as he could remember. To Ron Previn, the caliber of a weapon didn't make much difference. What counted was the feel, the way it handled, the balance, the heft of the gun. Not so much if it would blow a man to pieces because . . .

He turned to Mike. "I got a problem. I know guns."

Mike nodded sagely. "I know you do."

"But I never killed a man. I never tried to kill a man. I never even pointed a goddamned gun at a man in all my life."

"You'll learn."

"I don't know if I want to."

"Bullshit. If you didn't have it in your head, you wouldn't be here right now." Something about that remark stunned Ron, but he let it pass. Mike glanced at his watch. "Let's break for lunch."

Ron toyed with his food. What the big man had said bothered him. Why? He fought against the insight that was bringing his thoughts into focus. Because what Mike had said was right. The moment Ron started moving among those gleaming weapons, a strange fascination had begun to come over him. No problems with conscience, no guilt complexes weighing him down. Could Mike really be so discerning that he saw something in Ron Previn that Ron himself didn't yet comprehend? That he was only waiting to unleash something that *wanted* to kill? He pushed the thought out of his mind. After a fast lunch Mike took them back to the tent and showed them how to operate a variety of radios—large equipment and portable walkie-talkies, radios you wore on your belt and to which you listened with earpieces so tiny that the sound wasn't audible to anyone else.

Then there were more weapons. The mortars, the recoilless rifles, the special rocket launchers, white phosphorus, the poison gas distributors, the antipersonnel bombs you could fire with a rifle that exploded above ground and showered hundreds of tiny poisoned darts outward with rifle-bullet speed. Finally, Ron leaned back against a case of nitro and slid down to the hard-packed dirt floor. He turned off. It was that simple. *I've overloaded the circuits. Saturation. I'm a fucking monster trying to choose his magic wand of death.*

Mike sauntered by, leaned against a nitro case, and began picking his teeth with a bayonet. "Decide what you want?"

Ron shook his head.

"Better for you to select it than for me to do it for you, little friend. Think about what you want to use, how you'll use it, what it's going to be like to carry it. That's important. The more confidence you got in your piece, the better you'll use it. That's good advice. Take it."

Ron felt himself give in, accepting what it was all about. This wasn't going to be some silly hiking trip in the thickly forested hills. It was serious business. He took Mike's advice.

"I'll take the gelpacks," he said finally.

Gary echoed the selection. "Me, too."

Those were the fire bombs, harmless-looking little bundles of plastic straws.

"Let those go for now," Mike intruded. "Pick the weapon you'll carry for all your jobs here."

That brought Ron up short, but he ignored it. He hefted a small gun in his hands. It felt good, felt right. It *was* right. "This is the one for me," he announced. "What the hell do you call it?"

"Spaghetti gun."

"Why?"

"Man, it squirts."

Ron studied it carefully. It was a beautiful little gun. A 22 caliber. He never would have believed it. Twenty-two caliber, with all those bigger things there for the taking. But it was a .22 *magnum*. One of the reasons he selected it was its construction of wood and steel. No plastic. He hated plastic in guns. Whoever had made this weapon was a craftsman. He'd created a beautiful piece of art. Strange way to think of a killing device.

Gary didn't like the .22 magnum. He was much bigger than Ron, with bigger hands. The artistry of the spaghetti gun wouldn't appeal to him—too subtle.

Ron left Gary to feel and touch and handle while he again studied his own selection. She was light and beautiful. He was astonished to discover that each individual magazine was prepacked in the factory with *two hundred rounds*. Holy shit. You fired it and then snap, *out*, throw away the empty magazine, and snap, *in*, just like that, and you had your second magazine for another two hundred rounds. With this thing in his hands, one man could wreak the havoc of twenty. Once more, Ron pushed the thought out of his mind; it was getting easier and easier to do.

Gary held out his choice. "This one feels right," he said, his voice somber, as if for the first time he too realized what was happening, and that it was beyond his control, as if he were sliding a slippery chute and there was no stopping. His auto-rifle fired 30-caliber slugs from a clip that held thirty rounds. It was a roughhouse kind of weapon with a piece of thick, strong wire in the back that could be folded forward, hinging up against the barrel to reduce its size and bulk for carrying. It was the kind of weapon paratroopers or commandos would use, and Ron was convinced that was why Gary had picked this particular gun. It had a soldierly dash and flair that would appeal to Gary—something out of some stupid romanticism from wars past. Ron knew this was true even if Gary would never be aware of it himself. Gary had never been around guns; he didn't know the first thing about them, and he'd never even thought about killing anyone for any reason. So here was this gun with the right size and feel and heft; and it evoked dim memories of German storm troopers and American paratroopers, and it ignited some kind of flame inside him, so he picked it. Simple.

Mike led them to a broad table. "School, people. We learn about your pieces. Not just how to shoot them, because any idiot can do that. We take them apart and we identify all the parts and we put 'em back together again; then we use training rounds and cause jams and fuckups, so if it happens to you in the field, you don't waste your time being stupid and getting yourself killed."

They went through the drill again and again. Ron got it down pat on the first try, and he saw a deeply approving look on Mike's face. He spent the rest of the time helping Gary, and although Gary didn't know guns, he was a mechanic and a welder and he knew machines, so he went through this crash course faster than they'd both expected. When they were through, they put aside their weapons. Mike picked up a huge case of plastic explosives and gelpacks, nodded them outside with a toss of his head, and said cheerily, "School's on again."

They went to a remote clearing to learn how to use plastic explosives and the incendiary charges. It was war play on a devastating scale, complete with shattering explosions, concussion waves that knocked them flat and set their ears ringing for days, and fireballs soaring hundreds of feet into the air. "Some of these things," Mike said in a laconic fashion, "they got a watch inside, a clock, sort of. A timer. They got time fuzes that start when you pull apart two wires, like this. It'll go off in ninety seconds. You can also set them for ten or twenty or thirty seconds. Anything you want. Now, take a good look at this area."

They looked. Trees of all sizes. Small hills, heavy growth. Solid. Untouched for God knew how many years.

"We're gonna change all that," Mike said. "See those big trees over there? They're really trunks clustered together. They'd stop a bulldozer right in its tracks. The biggest tank you ever saw would bust itself open trying to damage that stuff. It's even too big for a regular charge. You may as well find out from the start what this stuff can do. Let's go."

They did precisely what he told them. "That's it. Get that primer cord around the trunk and then through those spaces. You want the punch from inside as well as out. We'll set that off with an electrical timer. We'll pull the switch same time we pull the fuzes on the gelpacks. See? The idea is to blow it apart and also make sure it's all burning at the same time. That way you get a double action and you keep the opposition busy *after* your blast. When it's all ready, we pull the wires and we run like hell."

Gary showed an unhappy face. "Why don't we just unreel some wire? You know, get to a safe place. Behind cover, and then detonate it."

"That kind of shit's too heavy to carry for miles. Whatever weighs one pound when you start out feels like ten before you get where you're going. This stuff gives you the biggest bang for what your muscles can carry fast and long, that's why."

Gary sniffed about him with naked suspicion. "I don't

like it. You mean we pull this stuff and we got just ninety seconds to get to safety?"

Mike nodded. "Right on. You know how far you can run in ninety seconds?"

"I never counted," Gary said darkly.

"With the devil snapping at your ass, friend, you'd be amazed." Mike surveyed everything. "Okay. This is a max charge. Otherwise I never use more than thirty seconds. Now, Ron, you get set by the gelpacks. They're all rigged on the same line. Gary, you take the primer. I'll count down from four. When I say pull, you mothers pull, and then you shag ass. We go for that small rise over there, and we get behind it and lay flat, and we watch." They didn't expect him to keep right on talking and counting. "You got it, boys. Four, three, two, one, *pull the sons of bitches! Go!*"

They pulled and at the same instant Mike's feet thudded heavily against the ground. He was off like a charging rhino, bending into his stride, not bothering to look back. They stared for one startled moment, then Ron was off like a startled deer, covering ground in huge bounds, Gary running like hell right behind. They hit the other side of the rise in fifty-eight seconds flat, dropped to the ground, crawled up so they could see, and watched the world blow up in their faces. The blast was incredible. The primer cord pulverized the tree trunks into chunks and shreds that at the same instant were set violently aflame, ripping upward through the air, tossing and tumbling in slow motion, setting off a steady rain of large and small objects. The explosion slammed all three men against the ground, lifted them up, and slammed them down again. When the dust began to clear they saw a huge smoking crater.

"Let's go," Mike said. "We'll try different size charges now and let you boys get sharp at it." He smiled at them. "You'll know when you know enough—when you trust yourselves. I won't have to tell you."

Two hours later the forest looked like a battlefield from the First World War. Craters heaped upon craters, the ground smoldering, and not even a tree stump left standing.

"I'm hungry," Mike said.

Obviously this part of school was over. The big man pulled his microphone from his pocket, unreeling it from an inertial pack. He spoke briefly into the microphone, listened through his earpiece, replaced the microphone. "They know we're coming," he said. "They'll disengage the booby traps and mines when they see us."

"What happens next?" Gary asked as they walked back to the jeep.

Mike climbed in behind the wheel. "Tomorrow you learn how to read jungle maps and find your way around the local real estate. Move it, willya? I'm hungry."

8

Somebody, thought Ron Previn, kept some kind of crazy miracle machine hidden away in this jungle. A machine that cranked out devastating weapons, cases of scotch or bourbon on demand, and at this moment a magnificent turkey dinner. He couldn't believe it. They followed their humongous guide out of the jeep and into another tent, actually one big tent covered by another, so that the outer covering layered the air, keeping the inside cool and dehumidified. It was the first air-conditioned tent Ron had ever seen; it reminded him of the Arabian Nights.

After eating from tin cans for so long, the only word he found to describe the meal was *fantastic*. Surrounding him and Gary was a horde of giants, more or less of the same muscle-bulging stature as Mike, many of them with bizarre tattoos, fierce moustaches, solid biceps, and an air of what Ron had come to identify as a killing confidence. Each one of these men was a professional killer who had, on many past and secretive occasions, done in more human beings than he could probably even recall. Yet here they were, pleasant enough, convivial, digging into perfectly done turkey with stuffing, mashed potatoes, cranberry sauce, a half dozen vegetables, fresh bread and rolls and butter, milk and wine and any hard liquor a man wanted. Cigarettes, cigars, even some joints if you so desired. Ron didn't care for a toke, but he did surrender to some beautiful Cuban cigars with his coffee and brandy. He could hardly move when they finished. He felt like a swine who'd died and ended up in gastronomical heaven.

Afterward, he and Gary went to a tent that was assigned to them. Zippered entrance. Waterproof sidings. A small bathroom facility with fresh running water—for Ron that was the greatest rarity of all. In the back a communal shower with scalding water and soap and shaving gear and fresh clothes.

Gary tested his cot. "Would you believe it?" he said, bouncing up and down. "It's got a mattress and *springs!*" He pulled back the blanket. "Holy Jesus. Sheets. I forgot these things existed."

Ron sipped brandy from a bottle and let out a mouthful of cigar smoke. "Sacred lambs, that's us," he said.

"What?"

"Sacred lambs, I said."

"What does that mean?"

"I have a clear picture in my mind of a sacrificial altar."

Gary's expression was one of instant sobriety. "Spell that out."

"Every man in that tent tonight was an expert, veteran, professional killer. And they've picked us because they *need* us?"

Gary showed a nervous tic in one cheek. "I never thought of that."

"I didn't think so." Ron put away the bottle and dropped the cigar in a can. One thing he'd always had in his favor. He could turn off. He was sick of the whole subject now. Piss on it. "Good night," he said.

Gary stared at a sleeping man.

In the morning they found themselves alone. They dressed, had breakfast in the large tent, went back to their tent, wasted an hour. Ron chewed on another rare Cuban cigar, warmed his insides with brandy, fretted, started getting pissed at the world. He picked up his spaghetti gun and six magazines and stalked outside, Gary hurrying after him.

Ron went into the big tent, saw a stranger in starched fatigues and no insignia. "Where's the firing range?"

The stranger smiled. "You're right on time. Hundred yards to the right. It's got a safety wall behind it. Have fun."

Ron didn't like his behavior being predicted so neatly. He offered no response but turned and walked away through

a small grove to another clearing. An earthen wall indicated
the backdrop for testing weapons. The area was filled with
cardboard silhouette targets, dummies on the ground and in
trees. There was a thick concrete block wall with dummies
crouched behind it. Ron ignored it, slapped a magazine into
his weapon, cocked it, and in a single spinning motion whirled
about, crouched on one knee, and squeezed the trigger.

Something tore the sky in half. It wasn't the sound of an
automatic weapon firing. He heard an ear-stabbing *RRRIPPPP!*
and, just like that, two hundred rounds tore away from the
terrible weapon in his hands. He was taken completely by
surprise. The target at which he'd fired was a mass of cardboard fluttering through the air, and beyond that branches
and leaves were still whirling crazily. Ron stared in awe at
the lightweight buzz saw of death in his hands. He released
the magazine, shoved in another, waited.

Gary, beside him, had selected a dummy of a man and
squeezed off several bursts. His rounds went wild as the
submachine gun bucked and roared in his hands.

"You'll kill *us* if you do it like that," Ron said. "Here,
hold it like this." He demonstrated. "Now, just before you
fire, start leaning into the thing. That way your body mass
will take the recoil. Squeeze off only a few rounds until you
get the knack of it."

Ron sat on a tree trunk and watched Gary learn how to
kill. When he was done, he was still something less than a
pro, but there was no question Gary could do a lot of killing.
At close range, his auto had a lot of punch to it. Gary sat
down beside him, nursing a bruised shoulder. "I never realized these things were so loud," he said. "My ears hurt."

Ron didn't answer. He'd been studying the wall of concrete blocks and the crouched dummies just beyond. And
then he understood. Still sitting, he opened fire at the wall.
The small bullets, traveling with tremendous velocity and
tumbling, sliced through the wall as if it were butter and cut
four dummies in half on the other side of the wall.

"Holy shit," Gary said.

Harry and Al waited for them in their tent. They studied
Ron and Gary as they came in. Harry, the talker, nodded as if
he understood everything. "You get your workout with the
maps this afternoon. Memorize everything you can. We've

found where the girl is. You two are part of the three-man team that goes after her. You two, and Mike."

Ron nodded. No one expected pearls of wisdom from him, and Gary was still running to catch up.

"After map work, let your mind rest. No more effort. Stay up late tonight. As late as you can. All night if you want because we want you to sleep tomorrow. You go out tomorrow night, and you'll be on the move all night."

They were gone. Twenty minutes later Mike came in with the maps. He taught them to recognize certain landmarks. "The main thing is to stay with me. Having a compass to find your own way back ain't worth a shit. You think you know that jungle out there, or the hills or the fields. You don't. You know only what you see, and that's just a cover. You want to come back with me, you stay with me. Got it?"

"Got it," Ron said.

"Good. Read the maps some more. Take your time. Let it sink in. Then quit or you'll get confused. See you later."

When it got dark, they wandered along the row of tents until they saw two men inside one tent reading magazines. One of the men called out, "Hey! You guys play pinochle?"

Ron and Gary went inside. Ron was still carrying the spaghetti gun. He laid it on a bed, moved a chair to the table between the two cots. "You got a game. Deal."

They played until five in the morning and Ron felt he needed toothpicks to keep his eyes open. He stumbled off to sleep.

Something stung his eyes. Ron cursed and rolled swiftly from the cot, the spaghetti gun already in his hands. The only sound he heard was Gary snoring. Jesus. He looked at his watch. Noon. The heat had awakened him. Sweat poured from him, soaked his clothes. Then he heard other sounds. Birds. They were always making noise. He heard voices and the sound of engines. In the background was the deep throbbing of a big helicopter. It faded away. He looked again at his watch, decided it would be wise to eat well now and eat lightly that night so he would have an empty stomach and a clear head. He nudged Gary with the spaghetti gun. "Get your ass up. Time to chow down."

Harry and Al showed up at five that afternoon with maps that were marked with lines and circles. They indicated a trail on the map that led from their camp around hills and through thick forests. Harry's finger tapped the map. "The girl's here, in this village. I can tell you more now. You already know she's only eleven years old. What we didn't tell you is that she's blonde, her name is Nancy, and she's the daughter of a high official in an oil company. Her parents have been here about six months, and her father runs a major oil distribution system."

"How'd they get her?" said Ron.

"The family had no reason to be suspicious. They went to a local village to shop. They'd been going there for months and they knew the locals. They had friends there. While they were in the market they became separated from the girl. The mother never saw her again. She started getting frantic when nobody she asked admitted to even seeing the girl that day. That's when she knew the child was kidnapped. After the mother returned, we put out feelers, used our contacts, and confirmed that the girl is here."

"How come it took so long?"

"Because we had to be absolutely certain. If we went after the kid and hit the wrong village, we signed her death warrant." Harry pushed away the map. "Clean your weapons. Mike will have extra magazines and your other stuff. He'll also have a change of clothing for you. No identification anywhere. You have rings, watches, anything, leave it here."

They emptied their pockets and stowed their personal belongings. Ron thought over everything he'd heard. "Question," he said.

Harry nodded.

"Still no shot at a ransom?" Ron asked.

Harry shook his head. "No, and it scares us. Okay, Mike will be here within the hour. Good luck. I mean that. For you and that child."

The two men left. Ron and Gary waited in silence. Mike showed up with a different look on his face. He brought them their changes of clothes and distributed weapons and small flashlights for map reading. By the time they were ready, it was dark. They could hear the insects bombarding the high lights.

"Let's go," Mike said. "We got a long walk ahead of us."

In sixty seconds they were completely lost. Mike set a steady pace without ever looking at a map. He walked like a machine, a giant phantom completely at home in the dark. They were stung by insects, and branches whipped their faces, but the giant never broke stride, never hesitated. They walked for miles, muscles cramping. Ron marveled at the big man. He seemed to know every inch of the local terrain. They followed him single file, Ron in the middle and Gary taking up the rear. It got worse the longer they were out. The jungle stank from rotting undergrowth, from animal wastes, from vines and creepers and the damned bugs and soft mud they couldn't see. Mike stopped after two hours. They remained silent, breathing heavily, sipping from their canteens.

Then they went on, crossing hard ground and boggy ground, trying not to curse aloud. Ron carried his spaghetti gun and a bunch of gelpacks. His had the plastic connectors with thirty-second fuzes. Gary carried the ninety-second gelpacks. He was big enough to carry twice as many as Ron could manage. They didn't know for sure what Mike carried, but it looked big enough to be a 50 caliber, and strange grenades hung from a couple of belts and bandoliers. They didn't ask. They were busy enough with their own.

They had agreed on their own weapons from the start, and they agreed always to carry the same kind of gelpacks, Ron with the thirties and Gary the nineties, so they would never make a fatal mistake by mixing them up. Ron mused on that as he fought his way through the stinking jungle. He and Gary had slipped into their new roles as if they'd been trained for years to do this job. They didn't question anything anymore. He didn't understand how he had flowed into this new role, but there it was. Only an occasional flicker of something—conscience, regret, guilt—reminded him from time to time that he had once been a different kind of man. These he ignored—it was becoming easier all the time.

Ron nearly stumbled into the motionless form of Mike, who stood rock still, studying the gloom. Then he pointed, and Ron could barely make it out. The village.

9

It seemed to materialize out of thick jungle. One moment they were on a narrow trail immersed in dense undergrowth, breathing in millions of tiny gnats that buzzed in their ears and noses and eyes and mouths, the world barren of all human life; the next instant, there it was. They were acclimated to night vision, and against the skyline they could make out the thatched huts of the isolated community. What helped their vision were open clearings just off to one side. Light that barely trickled from the sky reflected off rice paddies. Ron concentrated on the village. It was exactly as Mike had told them.

The huts that made up the village were in a long row. At the end of the row he saw a clearing. Just beyond the open space loomed a hut by itself, with a higher top than the others and open on two sides. This meant it always had an open entrance and it could be used as the village communal center, for eating or talking or holding meetings. Mike studied that hut with extra care. Ron noticed one additional structure. He'd been briefed on what to expect, and he knew that this was the only building in the village that wasn't a hut for living or eating or sleeping. It was a communal shack where the villagers stored their meat, fish, or vegetables, or whatever they ate. It was made of logs and stones and sandbags to keep it cooler than the outside air. They had no ice, no electricity, nothing. Just what they could devise by understanding nature. They could have been living this way for a thousand years, in the middle of nowhere, in the center of nothing.

He couldn't see it from his present location, but Ron knew that beyond the row of huts was a canal, maybe six feet wide and five or six feet deep. It was always at least that deep, and old village lore enabled the Vietnamese to build the canal so that the tightly packed sides and walls of the embankments didn't cave in, even when torrential rains pounded the country. Extending outward from the canal were farm squares. Like rice paddies, all interconnected. There were perhaps ten of them.

Ron was surprised at how much he could see. He'd learned since arriving in this country that as long as you were out from under heavy growth you could see at night. It wasn't like anything he'd ever known back in the States. There, when the moon was full, you could see for miles. But this jungle land was always hazy. With or without a moon, it was like looking through a veil or a mist.

Ron already understood many features of the Vietnamese villages. He'd learned certain things from talking to other men, and Mike had filled in the details. One thing offended him; these people had no bathrooms. They could have built them, but for some reason they never did. When they had to go they just went to that trench, their irrigation canal. A man had to take a leak, he pissed in the canal. The women squatted with their backs to the canal and pissed into it. Everyone did that. When they had to crap they squatted over the canal and let go. They'd been doing it like that for centuries. What shook Ron was that they used the same canal for their drinking water. They just dipped a container into the canal and drank the same water into which they had released their body wastes. During daylight, they used discretion, or maybe it was optimum utilization. When they had to take a shit they went out to the rice paddies and let it drop in the irrigated sections. It was instant fertilizer. They moved from one paddy to another to crap. The whole area was filled with bugs feasting on human excrement.

It had always been that way. Somehow, the water never seemed to bother them, never made them ill.

Ron forced his attention away from the stinking canal. There was one hut in particular he had to pick out. The back of the village always had one particular hut. "That's where the head honcho lives," Mike had explained before they started out. "He's the boss man, the chief. He has the power of life and death over his people. All the villages are set up the same way. So we got to get where this one special cat lives."

Now they stood like statues in the night, providing warm and wet feast for the clouds of insects swarming over them, talking in the lowest of whispers. Mike pointed. "That's it. It's slightly apart from the others, at the end of the line." They had the chief hut in sight.

"There's no lights," Gary said in a hoarse whisper. "No lights anywhere."

Ron felt his eyeballs straining. He froze, pointing, trying to whisper in Mike's ear. "Over there. To the left."

"What is it?"

"It's a fucking dog, that's what." It bothered Ron. Watchdogs upset him. He felt a sudden urge to kill all watchdogs, silently and swiftly. Once, when he was a kid, a big damn dog had come rushing out of a neighbor's house at night to attack him. Ron had managed to get into the house and slam the door behind him, but he'd been badly frightened and had never gone near that house again. He felt no fear now—only an urge to kill. But this damn dog was tied up, and at the moment he looked asleep. That didn't matter. The animal could come awake and have the whole village roused before they got near it."

"Okay," Mike said, voicing his new decision. "We stay out this far to get to the other end of the village. Then we move in. Go."

They went as quietly as three men could move in the night in open fields. They were halfway to their goal, moving along the canal, when that bastard dog came awake. It barked a couple of times, and Ron wanted badly to kill it, but then he noticed that the dog didn't bring anyone outside. He breathed a sigh. Of course; there are dogs that bark at frogs and birds and the moon and the wind in the trees, and no one pays much attention to them. Especially in a village removed by distance and time from the rest of the world. "Dog don't even know we're here," Mike said. "Keep moving."

Sure enough, the animal flopped down again. Mike tapped Gary on the shoulder and pointed. "Take up your position back where we came from. The other end of the village. You know what to do?"

Gary nodded and left. He would lock into position to set up a cover of machine-gun fire if Mike and Ron had to come hell-bent for leather out of the village. Anyone following would move directly into Gary's line of fire.

Mike motioned to Ron; that meant for Ron to go to the opposite end of the village from Gary, the spaghetti gun in his hands ready for anything. Ron didn't know what was going to happen or even what he was supposed to do except keep that lethal machine at the ready. He bent to one knee so his body wouldn't shake as badly as it had been since he'd seen the dog. Mike went ahead, a water buffalo of a man, crouching down, without making a sound. Ron could hardly believe the way the big bastard ghosted through the night. And he was carrying a big and heavy machine gun with him, something with a short barrel. Ron didn't know the model except that it was obvious it would stop a rhino at short range.

Ron lost sight of Mike in the shadows. The only sounds he could hear were those insects: tiny ones in a cloud around his face and bigger ones in the thick undergrowth. The dog was quiet, Mike was quiet, and except for the background of the insects there was a heavy and wet silence over everything. Ron felt nervous and itchy. And then a terrible blast erupted from the end of the village, a deep ripping sound that shattered the night. That was all. One blast and its crashing echo across the fields and against the thick jungle forest. Ron didn't breathe. He had tensed as tightly as a coiled spring, his mind blank.

Mike moved slowly and deliberately from the hut. Ron saw his silhouette hulking through the haze. The big man motioned for Ron and Gary to move after him, and they took off at a dead run, as fast as they could move through the sloppy footing. Ron groaned. Goddamn Gary. He was running *toward* them and leaving open his position at the opposite end of the village. Mike had a look of mild disgust on his face when he and Ron came up to Gary, but he dismissed it. The three men ran steadily through the slop and excrement, splashing and sliding, until Mike motioned for them to stop. They hunkered down, turned back in the direction of the village. Voices carried across the field, and screams, and cries of rage, and they could see people streaming out of their huts, some lighting torches or flashlights, milling about in confusion.

Mike nodded to himself but spoke aloud. "Good. They're too confused to think of coming after us."

Gary looked doubtful. "They won't stay that way for long."

Mike glanced at Gary as if he were an annoying insect. Mike didn't answer but sat quietly, waiting. He had told them earlier that they'd go back along a different route. Ron didn't want to bother him, but he had to ask. Because he knew what that ripping burst had been. He could still smell the stink of the the heavy machine gun that had been fired in that hut, and he wanted to know what had happened. How many were dead in there? Jesus, they'd come to rescue a young girl . . .

"Mike. Where's the kid?"

Mike looked blankly at him.

"The girl," Ron persisted. "Where the hell's the girl?"

He never changed expression. "She wasn't there."

That's all? "For Christ's sake, Mike, I heard you cut loose inside that hut with that cannon you got. There had to be a reason! We came for the girl, damn you!" He tried to say more, but the words wouldn't come; suddenly, he knew, and it didn't take a genius to figure it out, that people had been chopped to hamburger by that heavy machine gun.

He didn't ask Mike again. Then the world lighted up with a great warm orange flash, reflecting off the hills, shining on the paddies, and making the night mist glow. It sent birds fluttering into the air and spilled fire along the row of huts. It lighted their own faces and equipment, glinting off the deadly metal they carried, and Ron understood. Delayed action charges. The people were outside now, vulnerable and naked. After the deep WHOOM bounced off into the distance, the thin screams became louder and ever more desperate.

The giant's expression hadn't changed, but he jerked a thumb in the direction of the village. "They'll look for us now," he said, and then he pointed in another direction. "We go that way," and without another second's hesitation he spun about and was off at a steady run.

Ron didn't want to stay there and get torn to pieces by

those villagers who were still alive. He cursed and ran after Mike, and he heard Gary start up behind him like a startled elk. And he knew with a burning in his throat that this whole thing was a lousy, stinking setup; they'd been used for murder. He and Gary were just two more items—human weapons—in that arsenal back in the camp.

10

His feet thudded against grass and into mud, slipping on
rock. He splashed through water, cursing the branches whipping his face, and he breathed in and out the tiny gnats that
accompanied him in a foglike swarm. Sweat poured down his
body in rivulets and dragged clothing against his skin. The
spaghetti gun smacked against his arms and chest, the extra
magazines banged against his hips, and the gelpacks had
become dead weights that were getting heavier every minute. He ran across fields and into thick growth and along
trails, moving through the nocturnal mists like an animated
wraith, and all the time he ran he cursed, a steady, unrelent-
ing stream of quiet profanity. Ahead of him Mike rolled
through the night jungle and over the fields like a great
boulder, unstoppable yet fluid, carrying his heavy machine
gun with no more effort than he would carry lunch in a paper
bag. Behind Ron came Gary, more winded than the other
two, silent, sucking air through his nose and his mouth,
caring only about getting the hell out of this loathsome jungle. Gary remembered George's body whirling madly through
the air and the blood all over the bulldozer, and he thought
of traps and knives and a dozen ways he might be killed. He
focused on nothing more than following that giant who had
brought him here.

Ron didn't think that way. He ran behind Mike because
staying here would have been stupid, but for long moments
his eyes burned into the back of the man running before him

and he felt the urge to unleash a magazine into the son of a bitch. The girl. *The girl.* He wanted to scream and shout and shake the man's throat between his hands and kick the answer out of him. *The girl—where the hell is that girl!*

There hadn't been any girl. He could have asked for proof. He should have done that instead of swallowing—like some stupid country hick—the story of a kidnapped child told to him by men whose names he didn't even know, by strangers who toyed with the destinies and lives of other men simply to meet whatever killing purpose they had in mind. This was just that—an old-fashioned hit. Mike had gone into that hut and he'd wasted God knew how many people, men or women or kids or maybe some of each. Then his delayed charges had gone off, and he'd killed even more. There were going to be people with the skin burned off their bodies and their eyes flayed to searing hell, and *they'd* been killed only as a delaying action. They weren't even a target. They were convenient, like a smoke screen or a ditch or a fence of barbed wire.

And Ron and Gary had walked right into it. The whole thing had been a sham. Their call to arms, that rot about serving their country, the decency reaction to the plea to save the child. How could he have been so stupid, so blind? Look at that big son of a bitch. He was a killing machine, and he was running at a reduced pace so Ron and Gary could keep up with him. Why the hell did he need two people along to slow him down? Ron and Gary were liabilities. Mike was big and strong enough to carry enough weapons and explosives to tear that village to pieces and take off at a dead run and keep going all night like some fleet-footed water buffalo. So why did he need—

Because you two assholes are now full accessories to mass murder. Because you two dummies are as guilty as that big son of a bitch. You were there. You carried weapons. You're his witness to complete secrecy. No one can accuse him of doing what he did because you two won't admit, can't admit, you were involved, and so long as you need to keep your silence to protect yourselves, you've given him the perfect alibi. Just a long walk through a night in the Vietnamese jungle. Nice and calm and quiet, you stupid mothers.

Ron found it tough to turn off his mind this time, but he tried. He railed and cursed at that inner self that wouldn't let

go, that clung grimly to whatever knob of conscience bobbed
about within his skull, because the truth was that, no matter
how you cut this stinking mess, he and Gary were just as
responsible as the man who'd pulled the trigger of that machine
gun and set those flaming gelpacks and explosive charges.

There had never been a girl. Oh, those rotten sons of
bitches, they'd led Ron by his nose. Forget Gary, he's just a
follower, can't hold him responsible. But Ron was old enough
to shake the water off his own lily, and he didn't need anyone
to help him up and down with the zipper on his fly. It was
he, himself, who was the perfect asshole for this whole caper
because he could at least *think*. But those guys had played his
emotional strings as if he were some walking violin. What was
happening to him, to his reason, his humanity? Well, the girl
was a fake, but those dead people weren't. And this stinking
jungle wasn't any fake either. On top of all that, Ron was
losing his wind.

It was one thing to set a steady pace and hold it, but
Jesus, this was insane. Ron was five feet eight inches tall and
he weighed 160 pounds, which kept him in the lightweight
class next to Gary, and compared to Mike he was no bigger
than a bantam cock. He was wiry and as taut as spring steel,
but he simply wasn't in shape for this. They pounded along
and he had to run while the others held a steady trotting
pace. He couldn't even concentrate on what he was doing
because of the shame that burned within him, as if he'd
poured rotgut alcohol down his throat. It twisted his insides
and cramped his gut and made it tougher to run, and he
couldn't cleanse himself in any way because he couldn't shout
at Mike and he couldn't beat him half to death and he
couldn't shoot him; he needed the big bastard just to get back
to the coastline.

They ran well beyond the village until it flickered and
danced eerily on the horizon of the trees. They stopped by
the canal, which was at this point five feet from one side to
the other.

Mike pointed at the canal. "We cross here." His arm
lifted. "And then we move out that way. Stop gawking like
chickens. Jump this goddamned ditch now."

He spun about and his body was that of a huge tawny
cat, a mass of bone and muscle that levitated before their
eyes. Just like that he was on the other side of the ditch.

Gary ran back several steps, turned, and ran madly for the edge of the ditch, throwing himself across. He landed in a clumsy heap, but he'd made it. Ron also ran back and turned, steadying himself, judging the run he would need to make the jump. It was difficult getting a running start in this muck and in the dark, but he tried. He ran like hell and he jumped, and just as he made his leap, one foot twisted in sloppy mud beneath him and threw him off. He fell, cursing grandly, into the stinking mess of the canal. He would have sworn that Gary was grinning as he leaned forward and extended a hand. Ron reached up for the hand; God, he was pissed; he was burning with new shame. The water brought strange movements within his clothes and he knew he was host to hundreds of crawling insects. He could hardly bear his own stench. Rage swirled headily through his skull, but he forced himself to stay with the program—to get the hell out of here in one piece—and he braced himself, half turning, to set his feet for support and be hauled up by Gary's grip.

Half turned, looking back, his face went rigid, and in an instant rage was banished from him by an icy coldness that engulfed his body. He couldn't move; his eyes were locked in their sockets; his lungs were unmoving, his brain numb.

Frozen. Unreal. Staring.

Total shock.

There was the body of the girl. That eleven-year-old kid. Lying like a discarded rag doll on the side of the canal. Not in it, but on the side. She'd been there all the time. *Jesus, oh Mother of God* . . . He clambered through the filthy water and crawled and slid and struggled to reach the girl. His lungs were working now, and he sucked in air that went down into his lungs like burning sulfur. He heard Mike and Gary come toward him.

She was bleeding from her nose and her mouth and her ears and her eyes and between her legs and from her buttocks. They had raped her. God in heaven, they had raped her everywhere. Maybe all the men in that goddamned village. They had beaten her everywhere. They had kicked and punched out every tooth in her mouth, and when they'd rammed their organs into that bleeding orifice they ripped her lips and split them, and they'd grabbed her ears to hold her, leaving those ears ragged and mutilated and draining blood and yellow fluid. She was a mass of bruises and her groin was torn and bloody and Ron knew she was dead, please God, make her dead from what had happened to her. But she was breathing; with that first horrified look they knew she was alive. In a single motion the big man tossed his machine gun to Gary and reached down with an awesome tender strength to pick up that shattered little body in his arms. He never said a word, but he turned and he ran and jumped the ditch and they went after him, each man clearing the ditch easily. Mike was now running at a steady pace, Gary right behind, Ron taking up the rear guard position. They ran for two hours and the whole time Ron hoped and prayed that some of those filthy bastards from that village would come after them and he could use that killing thing in his hands. Something had snapped inside him.

11

It was more than running for safety or to get the kid back with the scant hope that they might save her life. It was broken field running in a hellish jungle forest along barely seen trails. Mike had warned them before they started about punji stakes with human excrement to penetrate the body and snares and pitfalls and every kind of vicious trap man could devise. So they ran carefully behind him, twisting and turning to follow the giant with the broken child cradled in his massive arms. Mysteriously, as if he could see things invisible to them, Mike would leave the trail and take thick forest or open fields to go around areas that he considered lethal. They had blisters all over their feet and they were covered with sweat; Ron's covering of human excrement from the canal was suffocating, oozing up into his nostrils. Then Ron almost ran into Gary. Both men before him had stopped.

Mike stood silent, studying the night, sniffing like a predator. He turned back to them, and his eyes were glowing like soft coals in the dark. He nodded to one side of the trail. Gary laid down the heavy machine gun and brought up his own weapon. Ron dropped to one knee and flicked off the safety on the spaghetti gun, holding it ready for anything. In that strange hazy night they finally could make out what Mike's experienced vision had shown him at once; the edge of another village. The world began to shimmer before Ron's eyes. *Another village. More of those murderous scum . . .*

"We got to get through the village," said Mike. "We can't

71

go around. They're set to bushwhack us on any trail we could take. It also means that every man who can fight is out in the jungle or set up for an ambush. The last thing they'll expect is for us to go right into that village and right on through it. We can't hide and we can't just walk. We punch through. Gary, you take this kid and you take her carefully." Gary put down his machine gun. Mike slung it over his left shoulder and held the heavy machine gun in both hands. He looked at Ron. "I'll be on the left and you hold position about twenty feet behind me on the right. Gary stays between us." He looked at Ron's weapon. "Use it. Use everything you got. It's our only chance."

They started walking through low brush, and suddenly they were on the hard-packed dirt of the village itself. Pale faces showed from behind a hut. This was it. The heavy machine gun crashed and thundered, and bodies tore apart and flew through the air. More forms moved in the darkness. For the first time in his life, Ron Previn squeezed a trigger to kill. The spaghetti gun screamed shrill under his hands, and he saw bodies toppling and jerking aside. He saw people running into huts and he sprayed the huts; he heard screams from within and knew those small and terrible slugs were cutting apart everything they touched. To his left and front, Mike moved slowly and steadily, the heavy machine gun a terrible scythe in his hands. When he ran his clip empty Ron took up the firing, and, that quick, Mike had reloaded. Ron grabbed gelpacks from his belt, pulled the timing detonators, and flung them to his side and behind them. Thirty seconds after each motion, flame mushroomed upward and sideways through the night. Everything that moved before them brought roaring blasts of death from their machine guns. Mike was lobbing grenades hard left and right of their pathway, well over the huts into the thick growth and the fields beyond. Ron felt wet things hitting his body and splashing against his face, and he thought they might be pieces of bodies, but none of it bothered him because between himself and Mike's killing form was Gary, walking absolutely erect with that child in his arms.

Then they were through the village, and no one moved before them or to their sides. Mike turned slightly and took a wide trail. He seemed to know that there would be no one to oppose them, but he played it extra safe, and if anything moved or twitched in that pale darkness it was answered with a short burst of machine-gun fire and a grenade that crashed well beyond them. Finally, he didn't fire any more. They slowed to a walk, and Ron noted with surprise that the sky was lighter; they'd walked right into the first light of day. Soon he could smell the salt of the ocean and then they emerged from the thick forest and into the camp they'd left that very same night. It might have been a hundred years ago.

News of whatever had happened during those incredible hours had reached the camp. Men rushed forward, and Ron recognized the same doctor who had pronounced George dead. The doctor paused a moment to study the little girl in Gary's hands, and Gary stood weeping, not saying anything. The doctor swore. He reached for the child as a jeep came roaring up from nowhere, and two men helped him into the vehicle. It drove off, not in that sand-spinning rush that jeeps usually make, but carefully, very carefully.

By the time Ron and Gary realized what had happened, the girl was gone. And so was Mike. He was nowhere to be seen, and they were never to see him again. Another man came to them, opened a bottle, and held it out to them. Ron wiped the sweat and dirt and stink from his mouth. He took the bottle and swallowed a half dozen times until he could feel the fire going along his throat and through his belly. He held out the bottle to Gary. "Here," he said.

Gary was like an automaton. The bottle came slowly to his lips and he drank a long, deep swallow. Then, as calm as you please, he eased his body to the ground, crossed his legs beneath him, and drained what was left. He sat stupidly, staring into space. Ron and the stranger picked him up. "This way," said the third man, leading them to a tent. By now Gary was glassy-eyed, and they laid him out on a cot. They looked at him for a while. He was asleep with his eyes open. The man leaned over and used his fingers to close Gary's eyes; then he stood. A shudder passed through him.

"I saw the kid," he said to Ron. "What in the name of God happened out there?"

"Shut the fuck up."

The silence held heavy. "You need sleep."

"Get me some whiskey."

"Will you stay here? I'll be right back."

Ron nodded assent and the man left. When he returned several minutes later with an open bottle, he helped Ron to the second cot. Ron sat on the edge and let the spaghetti gun slide to his feet. He took a long swallow.

"We'll keep someone in front of the tent so you won't be bothered. Can I get you something? Can I do anything for you?"

Ron looked up. His voice was quiet. "Get out."

"All right," the man said, and he was gone. Ron took another long swallow. It seemed a year before he could turn his body enough to lie prone. The bottle slipped from his hands and he heard whiskey gurgling to the tent floor. It was too far away and too heavy for him to retrieve it. He wanted desperately to slip into darkness. Sleep. Or unconsciousness. He didn't care. He didn't care if he never woke up again. His eyes blinked several times, and the sweat beaded on his lips and his face and pooled about his body. He realized the sun was up. He couldn't sleep, but he floated along in a bubble of illusion-reality, a strange out-of-body transport that glided through the past and in and out of the present but never quite cut the last fragile hold on this moment. The sun. Thank you for the sun. He could ride that golden light away from this stinking, terrible moment. Sunrise. Golden light washing down on the world.

Remember that other sunrise, Ron?

Remember it?

Remember it, Ron. Clasp it to you. That's it. That's it, fella, let it carry you. Ride the sun. Let it go, let it all go, man. Just let it all out. You want to wake up sane, you have to let go. Hang on to yesterday. Hang on to the sunrise. You remember . . .

The sun across the mountains was warm and friendly. He watched it spinning silent beams through the sloping hills, spilling and racing down the thick forest coverings. Far below, the valley lay wreathed in its early-morning mists, waiting for the sun to release the last shadows. He loved mornings like this, on the farm. People who didn't live here never really understood the beauty of the Catskills at such moments. Long ago this was Indian country, and he felt a kinship with those who had lived here and stood on this same hill. He was twelve years old and he would meet

Cynthia here in the mornings before they went to take the big yellow bus to school. Theirs was a wonderful shared secret: watching the sunrise together, while all across the fields and valleys they heard the crowing of cocks, the sounds of barnyards stirring and tractors coughing, and sometimes even the drumming hoofbeats of horses let out to pasture in the early morning. They would watch the sun climb the hills and spill gold down slopes and sides and flanks and then, because far in the distance they could see the dust following the yellow school bus, they would start together down the hill to join the other children, his hand in Cynthia's. It was a daring thing to hold hands, and his hand slipped in hers because of the blood pouring down her arm and he turned and watched in horror as her teeth flew in slow motion from her mouth and her lips split grisly and foaming and her clothes were ripped away and a frenzied maniac rammed his member into her anus and she screamed and . . .

Ron jerked upright on the cot, choking, coughing madly, his eyes burning with tears, one hand outstretched as he begged the nightmare to end. Gasping, he sat up. Drenched in his own perspiration and his stink, he swung his feet to the floor, groping for the bottle and bringing it to his lips, not caring or even feeling the dirt and the sand. The searing liquid poured into his throat and gut and blew away the last fog of that horrifying nightmare of then-now.

He didn't dare lie down. The nightmare hovered on the edge of his subconscious, waiting to snare him once again. He took another drink, and this time he held the fiery liquor in his mouth and swirled it about until finally he brought the fire down into him.

Who am I?

The question leaped unbidden to the forefront of his mind. *Who, indeed?* Well, that was a bunch of highfalutin shit. He knew damned well who he was. He was Ron Previn and he was five feet eight inches tall and he was 160 pounds and twice as strong as he should be for a man of his size; he came from upper New York State, and he was born in the late summer of 1943 on a farm in New Jersey, and he had a wonderful mother and a strong father; there was a whole bunch of blond and blue-eyed brothers and sisters, and in 1949 they moved from New Jersey into the Catskill Mountains in New York. What the hell was so unusual or wonder-

ful or special about that except that they were good people?
They didn't move to a city or a town but to a sprawling tract
of land without even a single shack on it. They lived in an old
school bus and they washed and bathed in a cold-running
stream, and his father was a master craftsman. Everybody
pitched in and with loving care they built their own white
two-story house of five bedrooms on the slopes of a hill that
looked across wonderful country. Ron Previn knew who he
was—a Norman Rockwell painting come alive, so goddamned
rural America that he was an intrinsic thread in the woven
tapestry of his land. His father earned his living as a carpen-
ter and his mother was a waitress, and all the kids did odd
jobs, ran errands, and learned how to hammer and saw and
nail and wire and weld.

Yet *he* was different. He'd always been different. The
one loner in the family pack who liked to cut and run through
the fields, mile after mile as he knew the Indians must have
run. He ran and walked and sat on the banks of rivers and
streams and chewed a long piece of straw; and he wondered
about things, even if answers were often wanting. *Who am I?*
The question shocked him because he thought of all his
friends from when he went to school and he was growing up,
and he couldn't remember any of them, not even Cynthia,
just a dim memory of holding hands and talking about what
they'd do when they grew up—and a kind of dim remembrance of the pain of losing her. Not a single solitary friend
had managed to survive that transition, that giant step from
boy to man. He had made the trip alone, he realized. Was
there a plank in the wall of his character that had been loose
all this time? Now, hovering between the safety of long
remembrance and the stalking insanity of accepting where he
was, stinking and sweaty and bloodstained on a beach in
some shit jungle called Vietnam, he wondered if there was
something missing in himself or twisted inside him that kept
him from seeing things clearly. What was so wrong in being a
loner? He'd tested himself. He would take to the fields with a
pack on his back and a .22 rifle in his hands and he could live
off that rifle and his backpack and his own lore. He'd learned
to hunt and even managed to kill game and skin and dress his
kill. He cooked and ate it because he would have gone
hungry for the week if he hadn't, and because it was a goal
he'd set for himself. He became a young Daniel Boone behind

a trigger, but he never abused that skill, and it never occurred to him to do so. And the killing always bothered him, even though it was for food. Now the thought calmed him, and he forced into sharper focus homelife, rural life, small villages, the farmhouses that dotted the hillsides, rested against the winding dirt roads, and every now and then gathered in little knots they called hamlets and centers. The houses were painted and sometimes weathered and lined up in a neat row. He could see them now, in his mind's eye, and the sight calmed him. He watched one house that fascinated and seemed to hypnotize him because the wooden shingles on the roof dissolved slowly and shimmered in that mind's eye until they came back into focus as the thatched covering of a hut, and he saw his own hand reach out and pull the detonating timers and fling the gelpack away from him, the thirty seconds already ticking, spilling down the hourglass of life-time-existence, and then the *WHUMP* of flame shooting outward and upward and the ripping explosion that etched the flame into anything and everything within its reach, as more gelpacks sailed away and flame blossomed, enormous red roses writhing upward. The spaghetti gun bucked and hammered in his hands, and bodies crumpled and were hurled backward and pieces of flesh smacked wetly against his face . . .

Look at the girl. Look at her. Don't blink your eyes, not here, not inside that damnable stupid skull of yours. Look at her on the ground and see what they did to her. A child, defenseless and helpless. Death would have been nothing, but they made sure she would feel it all until she was insane and she may be insane right now if she's fortunate.

Good. Oh, that's goddamned good; that blew away the nonsense in his mind, and there was that tiny picture of fire hissing about and through and enveloping a hut, and he was glad. The fire mushroomed silently in his mind's eye and it boiled all the way from one side of the sky to the other. Then it began to contract, narrowing down, roaring and thundering and hissing until it became a bright eye-stabbing light. He studied it carefully, squinting to see down the thought canal along which he was treading so carefully. There it was. A welding flame. A welder's torch. Ah, that was better. He was at home here. The welder's torch, cutting along metal, bonding metal, joining it together. A beautiful flame, strong, helpful, and Jesus, it looked just like the flame that came searing and hissing with a dragon's roar from a gelpack and it exploded in all directions and the night recoiled like a billion dark snakes and . . .

STOP IT! STOP IT, GODDAMN IT!

His fingers squeezed into his eyes and he rubbed furiously and sat up as if someone had jerked him upright by his hair. The flame was still there, but it was a welder's torch again, and there he was, see? He saw himself holding the welder's torch in his hands and he was building and creating things, and there was this pretty girl with brown hair, her name was Joan, and she stood in his backyard watching him as he assembled big metal objects from many small metal ones. She looked at him and smiled. "What are you doing?" she asked.

Jesus, she was pretty. Green eyes and pale red lips and a full bosom. She wore a starched white shirt that pulled back from her breasts, and it caught his eye. She lowered her eyes when she saw his look, but she smiled and that made it all okay. "Me?" he said. "Oh, what I'm doing. I weld," he said to her, brightening with every word because he saw she was really interested. "See this?" He held up the welder's torch. "It's like magic," he said to the lovely girl before him. "Really it is. It shapes metal and heats it so that it's soft and pliable, like putty. I love this. It makes my hands come alive, and I can make things." About him were beautiful works of art. He'd welded an airplane in a free-flowing sculpture because he loved flying—he'd learned in a wonderful yellow Cub. But he'd also made parts for cars and boats and gears for machinery, and he showed them to Joan. He wanted to show her more so that she wouldn't walk away, out of his life. "See? You hold it like this, and you open the flame . . ." Orange flame and blue flame. He laughed. "Look away because it can hurt your eyes." She waited. "All right. See how the metal glows now? For a little while it's soft, and this torch does it all. When you hold it this way it spits out hollow points at way better than a thousand feet per second, and it'll cut right through a stone wall and slice a human body in half on the other side of the wall like it wasn't even there, and you'd never realize a single round into a man's head can explode the eyeball and splatter brains for fifty feet in all directions, would you? and it makes whipping jelly out of a man's intestines and . . ."

NO! NO! NO! Think of Joan, you son of a bitch! He railed at his own weakness for slipping back to now, and he told Joan of all the marvelous things he was going to do, how he and his friend Henry were going to open a speciality company. "Artists in welding," he said to her, "and we'll create and build and make the world better," and it was the first time he'd felt anything for a girl since the long, slow sadness of Cynthia's dying and then missing her so. Now he felt that warmth that was love, and he thought again of all the beautiful things he could make for her with his welding torch and two hundred rounds in a single plastic magazine, and just throw it away after that tremendous explosive spray of killing machine-gun fire . . .

He slapped himself across the face. Hard. Again. His ears rang with the blows, but it pushed the other stuff back. He grabbed the bottle, but the goddamned thing was empty, and he let it slip from his fingers.

12

Gary cried out from his own tormented sleep, and that jerked Ron's attention to his friend. Which was just as well—there was no getting away from the nightmares. Ron thought back to how he had met Gary in the hiring office of Delco Marine. They were hired together after showing their stuff to a big black man. "My name's George," he told them. "You're the best I've seen in a long time, and I know because *I'm* just about the best." George grinned and they all shook hands. "Trouble is," George told them later over coffee, "you never know how long your job is here. Delco has contracts; they come and they go, and that's the way it is with people like us. They got a good contract, we got a good job. They got no contract, we got no job. Simple."

"Well, if that's the way it is," Gary had said, "why don't we pool our expenses, live together, and save everything we can, so that when we get our asses fired we won't be busted?" They thought that was a great idea, and they shared an apartment. They shared the cooking and the beer drinking, and they did pretty damned well. Sure enough, a contract came through from Delco Marine and they went right out with it. Then they got a job at Delco Remy and another at Chrysler Air Temp; later there were some steel mills, and pretty soon they'd earned a reputation as the best welding machine in the long stretch running from New York well into Ohio. But they didn't like bouncing from one job to another; it kept their lives jumbled, and they felt appreciation for their work was lacking. Then Ron saw the newspaper ad that would change their world forever. They called the number in the ad and made appointments for the following week. They went to the address in the ad, and they felt strange standing in an office with one desk, one chair, one telephone, and one man. That was all.

"Do you know where Vietnam is?"

Gary stared blankly. "Who?"

The man behind the desk, even sitting, was so tall and thin he seemed to sway with the slightest breeze. Ron almost laughed aloud. If anybody were trying to cast a true-to-life Ichabod Crane for a movie, they were missing out by not visiting this office. His name was almost as crazy. Art Hinkler. It might fit anyone else, but on this scarecrow it seemed ludicrous, almost fabricated.

But there was nothing wispy about his character. His eyes drilled into them before he spoke a word, and Ron felt as if he'd been stripped on an examining table and then permitted to stand again. It was unsettling. But Hinkler was patient as he watched the vacant stare on Gary's face.

"Not who. *Where*," Hinkler said.

"I know," Ron mumbled.

"What?"

Well, shit, two can play that game. "I said I know!" Ron shouted.

George winced, and Hinkler offered his own stare.

"You deaf?" Hinkler queried.

"No. You're just pushy," Ron told him, and he swore he could see the tic of a controlled smile on the man's face. "It's the old French Indochina, and it's on the coastline below China."

"How much else do you know about it?" said Hinkler.

"You got it," Ron said. "There's a lot of stuff in magazines and newspapers I remember about the French in a war there. The natives are supposed to be real special at jungle fighting, and they ran the French off."

Hinkler nodded. "True."

"*You* know much about the place?" Ron asked.

The eyes narrowed. "Enough. Why?"

"Just puzzled. Like I said, there was all this stuff about how the Indo-Chinese—"

"Vietnamese," came the correction.

"Whatever. But the papers said how wild they were and that they threw out the French. If they're so great, how come they didn't throw out the Japanese during the Second World War? I know about that because I had an uncle who was in Burma and he didn't think the locals were good enough to clean his shoes."

Hinkler leaned back. "We'll talk about it sometime. You guys here to answer the newspaper ad?"

George held it out. "This is the one, right?"

Hinkler didn't bother to look at it. "This is the one. I'll lay it out clean for you, but before I do, I want you to understand that this interview is confidential. If it goes well, you'll all have jobs before you walk through that door. Jobs with an ironclad contract and a security oath for your government. If you can't handle the oath, say so now. Once I start talking, you're bound to silence."

He looked at each man, one by one, and appeared satisfied with what he saw. "We're working with the government of South Vietnam. The country is carved into the North and the South. Like Korea. The North is Communist; the South works with us. We're there to bring out oil. It's as simple as that. Everything about this whole affair is in the best interests of your country, but for certain reasons that aren't important here we're not advertising what we're doing. I can't emphasize too much that the *why* really isn't your concern."

Ron shifted on his feet. "Is it clean?"

"Absolutely." Hinkler's response came immediately and without the slightest note of anything faked. "It's clean, it's legal. You won't be asked to do anything against any law, ours or anyone else's. We're hiring good men to go to Vietnam to teach the natives how to handle equipment, how to weld, how to lay oil pipelines and keep them running. We also want men there who can do the work themselves in an emergency. Our office is in Lima, not far from here. You interested?"

George gestured. "You don't do the hiring?"

"Uh uh. Just the firing."

"You mean you're passing on us one way or the other, right?"

"Right."

"We pass?"

"You pass. You're exactly what we need."

"You seem sure of that," Ron said, "without knowing very much about us."

"We know more about you already than your mother does, Previn. You and your friends. This interview is over. Deal?"

They dealt. Damned right they dealt this hand. It was the answer to all their hopes and dreams. They went to an office in Lima, Ohio, that could have been any office. It sold tractors and farm equipment. That's what the signs said, anyway.

They filled out forms, and they were questioned by a woman who filled out her sweater so well that they were hard pressed to pay attention to what was going on. But she took their forms, and they relaxed, smoking cigarettes until they were called into a private office furnished with thick carpeting and plush sofas. A big man was seated behind a desk. He wore a dark suit and a thin tie and looked as if he didn't care about *anything.*

"You're in," he told them without salutation. "You're down on paper, and you know all about the security oath you signed. From this moment on, you have no contact with anyone." He held up a meaty hand to forestall the expected complaints. "We'll get in touch with your families or anyone else you want, but *we* do the explaining. It will be clean and warm and polite, or however you want it, but we do it. From this moment on, you're working. If anyone presses you, you're working for Arizona Mining and you're on a geological survey, and that's all you say, and whoever presses we want to know who they are, and right away. Got it? We'll take care of all your bills and all your needs. Let me review. You're under contract for one year minimum. You get thirty grand each and you get to keep it all. No expenses and no taxes and that includes clothes, food, medicine, or whatever. You'll go to—"

Ron waved his hand in the air. "I don't care if it's the Gobi Desert or the Antarctic."

"You're sure of that?"

"Man, we could work our asses off all our lives and not come back with what we get with you for one year. Damn right I'm sure."

The big man stood up and smiled. "Then all you need to do is go through that door to your left. Good luck."

And they'd gone—without asking a single question.

They had walked across the thick carpet and stepped through the door to another world. Four hours had passed from the moment they entered the "farm tractor sales office" until they left. A station wagon waiting outside drove them to an airfield they didn't recognize. "One thing's for sure." Gary had spoken after a long silence. "I don't know where we are or who flies those planes," he said, pointing to rows of large transports, "but they're military."

"No markings," George corrected him.

"But he's right," Ron said. "They painted over the markings. You can see where if you look hard enough."

George looked. "You're right. Cargo ships, but they could be anything. You can tell by the doors."

"Tell what?" Gary asked.

"They got both types. Jump doors for paratroopers and big doors for loading heavy cargo."

The station wagon pulled up by a battered old twin-engine ship, its cockpit high in the air and its tail close to the ground. "Gooney Bird," Ron muttered. "Jesus, they must be running anything they can get into the air for this job."

Indeed they were. They didn't fly west to Asia. George spotted that first. "Look at the sun. Sure as hell we're going the long way around to get to this place. We're flying to the northeast. Sure as shit ain't to the west."

They fell asleep, woke up in Canada, and moved groggily into a mess hall on a field where they couldn't see anything. They ate and were issued cold-weather clothing, and then they were led to another airplane—this one with four big engines—standing on tricycle gear. They took off in darkness and fell asleep again and when they awoke a crewman brought them doughnuts and hot coffee. They looked down on a canopy of thick clouds. They could have been anywhere. They asked the loadmaster where they were. "Shangri-la," he said with a thin smile. "Sorry, guys. Orders are no questions and no answers."

"You got any cards?" Gary asked.

"Coming up."

For the next seven hours they played hearts and ate

sandwiches and drank coffee. The loadmaster came back. "We're going down," he said. "Buckle up."

Gary looked doubtfully at the clouds alive under the moon. "What the hell's down there?"

"A field, I hope," came the answer, and he was gone. They felt the power coming back and the props changing pitch and then they were in the soup and being bounced around. They felt the flaps grinding down, the gear clunking into down-and-locked, and then a squeal of rubber on hard surface. They looked through the windows, and in the first light of day they could see mountains and snow and ice. "Jesus Christ," Gary said, "I think we must be near the North Pole." Already ice was forming on the windows and the wings.

They didn't leave that plane for three days. Doctors came aboard, examined them, and stuck needles in their arms until they were dizzy and groggy from all the shots; other men brought them green jungle fatigues and thick-soled boots. They slept on cots aboard the plane and they used the plane's bathroom facilities and they ate meals cooked on the plane. They watched men loading generators, welding equipment, refrigerating units, cables, tools, and unmarked crates. And no one told them a thing. On the morning of the third day, thunder hammered at them and they rushed to the windows and stared at a dozen jet bombers, painted dull black, all of them emerging from some invisible cover on the airfield. The giant black ships lined up at runway's end and poured back thick black smoke, and the thunder rattled the earth and sky and vibrated through their own plane. Then the jets were all gone.

An hour later another flight crew came aboard, the loading doors were sealed, and they were told to belt in. The big transport groaned with the weight of its cargo as it wheeled to its take-off point, and they looked with misgivings at a leaden sky above them. Minutes later the world was turbulent gray, and rain slashed at the plane. They broke out finally on top of a white cloud mass, white below and blue sky above, and the only way they knew in which direction they were headed was by the sun. Hour after hour of fitful catnapping and coffee and sandwiches and pinochle and gin and hearts, and then they were on their way down again.

"We're in Canada," Ron told the others. Easy enough to

tell. Radar installations, missile sites, fighters and bombers with Canadian markings. American planes. Others without markings, gray and black and not a number anywhere. They tried to leave the plane but were told politely and firmly—at gunpoint—to remain where they were. They didn't stay long. Just enough to refuel and change crews. But they had enough time to figure it out.

"It's like the Berlin Airlift," Ron decided. "Look at the way those planes are lined up." He pointed to a long row of transport planes that went on until they simply faded from sight. "I can tell some of them. Globemasters over there. And Skymasters. Jesus, they got Connies and—" He shook his head. "It looks like they're moving everything they can fit into these things."

They slept for the next eight hours, landed at a desert field that was surrounded by mountains, refueled, and took off again. Ron recognized the lights of San Francisco far below them. "The Pacific this time. A dime gets you a buck the next place we see is Honolulu."

It was. They landed on a remote field in the Hawaiian Islands, took on more fuel and a new crew, and were back in the air an hour after their wheels touched the ground. They saw other transports landing, refueling, taxiing, taking off; they caught sight of them in the air, a loose and far-stretching stream of winged metal beating its way across the Pacific. Another island below them, waves breaking across a coral reef, and another landing. This time four armed men came aboard the transport and remained aboard when they once again thundered into the air. They didn't care. They were punch-drunk with engine roar and propeller vibration and living more than a week inside metal cocoons. They were asleep when the transport landed a final time.

When they finally stepped off the plane, they stepped outside to a different planet.

13

Hot. Sticky. Eye-stabbing sunlight.

My ears! My God, they hurt. I've been hearing engines for a solid week, all that prop noise banging off the sides of the cabin; I feel like I'm deaf. Whoof; my ears feel like I'm a hundred feet underwater.

It's tough breathing. What the hell is this? My nostrils are clogged. I don't understand what . . .

Tiny insects, like gnats. What they call see-me-nots in the States. There were millions of them, and the guys who'd been here a while called them shitflies. They drove in a swarm about a man's head, clogged up his nose and his ears, sat on his eyeballs, and flew into his mouth. If you took a breath a cloud of them flew into your mouth and went down your throat and into your lungs. They were like a mist. Evading them was like trying not to breathe water vapor in a fog.

Gary swatted wildly and ineffectively. George was more of a survivor. He grabbed a man who was standing near the plane. The man wore a stupid-looking rag on his head, the four corners tied in knots. "What's that do?" George asked.

"You soak it in kerosine and wear it on your head, and the shitflies don't bother you none," came the reply.

Score one for the first survival lesson. Everything was a bit confused for a while. Someone tossed their duffel bags to them, and they walked to a large square building made of galvanized tin that reflected sunlight painfully. Inside, the

87

place was steaming. Someone led them into an office where the air conditioning was blessed relief. A military man sat behind a desk. They noticed he had no insignia, just a uniform without a mark on it. He picked up a clipboard. "Names?" he asked.

They told him, and he made check marks and pulled folders from his desk. He made a terse phone call, hung up, and studied them. "A jeep will be here in a few minutes to pick you up. Welcome to 'Nam. The dancing girls are great." It wasn't difficult to figure he'd been here for some time.

When they went outside again they felt the renewed impact of their new home. Stepping out from the arctic office air only made the heat worse. The packed dirt beneath them scuffed up the dust. They had been so sun-blinded when they first came off the plane that they hadn't noticed how muggy, humid, and hazy it was. Visibility was lousy. It was like being in the Big Smokies, in a funky blue haze with rippling waves of heat. And the swarms of bugs were already driving them to near distraction.

"You know," Ron said slowly, "what's always going to stay with me as my first impression of this place?"

"The bugs," Gary said flatly.

"I'll try the heat," George offered.

Ron shook his head. "Uh uh. None of that. Stop for a moment. Now, sniff. Smell it? It stinks here. A stink of rot. Wet jungle rot, like opening up an old tree trunk that's been lying on the ground for twenty years and stuffing your nose in the middle of it."

"You ought to write folders for the chamber of commerce." Gary grinned at him.

They broke off conversation as a jeep pulled up. A man in a T-shirt and a hard hat stopped before them. "You the three guys just got in?"

"We win the raffle," George said. "You come for us?"

"Yeah. I'm with the oil company."

"Which one?" Ron asked. "There's a dozen of them here."

"Don't matter none. They all work together. Hop in. Toss your gear in the back."

They were driven to their huts. The driver explained how the system worked. "We fly these to the base camp by chopper. The heavy gear gets trucked in to you. Right now, stow your stuff. Pick the hut you want, then c'mon back right away. It's time to get you guys started. We're way behind schedule."

A tall black man who was built like a tree trunk met them in an orientation room. "Name's Dudley. Walt Dudley," he told them, shaking hands all around. "I brief you, tell you what you need to know, answer your questions. Okay? Let's get started. First, you're here to weld pipeline and to teach the gooks how to weld more pipeline. We're not looking for anything pretty. No inspections. We ain't got time for no pretty shit. We want lines that carry oil, and if they leak a bit we don't care. You can lose 10 percent of the crude those lines carry and the other 90 percent makes you heroes. The lines you got to extend are already six miles long. We want 'em longer for some wells we got inland. We need to keep things moving, like I said, so as fast as you need pipeline we bring it to you by them choppers. You lay five sections at a time and you lay them on steel cradles. You got any bad bumps or depressions, you straighten it out with a dozer blade." He looked up. "I haven't checked your papers. Any of you guys good with a dozer?"

Gary raised his hand, and Dudley nodded. "Okay, that takes care of that. The next thing is to pick up where the crew working here—before you—left off."

"What happened to them?" George asked heavily.

"They couldn't take the heat, the bugs, and the country." Dudley said it matter-of-factly. It was obvious he hadn't thought much of the crew. "All that counts is that you're here." He glanced at his watch. "Okay. Now we watch movies for a couple of hours."

Ron peered at him through narrowed eyes. "What kind?"

"You'll love 'em. Especially the one on snakebite. Did they tell you they got some kinds of snakes over here that the snakebite kits don't work on?"

Gary was gray. "No, they didn't. What kind are they?"

"Hit and run."

"What the hell kind is that?"

"Snake hits you and he runs like hell because you're gonna fall over dead before you can take one single step. The snake don't want you falling on him, see? But there are other kinds against which the kit works pretty good."

"You mean," George said with arched brows, "if we're lucky, we get bit by the *right* kind of snake?"

"Uh huh." The words came with a broad grin.

"Sounds to me," George went on, "a machete is the best kind of snakebite kit there is."

"Sure," Dudley said. "A machete or a shotgun. You kill the fucker before he nails you; even the best of them are lousy."

"Charming," Ron muttered.

Dudley thought the remark was hilarious. "Okay, couple of things before we go on. Later we'll check you out in some six-by-six trucks. The road going out to your work site is pretty well overgrown by now. Been a while."

"How much is a while?" Ron pressed.

"Too long. Come on, guys, we got a lot to cover. Let's stay with it, okay? The one thing I want to warn you about is worse than the snakes. You get machetes and medical kits for them, but for this other problem, you got to use your noodle." Dudley leaned forward, and there was no question about how serious he was. "Watch who you mess with in this camp. I don't mean the company people; they're okay. I'm talking about most of the workers we got here. They're trash. The bottom of the barrel. We need a lot of bodies to do basic work. You know, ditchdigging and garbage detail shit. We got people here who'd cut your throat for a nickel. Don't go around this camp at night on your lonesome. Do it in pairs, or even better, make sure everyone knows the three of you are a team who watch out for one another."

"Sounds a lot like Harlem," George observed.

"Worse." Dudley and George exchanged glances. That was good. Heavy eye contact said more than words. "There's a lot of guys here who are the fucking lowest. We got them from the bottom of God knows what barrels. Roustabouts. Itinerants. Ain't got no fucking brains and they'll steal anything that ain't nailed down. So don't leave nothing lying around. Don't get into any card games with anyone you don't know. That could be trouble."

Ron shook his head and smiled. "A real high-class hotel."

"Yeah."

"Anything else before the movies start?"

"Yeah. Don't ever drink any water here."

"That mean bottled water also?" Gary asked.

"That means any kind of water. There's no water here that's fit to drink unless you, personally, boil the absolute living hell out of it, and even then *I* wouldn't drink it. We carry guys out of here all the time who drink the local water and they come down with stuff no one can even identify. Drink beer. Got it? Beer. You can drink all the beer you want when you're working and you won't get drunk. The temperature out there is a hundred and twenty or thirty and the stuff goes through you as fast as you take it in. You'll sweat and piss like warthogs, but it's safe."

They wore head rags soaked in kerosine. They checked out on the trucks and the dozers, and they made a meticulous inspection of their welding gear. They got more shots, briefings, and lectures, and each went through his expected period of the screaming trots, remaining within thirty seconds flat of the nearest john. The helicopters carried their gear and their huts to the remote work site, and they got radios and medical kits and snakebite kits and identification charts of venomous and otherwise deadly creatures. They were instructed in basic sign language to deal with the Vietnamese who'd come to the camp to be trained in welding the pipelines. They confirmed why Dudley didn't want to waste time talking about how long the job had been abandoned. The elephant grass on the old trail towered twenty feet above ground—the trucks knocked it down in waves just getting to the site. "That tells us something," George noted. "Whoever was working this job got scared so bad no one else would come out here. You could say we're the advance troops of the new wave."

They made camp and discovered the small joys Dudley hadn't bothered to describe. At first they saw hardly any mosquitoes and counted themselves fortunate, but after they'd clanked about in the bulldozers and churned up the boggy ground, and after the first rain ended, they were enveloped in thick clouds of buzzing and snarling creatures endowed with long needles that could pierce clothing. They sighed, wore more kerosine-soaked rags, and splashed the kerosine on their clothes; it seemed to help.

They were *not* prepared for other visitors: inch-long black and brown creatures with white stripes running along their bodies. They came out of the ground and crawled up

legs and clothes, they fell from trees, they crawled into shoes
and beds, and if you left so much as a scrap of food, anywhere, you were asking for an invasion. The Vietnamese
leeches. They were like an inexorable tide that came out of
nowhere and everywhere, covering tables and chairs and
forming mosaics of black-brown-white whenever they could
pick up the scent of something edible. The men got used to
their uninvited guests—they never sat down until they banged
a chair against the ground or kicked a table, and they never
sat down to relieve themselves without checking everything
first. The leeches were bad enough, but you never knew
when a black mamba could also be there; one nip from that
mother and you'd be dead before your face whacked into the
ground.

"You know what this is? It's what we call string cable. I'll
say it slowly, so you'll understand, okay?" Ron wiped sweat
from his upper lip, rolled his eyes upward as a signal to
George and Gary, and turned patiently back to the Vietnamese
laborers who watched him with an improbable mixture of
stoicism and interest. "St-rinnng ca-ball. Got it? No? Well,
shit, it ain't because I ain't trying." Ron quit using words and
resorted to pointing and touching objects as he identified
them by name. The Vietnamese walked along, touching when
he did, trying to mouth the words. After a while, Ron said to
hell with it. Let it come slowly. *He* couldn't plow a field for
shit with a water buffalo.

He tried again the next day. "Okay, that's a cable reel
over there." He went to the huge cable roll, as big as a
bedroom, then tapped the cable. "We get the juice from the
base camp through this cable. Electricity. What makes lights
go on and off. Shitfire, I forgot, you guys don't have electricity, so how the hell can you know what I'm talking about? All
right, let's keep moving. See this thingumajig here? It's what
we call a stinger handle. That's right, pick it up. Get the heft
of it." He waited as each of the fourteen men shuffled forward
to pick up the welding stinger, heft its weight, feel the grab,
then pass it on silently to his neighbor.

"Watch me, now. *Watch me*. That's it." He motioned
the Vietnamese closer. "Okay, you take this stinger handle,
and when you're electric welding, you have two cables; you
have a ground and you have a stinger." He ran his gaze from
one impassive face to another. "Means a whole hell of a lot,

doesn't it? Maybe I'll get friendly with a water buffalo. All right, take a closer look at the stinger cable." He held it up for all to see. "It's about five-eighths of an inch in diameter. It's made of black rubber, with some chemicals in it. Inside this rubber is very fine braided copper wire. Now, how do you weld the pieces together? It's easy. You do it one at a time. Okay? You take a piece of pipe, like over here. It's twenty-one feet long, and we set it on these cradles so it will be level. It's four feet in diameter in some places, and other pipes are two feet in diameter. That's because someone screwed up and sent two different sizes. Watch what I'm doing, that's what counts.

"The next big question is where do you weld this stuff, and how do you weld together two completely separate pieces of pipe? What do you call this kind of welding?"

George's voice came from the side. "I would call it lousy honkie welding."

Ron looked up. "Honkie or nigger or gook, it's lousy welding. Shut up, George, they all think I'm smart. Okay, you guys. You bring two pieces of pipe together, and now we come to the best part. It's called arc welding. We melt metal together where the pipes join, so that when the metal cools it's all one big connected unit. You take these two pieces of pipe and butt them together. Some pipes fit one into the other, but not this shit. It's butted one end against the other, see? You bring them in close, and you take welding rods and put four of them, one on each half of the pipe, like this, see? Four of them into each half of the pipe, so you got a three-thirty-second gap, then you take that welding rod—here it is. It's a piece of steel about thirteen inches long. This steel has flux on it, and then the electrical charge comes into the steel. It's like taking two fingers and sticking them into an electrical socket."

"They don't know what that is, Ron," Gary said.

Ron ignored him. He was afraid if he stopped he'd never pick up momentum. "You set up your electrical charge, you have your contact, and that gives you a complete circuit. When you complete the circuit you create an arc. That's like a super spark. You melt a piece of metal—we're actually melting steel rod—into the steel pipe to form what we call a bead of weld.

"In other words, fellas, it would be a lot like taping it

together by wrapping tape about the butted ends of these pipes, except that our tape is metal and we're welding it all together. We make one pass around it—" While Ron spoke, his hands brought the machinery alive, and flame hissed and sparks flew, "and we make a Z weave. That's to keep the pressure inside the pipe from blowing the first time they send something flowing through this thing. Everything nice and clear. Jesus Christ, I need a beer."

Later, they reviewed their teaching techniques. "Don't kid yourself," Ron told George and Gary. "Those little fuckers are a lot smarter than they showed us."

"They did a lot of smiling and headshaking, but no talking," Gary reminded him.

"So what? They can't speak English, and we can't handle their lingo, so one's just as dumb—or smart—as the other. They smile a lot when we're teaching them. That ain't being dumb, it's being polite. They understand, they nod. They don't understand, they shake their heads. What they don't do is stay blank. They're picking it up, and I'll tell you something. Once you show them, slow and in detail so they can follow what you're doing, you never have to show them again. You remember that guy in the yellow shirt? One will get you ten he can handle that stinger all by his lonesome tomorrow. He had his eyeballs glued to everything I did today and he didn't miss a trick."

"He's right, man," George added easily. "They're smart. More than smart, they *work*. Couple times today I tried to move some pipe that was too damned big for me, and I hollered for help, and three of them little guys come running right over, and they know just what I need and they do it, just like that. They figure it all out in a couple of seconds." George sucked deep on a cigarette. "Do as much work as a big man. How'd you like to work barefoot or in sandals like them? You see those little guys burn their feet today? Shit, they're either barefoot or wearing grass slippers, stuff made from dried leaves. Sneakers is like heaven to them. I wish we could get them shoes."

The thought sobered them. Those crazy slippers were dangerous. Sometimes they caught fire right on the feet of the man wearing them. If they got smart and took off their slippers, that left their feet exposed, and once in a while a big piece of slag fell from a pipe. The stuff was red-hot molten iron and those poor bastards would step right on it. Jesus, it was hard to believe, but the soles of their feet were so thick that the tissue along the bottom of their feet *just burned*. The flesh was literally burning, and there'd be a god-awful stench, but the Vietnamese didn't bat an eye because he never felt any pain! When it was over, the molten slag had simply burned a hole into the foot, through that dark skin, as if it had been an old tire.

The Vietnamese thought the reaction of the Americans was humorous. But when George and Gary secretly welded Ron's steel-tipped shoes to a section of pipeline while Ron was engrossed in his teaching, they howled with open laughter as Ron tried to walk from his position and fell flat on his face. It was a moment of sharing, a lighter side they rarely showed. Unfortunately, it was just one moment—not a pattern.

Then the "new phase" began. Their Vietnamese friends, somber or smiling, failed to appear for work.

Equipment, tools, clothing, and other materials "disappeared" from the job site. Phantoms prowled the camp at night. Finally the generator and its bright light died and the bat-sized moths careened blindly through the field site.

They were cut off from the base camp. Then came that morning when George clipped the welding stinger to the pipe to short out the system so they could notify base that they needed assistance.

His mutilated body flip-flopped through the air and George bled to death on that pounding bulldozer plunge back to the coastline. And they buried him with their bare hands.

They've kidnapped a young girl. We're afraid what they might do to her. Will you help us? Don't you want to get even with them for George?

The long march through the night jungle. Ripping bursts of machine-gun fire, exploding gelpacks, the breast-heaving run through the night, splashing in that fetid canal.

The horror of finding the child in the dark. Raped, beaten, tortured, mutilated, savaged. Saving her life.

Tearing the village before them to shreds. Killing, maiming, destroying. He had never killed anyone in his life. Not before now.

And now he was a killer. Maybe, deep down, he was the same Ron Previn, but up front, here and now, he was a killer.

Mother of God . . .

*   *   *

They sat before the two men in their white shirts and slacks and gleaming shoes. Ron savored the deadly calm that had finally enveloped him. "I have questions and I want answers," he told them.

They nodded. "We know you had a tough night. But you saved that girl—"

"Stow it," he told them tersely. "That's history. Yesterday or a year ago doesn't matter. It's all behind me. I want some answers about tomorrow. Do you level or don't you?"

Nothing had changed. Al remained a numb-lipped dummy and Harry did the talking. "We'll level."

"I don't care about getting even. That's horseshit," Ron said slowly. "I want to know other things. I don't know who the hell you two are. I don't know who you work for. I don't know who I killed for. I don't know the name of the man who's president or king or whatever of this goddamned country. I've never *talked* with a Vietnamese. I've got to do that. I want to hear from one of them why we're doing this. I want to know what happens to me, why I should decide to stay here, or why I go home after everything that's happened."

"You can go home if that's what you want. If you break your contract you don't get paid. But you did a mission for us. We pay for that. Give thousand cash. No taxes, no questions."

"I want information," Ron said. "Then I can decide. I already know you want me to work for you. Not with a welder. With that spaghetti gun."

"That's right."

"That's all you're going to tell me?"

"That's all for now, Previn. You just set the rules, remember? You want information. You want to know what we're doing here, why you should stay, why you should work for us. Okay, by your rules, then. We'll set up a face-to-face with Ty Pum An."

"Who the hell is he?"

"A major. Vietnamese. He speaks his own mind. Now I have one question."

"Shoot."

"What about Gary?"

Ron turned to his friend and his eyes asked the question.

Gary nodded slowly. "He decides for the both of us."

Ron turned back to Harry. "When?"

"Now. The jeep's outside. Let's go."

14

They drove in silence for nearly an hour until they came to a military compound. Barbed wire stretched everywhere. Machine-gun towers loomed every three hundred feet. The place swarmed with armed men, and they saw tanks, tracked vehicles, helicopters, trucks, all kinds of powerful weapons. Four heavily armed men, two American and two Vietnamese, examined them closely. Harry showed his wallet to the first American. A barricade went up, and they drove inside and parked next to a tent. Harry turned to Ron. "The tent's a cover. There's an underground bunker inside. Major An is waiting for you; we spoke with him by radio. We leave you here. I don't want to influence in any way what happens between you and the major. When you're through, Major An will drive you back to our camp. Good luck."

He didn't offer to shake hands. Ron climbed from the jeep, Gary following slowly. Harry and Al waited until they went inside the tent, then drove off.

Several men who were armed with automatic weapons studied them. These men were short and wiry, a kind of Vietnamese Ron hadn't seen before this moment. "Please. Your hands in the air," one soldier asked. They were frisked swiftly and efficiently. The same man motioned. "Follow me, please," and they went down a flight of roughhewn stairs into an area where a single light bulb glared from a wire coiled down from the ceiling of thick timbers. The place smelled of human sweat and the jungle. Radio gear lined one wall, telephone switchboards filled another. The third was jammed with weapons. The fourth wall held a desk and several chairs, and behind the desk sat a lean, hawk-faced Vietnamese in a major's uniform. He rose to meet them, clasping hands with a grip Ron found astonishingly strong. Ron's own was the same, and the two men shared an immediate smile. Sometimes, thought Ron, being a lightweight as an American can have its advantages. He had a hunch that Major Ty Pum An was going to be somewhat looser in his mental posture than before he'd met Ron face-to-face. He was polite but somewhat distant with Gary. Men like An, mused Ron, size up their opposites at once. Gary was a follower; therefore An dispensed with any need to be more than polite.

Moving with quick nervous energy, An poured scotch into two tin cups for his guests. Ron took the chance to study the strange little man. His uniform was surprisingly neat; Ron spotted the old-line soldier's trick of sewing creases into trousers and shirts. The man cared for himself; that was a good start. Ron looked around the bunker. Every weapon gleamed. Another good point. A hunter takes care of his dogs before his guns, and a killer takes care of his guns before anything else. He was dealing with a professional.

"Your friends have spoken to me," An said without preamble, "about your problem. I will be glad to answer any of your questions. You may be as blunt as you wish. There is no false ego within these walls."

"Thank you. I'll be as frank as I can. Just coming here," Ron said, his eyes moving about the room, "tells me as much as any conversation. Something's wrong here. This is more than a military outpost. This place is a fortress, and I'm sure there's a lot more to this than I can see."

An nodded but kept his silence.

"Okay," Ron said with a deep breath. "I came to this country, major, to weld pipeline and to teach. I never wore a uniform in my life. I don't belong to any organization, unless," he broke into his own stride, "you want to count the Boy Scouts." He saw An's touch of a smile. "The point is, I was teaching the Vietnamese. Your people. Damned nice people, too. I can't handle their language and they didn't speak English, but we got along just fine. I mean that; we did. They learned fast. After a few lessons they handled tools and equipment better than I would have believed possible. And then—" he shrugged, "it began."

"It?" An echoed.

"Yeah. It," Ron repeated. "All of a sudden things started disappearing from the camp. Men who I considered to be straight out started stealing things. Tools, gasoline, equipment. And then they tried to kill us. They killed our best friend. George was a black man."

"I know," An said. He had made a steeple of his fingers and was observing Ron through his hands.

"He was a kind and gentle person who really tried to help those who came to him," Ron went on. "So they smiled to his face, and they booby-trapped our equipment, and they blew George into big bloody chunks." Ron pressed fingers against the headache that had leaped behind his eyes. "Okay, okay. It happened. Then we get this story about a kidnapped girl, and the two men who brought us here need our help. I thought we'd been suckered, but it turns out to be true; we found that girl and got her back and—"

An's hand went up. His voice was very soft. "And saved her life. I don't know if you were told that."

Ron showed confusion. "I'm not sure."

"Be certain, then. She is alive, and most important, her mind will heal as well as her body. The doctors have reassured her parents that the girl is responding well to treatment. She is able to talk about what happened to her. That is an extraordinarily good sign."

"Yeah, sure," Ron said impatiently. "But in the process, this big guy, Mike, he chewed up a village, and to get back to our camp the bunch of us had to tear up *another* village, and God only knows how many people we killed—" He stopped at the look on Major An's face.

"Some things are necessary. What you did was necessary. Many Vietnamese died. My people. But it was still necessary. You are blaming yourself, my friend. It is false guilt." The major was not smiling. "What was done to the young American girl should not have happened. What was done to save her was necessary."

"I can buy that," Ron said through his headache. "But damn it, we did a number on those two villages. I don't know how many we killed or—"

"Two hundred and fourteen dead."

Ron and Gary stared, speechless. A strangled sound came from Gary. "My God," he said finally.

"You must understand," the major said. "It is not simply numbers of dead. All things die. But that child was no one's enemy. She was mutilated and tortured as an object lesson. Yet even that is not so simple. If the girl had not been raped by the men of that village, then all the women of that same village would have been raped and abused by those of us who wear black."

"What?" Ron sounded foolish and he knew it.

"The guerrillas. The Cong. Those who live in our midst and do the bidding of Hanoi. They ordered the American child kidnapped and raped. If those orders had not been followed—" He shrugged, not finding it necessary to repeat what he had already said.

"I'll be damned if I understand," Ron said angrily.

"It is never simple," came the response. "You will hear much talk about self-government and communism and Saigon, our capitol, and Hanoi, and of the Cong and the regulars and the Army of Vietnam, and of the advisers from your country who are here, and of secret organizations, but it all comes down to a simple matter. You may spell it in one word, Mr. Previn. That word is *oil.* It is the dominating theme of everything that happens here. Your country needs oil. We walk on a vast sea of underground oil. We are willing to sell it to your government. To exchange it for weapons, technical assistance, training—everything we need to remain free of being taken over by the North. You support us, by our invitation. Make no mistake about that.

"But the Russians, and the Chinese, want very much to prevent that oil from getting to the United States. They cannot stop us directly. Therefore they pour weapons and money into the North, and they use terror as a weapon to break us apart. They have no scruples. They will do anything. Any horror, any atrocity to force our people not to resist them and even actively to support them. There are no rules to this kind of fighting. And it is difficult not to fight them on the same terms, for whom do we fight? They live among us and are a part of us."

Ron stared for a while before responding. "It sounds impossible."

"Nothing is impossible. Horrifying, perhaps," An said

with a thin smile, "and frustrating, and lethal, but not impossible. It is also very difficult because of the false front we must show to the world. Our face cannot be one of open cooperation with your country."

That remark galvanized even Gary into verbal reaction. "But why not? Why all the secrecy?"

Major Ty Pum An's look was one almost of pity, yet there was also scorn. "You are an American. You fought—your people fought in Korea," he corrected himself. "No state of war was ever declared by your Congress. Ah, but more than fifty thousand Americans died there. Do you know why?"

"Well, it's obvious," Gary said uncomfortably. "I mean, the North Koreans attacked—"

"Whom did they attack?" came the interruption.

"Why, the South Koreans, of course!"

"Of course," An said silkily. "Then why did you fight there? They did not attack *you*, the Americans."

"The hell they didn't!" Gary said hotly.

"Very good. Now, why did they attack the Americans?"

"Well, we were there; I mean, we were occupying South Korea, and we were going to give them their freedom, and—"

An was relentless. "And when it was all over after years of fighting, with punitive forces from that maggot they call the United Nations, what was the result? The lines were almost the same, were they not? The thirty-eighth parallel, ah, a wonderful demarcation. The Mason-Dixon Line of Asia, it might be called. If you were there to free the Koreans, my young friend, why did you quit?"

"The Chinese, they wanted to talk peace, and there was an armistice—"

"And you think that the tungsten mines just north of the thirty-eighth parallel, which were occupied by the Americans just before the armistice, had nothing to do with the final deciding line?"

Silence. Gary had never even heard of tungsten mines in Korea.

"It is much the same here," An said wearily. "Your government must work with us in covert operations. Your Congress would never permit another Korea. Fifty thousand dead Americans is not good for election. So your government, who understand all this, work with us and help us secretly. America needs oil. We have it. We need your weapons and your guidance. The Communists intend to prevent either side from gaining what they want and need. It is no more complicated than that."

"That's hard to believe," said Gary.

"I am a military man and a student of military affairs," An told him. "I studied at your War College for two years. Give me a concise and brief explanation of why your nation fought a bloody civil war for five years. And please, do not insult history by telling me it was to free slaves. They—and their problems—were far behind pride, cotton, and many other factors."

"I, well, I can't, I mean, that quickly—well, there are a lot of things . . ." Gary sputtered to a halt.

"Precisely," came the quiet answer.

Ron moved in. "Should we help you, major?"

An smiled. "That decision is yours. However, helping us is helping yourselves. Let us not build in more complication than that."

"You've told us what the people from the North do. How can we accept that? No offense, major, but—"

"None taken."

"But we have only your word for it."

"And you are the man who found that child?"

"That could happen anywhere and by anyone."

"True. But it was not an isolated case. It is part of a pattern. One the North considers necessary. Lives and pain are not important against their final goal of dominating my country."

Silence again. "Can you prove what you're saying?" Gary said. He was still smarting from being shown up as an oaf.

"I can. Understand this first. You cannot tell a North Vietnamese from a South Vietnamese, any more than you can tell a Pennsylvanian from a Virginian. Our people are short and dark and our eyes are slanted. Our only difference lies in how we think, exactly as there was this difference between your North and South in your Civil War. The prisons both sides kept speak very poorly for a nation that—well," he shrugged, "one day, perhaps, we can talk about such things. I have told you of the pattern the followers of Hanoi use here. I shall also show you. You will then answer your own questions and heed your own conscience. I am going to take you to a village. The Cong were there last night. There were no troops in that village, but they—the people there—are the center of a major area, and they were chosen to become an object lesson for all the countryside. That was their only crime: *they were available.*"

They drove for twenty minutes. It was a small village, and Ron knew he had all his answers without the need to ask a single question. Before they rounded a final bend in the jungle trail, he heard the sounds. Mixed but distinguishable. The moan of broken hearts and the buzzing of big blue flies.

Every female, including hand-carried infants, had been impaled through the vagina on sharp and jagged stakes. Every young male was dead after having his genitals cut or ripped from his body and jammed into his mouth so he would both choke and bleed to death. The elders had demanded more attention. Their eyes had been gouged out, their tongues ripped out by pincers, their stomachs slashed open, and then they were strangled with their own intestines.

Most of them had taken a long time to die.

15

"It's not the way you think. Forget your old contracts. That's all in the past. We start fresh." It was the first time Ron had seen Harry relaxed. Not really letting down his guard, but not pushing. It was a subtle but critical difference in their relationship. Harry knew they'd been taken to that village. He didn't have to sell anything to Ron. There'd been enough psychological pressure for Ron to decide for himself. Ron understood all this, understood as well that he'd been prodded and parlayed, but damn it, he agreed with his own decision. Despite his dislike of being maneuvered, he had no conflict with the final results, and he kept his own counsel. He watched Harry lean back, open an attaché case, and remove a long, thin cigar. Harry lit up before he spoke again.

"All the old rules are changed. Everything is coming out into the open now." He blew smoke quietly. "Maybe it's better this way. We were getting pretty tired of lying to the whole world about the military assistance we were giving the Vietnamese, but we had no choice. The North has opened the gates for us. We'll make certain that the Congress and the American public know what atrocities those people have been practicing here. It'll sway opinion just enough for us to do our job better." He smiled. "We won't advertise what we're doing. We'll maintain just the right facade—"

"Spell that out," Ron interrupted.

Harry studied him. "I guess you've only seen part of the picture. We provide assistance to the Vietnamese. But only part of it is military. There are hundreds of missionaries here. We've also brought in about two thousand experts in agriculture, mining, engineering, public health—the works. We've started an educational program that has nothing to do with weapons or oil. It's straight people-to-people. We'll concentrate the public spotlight on that, of course, and do what we have to do in the other areas."

"Which includes people like me and Gary."

"Right. Let's talk contract, and then if you're agreed we sign papers. The loyalty oath and the rest of that is on file. We can dispense with it." As Harry talked, the attaché case was again opened and two folders emerged. "You sign a new contract. Your title, for the records, is field adviser. It doesn't mean a thing except to provide a cover title. Any questions come to you, you answer simply, with the detailed knowledge of the fields in which you are expert: welding, steelwork, tools, machinery, and so forth." A finger tapped the paper. "Part of your contract is that you may never discuss your job. Any questions?"

Ron shrugged; Gary shook his head. "Good. You'll receive individual assignments, but you'll work as a team. Each mission—"

"Each hit," Ron corrected him.

"As you wish. Each hit will pay you, individually, five thousand dollars in American money. The funds can be banked for you in the States or kept here in a safe. No checks or any other means of handling. Strictly cash over here."

Gary motioned for attention. "We get five grand for each job? Each of us? I mean, that's ten thousand for a job?"

"That's correct. Each of you has a safety-deposit box in the main building at the camp. Five thousand dollars is in that box. You can take that money and leave here if you wish, right now, and no questions asked. Your new contract will be what we call open-end. Either party may cancel without notice and without prejudice. Anytime you want to quit, we'll fly you home, set you up with a cover story in the States, and you're back on your own. That's the deal. No pressure for you to stay. Men do a better job that way."

They signed.

Then they settled down to serious practice with the tools of their new trade. They fired a variety of weapons, but Ron found himself still favoring the spaghetti gun, which he could now disassemble and reassemble blindfolded. He learned how to throw killing knives and stars so perfectly balanced they were almost certain to strike their targets blade on. He practiced with gelpacks and napalm and primer cord and small rockets and different types of exotic and terrible chemicals. He memorized maps of the surrounding countryside, read aerial photographs. Gary was less intense; he had accepted in his mind what had to be done and what he had promised to do; he had become a stolid, thorough, no-nonsense killing machine.

Find. Hit. Destroy.

Find, hit, and destroy *what?*

They never chose the hamlets or villages or outposts or whatever their targets were. They were given maps and photographs and detailed briefings. For a while they worked with experienced men so they might learn the finer points of professional killing. They were being groomed to run their own missions. Their "hits." Sooner or later, they knew, Ron would take the lead on these jobs. He had a natural flair, an instinct, for murder on a mass scale.

But nobody called it that. Ron himself had almost ceased questioning it, had almost ceased wondering what had happened to him to change his nature so drastically. It was, he had thought, almost like a reverse lobotomy—whole new emotions and impulses had been opened up within his mind, a whole new side of his personality had developed. But strangely, he had come to accept that new side quickly and easily; he didn't dwell on stuff like that. He dwelled on his job—learning it, doing it. Action all the way.

They opened their newly inked contracts with a savage blow. Six men worked their way through the hazy jungle night by map, compass, and stars. "Sam" led this mission. Ron didn't know his real name, and it didn't matter; around here, names could just as well be numbers. Sam was an old hand, and Ron followed him without question. Learn; that was the key.

Sam stopped in a grove of trees within sight of the village. "This is a big one," he said in a hoarse whisper. "They've got guns in every hut. They also had a big party

earlier tonight, and most of the men are wiped out. So we got
a good chance to get everything set up just the way we
planned. I want max timers on the gelpacks. You guys got
ninety seconds from start to finish. Set 'em down and pull the
timers, and remember, you got sixty seconds to get them all
in place and thirty seconds to get the hell off to a safe
distance. Everybody knows his position and his route. Any
questions?"

No one spoke. "Move out," Sam told them quietly.
Crouching, they fanned across the last open field, spreading
through the village, laying down the gelpacks, and pulling
the detonators set for ninety seconds. They moved swiftly,
efficiently, quietly. At exactly sixty-four seconds, every man
was running like hell. They threw themselves onto the ground,
squirming around to look back. Silence and darkness.

An enormous movie screen a thousand feet wide and
over a hundred feet high exploded in blazing light. Yellow
and orange and white and red. "Holy shit!" Gary yelled.

"Stay down, you dumb bastard!" Sam yelled back. Without thinking Gary was rising to his feet, a dumbfounded
spectator. The gelpacks went off with their familiar shattering
roar, scattering their insidious blazing chemicals. Thatched
huts roared in flames. Anything that could burn was instantly
wrapped in swirling fire. Night was gone. They might have
been looking directly into the center of an oil refinery where
every storage tank and pipeline was erupting in all directions.
In the midst of the flames, silhouetted in Daliesque fashion,
figures large and small ran about, sometimes stumbling, pir-
ouetting, or twitching like wooden soldiers on tottering stiff
legs, hands clawing at nothing as the flames ripped up and
broiled their bodies and speared into noses, mouths, and
lungs. The fire was a hellish hissing roar, but the thin screams
and shrieks cut through it all like sirens in the background of
a tormented mob.

"Open up!" Sam yelled, and he was suddenly on his feet,
a heavy machine gun bucking and roaring in his arms. The
burning figures spun lazily and toppled and tumbled, bouncing off the ground, running madly and blindly into huts or
careening off one another. Dogs ran in their own form of
madness. Ron stood openmouthed, not believing what was
happening, the roar of the fire and the deep *whumping*

sounds of huts kicking off huge fireballs like rising roses, freezing him where he stood.

"For God's sake, Ron, shoot!"

Gary's voice. He didn't understand. Shoot what? Was this a mercy firing to kill those people burning alive? That was crazy! "Goddamn it, you dumb son of a bitch, *behind you!*" He felt Gary's arm smack him on the shoulder, throwing him to one knee, and it saved his life. Enemy, soldiers, Cong; he didn't know. But they came running from behind a copse of trees, shooting wildly, their eyes horrifying, reflecting the firelight. Ron squeezed the trigger on the spaghetti gun, held it, and two hundred rounds ripped away. He saw a head explode like an overripe melon, and pieces of bodies sailed through the air. There was crimson spray, and then only the hissing of the flames dying down.

Nothing moved. They stood back to back, searching everywhere. The only sounds were their own tortured breathing and the metallic snicks of magazines and clips being ejected and fresh loads being slammed into weapons. Still nothing moved. Sam stood erect, his machine gun over his head. "Stay off the trails. Single file. Matt, take up rear cover. Okay, let's move it."

Ron had become two people. The one who carried the spaghetti gun and walked through the valley of the shadow with that terrible scythe in his hands, who flung out his arms and scattered fire and brimstone and sulfur and napalm and hell in whatever direction those outstretched hands pointed. That was one man—the killer, the one they regarded as a "natural hit man." He did his work, and he studied his maps and kept his weapons in perfect working order, and he went out and burned and blew up and killed. His grisly toll went beyond any counting, but on the basis of past experience with other equally skilled men they figured his first four hits had killed over a thousand

A thousand what? Enemies? He wasn't in any goddamned war. *The* enemy? He didn't wear a uniform, and his own Congress didn't know or didn't give a shit. Who and what they were, he never really knew. Silhouetted forms, jerking and dancing at the ends of the ropes of fire he draped through their midst. He refused to think about it.

The other person, the Ron he had known all his life, crawled into a distant corner of his mind and wouldn't come forward. *Thank God for that,* something in his head said to him. *We don't want to talk with that fucker. He can't handle this.*

Besides, there was that first job with Mike leading him and Gary, and that little girl they'd found in the field. But her memory was dimming. Sometimes, a sense of the horror of what he was doing would force its way into his mind, but it never reached the front door; almost nothing touched him. Even Gary was held back by whatever stalked through Ron's soul and had taken command.

They got paid for each mission. The first, and then three more with the powerful fire-fight teams. That made twenty thousand for Ron and twenty thousand for Gary locked up in the vault. Four missions. Ron hadn't counted the money, had never examined it, just told the people in the camp to stuff the bread in his vault. He didn't talk much anymore. He didn't want to talk with the other men. Gary was a part of his past and his present and there really wasn't any future. So fuck it. All of them.

He walked into the tent, where he found Harry going through papers. Still in that short-sleeved white shirt and the creased trousers and the simonized shoes. "We're changing our operation," Ron announced.

Harry looked up. "Oh? How?"

"No more big parties. I work alone. With Gary. A two-man team. That's all."

"You're squeezing your chances, you know."

"I haven't seen you out there in the jungle, so if I want your fucking advice I'll ask for it."

No answer.

"Do we deal that way or don't we?"

"I want you to understand something. You can run your field operations the way you think best," Harry said. "My concern is a lot bigger than you or me."

"I'm touched."

"You're a valuable investment to us. You've become one of the best. Whatever it is, you've got it. We don't want to lose you."

"Oh, for Christ's sake, will you stuff all that garbage and answer me yes or no?"

"What if I say no?"

Ron smiled. He didn't even know he had done that, but he smiled.

"Okay, okay. You've got it."

16

They killed and they burned and they slaughtered. They studied the maps and learned every aspect of the villages they would hit, and Ron ran through their plans again and again until Gary started to complain. "You're turning into a goddamned general," he told Ron. "Ease off, will you?"

Ron leaned back in that cold armor he wore. "Stop whining. You whine instead of listening to me, you're dead, you know that? You're no good to me. You can't take it, shove that gun up your ass and quit."

"Well, I—"

"You won't quit. Five grand for every hit. You got so much fucking money in that concrete box you can't even count that high. The devil owns your soul, Gary, old friend, so knock off the crap and stay tight."

Gary flushed. "I never heard you talk like this before."

"How could you?" Ron said with a calm that astonished him. "I was never like this before. I'm a stranger in a stranger's body."

"Doesn't it bother you?"

"What's there to bother?" He curled his finger around an imaginary trigger. "You go squeeze, that's all." He held his hands about an imaginary gelpack. "Pull the little wires here, and throw it away, like a boomerang you know isn't coming back, and look, ma, no hands, see? They got no hands and no feet and no faces, so what's there to bother?"

"We're killing a lot of people, Ron." Gary's conscience was snagging him.

"I haven't seen you turn down any bread, baby," Ron said softly. "Or would you trade your five grand per job for a medal? Don't you want some medals, Gary? I mean, when you get home who the shit's gonna believe that big bad Gary is a trained killer, a professional assassin? Who's going to know you're a hero? What the hell are you going to say to people?"

"I don't think about that," Gary said sourly.

"Smart. Stay that way. Now shut up and pay attention. Tonight we got a different job."

"Like what?"

"Whole village is moving. We know the trail. Maybe ninety or a hundred people. They're setting up a new command post somewhere in the jungle we're not supposed to know about."

"Soldiers? There's only two of us, Ron—"

"Some soldiers. Maybe a dozen. They're moving the whole village as a cover. We're going to bushwhack them."

"But there's only two of us!"

"No, Gary. There's you, and that's one. And then there's me, and that's a hell of a lot more than one. Your muscles in good shape? You got a lot of cord to carry tonight, sweetheart."

They went to the trail just after dark. Ron had studied it for a long time. The trail came up from open fields and then narrowed into a wedgelike space through thick trees. Only one person at a time could move through there. They'd be loaded down, packed tightly together. Ron and Gary strung primer cord through the trees on each side of the trail at waist-high level. They rigged antipersonnel grenades higher in the trees, and then they laid down a long series of mines in the soft ground. These could be set off in two ways, on impact or by electrical trigger. Ron set everything up with a detonator system.

It was easy. They were a hundred yards away, behind a hill, when the trail was lined with people and Ron set off the charge. A thousand feet of primer cord went off like a blast of lightning. The concussion blinded and deafened everyone within reach and brought blood spurting and gushing from ears and eyes and mouths and noses. The physical impact and shock loosened bowels and bladders, and in the same shocking freeze of time the grenades went off above the trail and rained down chunks of metal that tore everything in their path to bits. To top all that, the mines in the ground leaped up three feet and then exploded, to send out heavy chunks of red-hot metal. Half the people in the column were killed instantly. Those that weren't took longer to die. Ron didn't even wait to see what had happened.

He didn't want to see. He knew. He could have described it in great detail. He knew every gruesome and grisly event from experience and from his knowledge of the weapons and the effects they had on the human body. It was the most perfect killing ambush he'd ever even heard about. All he wanted was to get away.

"That was a beautiful job you guys did last night," Sims said. Ron tried to remember Sims. Christ, he handled the money for Harry and Al and whoever. Curt Sims was his full name, a beefy man with hair sprouting from his shoulders and a thin greasy film that never left his face. He placed a stack of hundred-dollar bills on his desk before Ron and another in front of Gary. "There it is, guys. Fifty big ones each. You earned it."

Ron didn't touch it. "Stick it in the box."

Sims showed an amused smile. "Aren't you going to count it?"

The room went quiet. Ron and Gary exchanged glances, and Ron turned back to Sims. "Why'd you say that?"

Sims stiffened. "Hey, I didn't mean nothing. It was, you know, like a joke."

Ron pushed the stack of money gently with the nose of the spaghetti gun. The muzzle was pointing directly at Sims's belly. "Did you count it?" Ron asked quietly.

"Sure, sure! Of course I did. It's all there. I swear it!" Instant sweat, Ron noted.

"Then if you counted it, why the games?"

"Like I said—a joke, man, a joke!"

Ron nodded slowly. Then a thought hit him. "You said it was a beautiful job. How do you know? Your hands look clean to me."

"Well, I heard—"

"What did you hear?"

"Man, you got 'em *all*. I mean, no survivors, no one to tell what happened."

"All dead?"

Sims smiled in a frantic attempt to please what he now saw as a dangerous madman standing before him. "That's right, Previn. All dead."

"That's good. Maybe we even got the dogs." Ron scratched his chest. "Dogs. Yeah, the dogs. I don't like to see them wounded."

Sims was stunned. "Why?"

"You ever gut a dog, Sims?"

Sims shook his head.

"A dog wounded in the belly or the nuts screams like a woman, Sims. It isn't pretty."

"Sure, sure, I can understand."

"The shit you can. Who's got the word on the next job?"

"It's a village thirty miles northwest of here. Mountain town, like. Not many people, but it's being used as a base to hit our field agents. We need it taken out. It should slow things up. You'll probably be gone four or five days. A helicopter will drop you off nearby with your gear, and you can walk out. That's the safest way."

Ron didn't answer. He motioned to Gary and they went outside. "We've been promoted, old buddy," he said to Gary.

"How?"

"Until now, it's been jeep and feet, right? Now they're setting us up with a chopper drop. That means the big boys who run this detail think we're really hot shit."

"This whole thing stinks." Ron rested in the crook of a tree, his heavy gear on the ground beneath him. Gary was in another tree, uncomfortable, frightened, unhappy. "Yeah," he agreed swiftly. "Why don't we just let this one go? You know, get the hell out of here."

"What? And fuck up your pay scale, Gary, old buddy? I wouldn't think of it."

"Goddamn it, look at that setup," Gary hissed. "We can't get in close to set up the gelpacks. The place is spread out on all those little hills and hummocks. It would take a whole force to knock off this place!"

"No one said they'd all be easy. I guess it's time we earned our keep."

"You dumb bastard, this is *suicide*."

"Nope, it's just tougher. And I think I got it figured out." Ron studied the village. It wasn't like any of the others. The huts were arranged willy-nilly on a steep slope. There was no way to sneak up and hit the village full blast. That meant little or no warning, and from what they'd been told in their briefing, the people in this place were heavily armed.

"We don't wait for tonight." Ron announced his decision. "The men are out in the fields working, or they're off somewhere else doing what we're doing—planning to kill a bunch of people. That means their guard is down. The last thing they'll expect is a hit in broad daylight. We start from up here, and we go down there with the gelpacks and shooting, and we go right through them like shit through a greased goose. And we keep on going. You got that? We don't stop. We just hit and we run, right on downhill, and we disappear before they get organized. We keep moving, we'll be miles away ahead of a cold trail."

Gary was adamant. "Not me, buddy. Count me out."

Ron grinned a death's-head mask at his friend. "Have it your own way, sweetheart. I'll give your best to Broadway when I get back."

Gary's expression was incredulous. "You're going down there *alone*?"

"Can't do it with a man who's already quit me, can I?" As he talked, Ron was setting up his equipment. He made a lariat out of a long line of primer cord. That would give him an advantage no one would ever anticipate. Then the gelpacks from a standing position, and more as he moved down the mountainside.

"You son of a bitch, I'm in."

"Then do as I say. Set your gels for fifteen seconds. Got that? Fifteen seconds and no more. You pull the times when I say, and you start slinging them down into that village when the first blast goes off. Aim for the center area of the huts."

"Okay, okay, I got it. Fifteen seconds. But what first blast?"

"Watch."

Ron moved into the widest area he could find. He tied the end of the primer cord to a rock, swung it over his head, and began whirling it faster and faster about him. When he had enough momentum built up, he hurled it toward the huts. The weight of the rock carried the cord behind it like an arrow with a string attached. The primer cord draped over two huts, the rest of it lying on the ground. Several women looked around, startled. One screamed a warning, and Ron hit the electrical detonator. The blast tore the woman apart and killed everyone else close by as the two huts burst into flames. Seconds later, gelpacks, thrown by Gary's powerful arms, were raining down on the village. They slung off nine of them, one after the other, setting most of the village aflame, bringing people running madly into the open spaces. By then both men had scrambled down the steep slope, stopping at the edge of the village.

"Open up!" Ron yelled at Gary.

The heavy machine gun roared in the midst of hissing and crackling flames, increasing the terror and the screaming. Women toppled over in every direction. Ron waited until Gary's clip was almost empty. "Reload!" he shouted. "I'll take it now. Reload and set off the rest of your gels!"

He dropped to one knee, the spaghetti gun an acetylene torch of death, cutting down anything that moved. He fired into huts not yet aflame and heard screams from inside. Off to his right he saw men running madly from the fields toward the mountain hamlet. "The gelpacks! Get them off!"

Gary dropped his machine gun, fumbled frantically with the incendiary packages. His eyes were wide and frightened. One of the packs went off almost at the same moment he threw it, and the flames licked out and washed briefly across his face. He cursed, pawing at his eyes, forgetting everything. A young woman burning alive, screaming, rushed toward them, a machete over her head. Ron stared at her in amazement. He couldn't believe a human being could be on fire like that and still run. The machete was coming down and Gary was helpless, trying to scramble out of the way. Ron half turned, shooting from the hip, and put at least forty rounds into her. She stopped dead, the flames curling after her and roiling about her body. An arm fell off and then the side of her head dissolved in bullet-ripped flesh and fire. Gary threw up. Ron cursed and kicked him in the leg to get him up. Fuck the gun. He grabbed Gary's arm with one hand, held the spaghetti gun in the other, and shot his way through the maddened, flame-torn people around him. They ran and stumbled through the village and into the thick growth beyond. Gary was whimpering from pain. "Shut up," Ron hissed. "Grab my belt. Hang on. Keep moving."

They ran and stumbled and tripped and got up and worked their way halfway down the mountain, then cut off at an angle until they reached a thin mountain stream. Gary collapsed in exhaustion. Ron slipped a new clip into the spaghetti gun and ripped open a first-aid pack. Shaking from fear and pain, Gary clawed at the ground as Ron applied burn ointment to his eyes. "Oh, Jesus, I'm blind. I'm blind," he wailed.

"Shut up. Five minutes is all that stuff takes. Then we wipe it off and you'll be able to see."

The damn five minutes lasted forever. Ron wiped away the ointment, peered anxiously at Gary. "How is it?"

"I—I can see a—little. It's hazy."

"It'll get better. Now get on your feet. We stay here, we're dead men. We can't go straight back to the camp. They'll bushwhack us. We go the long way around."

Four days later, clothes in tatters, footsore, worn out, they walked into the camp. Everyone stared at them in disbelief. They'd been written off for dead.

Ron had a strange look on his face. He went into the tent to see Sims. "Where's Harry?"

Sims didn't answer. "Jesus, we thought you'd bought it for sure."

"Where's Harry? I had a long walk home. It gave me time to think. There's something we all forgot to do."

"Hey, let me get you to the doc. You look like you need it, and some food. Jesus, have a drink." He shoved a bottle to Ron.

Ron drank long and deep and wiped his mouth with his sleeve. "When does Harry get back?"

"Not for a couple of days."

Ron turned to Gary. "Get another weapon."

"I'm going to the doctor. My eyes."

"Get another weapon. Get it now, and get your ass back here, and don't stop for anything or I'll blow your fucking head off."

Gary stared, nodded, and left. Sims's eyes were wide.

"The money," Ron said. "Lay it out."

Sims opened a safe and placed two stacks of money on the table.

"Good. Later, when we get back, you stick it in the boxes for us. Okay?"

"Sure, sure."

"Harry ain't here, so we got a job for you. You're the moneyman, the big man in town, right?" Ron didn't give him a chance to answer. He waited until Gary came back with a new machine gun.

"That thing loaded?" Ron asked.

"Uh uh."

"Put a round in the chamber and take off the safety."

Dumbfounded, frightened, Gary did as he was told.

Ron turned back to Sims. "Let's go. Get two or three other men, and let's go to the equipment tent."

"I can't leave here."

Ron thumbed the safety off. "Sure you can," he said quietly.

Sims turned white. He moved ahead of Ron and Gary to the equipment tent. "You three," Ron said to three men in the tent, pointing the spaghetti gun at them. "Get four shovels and a big sheet of canvas. Now."

They looked at him as if he were crazy.

"Three seconds," Ron said lightly. "One for each man. Then I open up with this thing."

They scrambled for the shovels and the canvas. "Now, walk ahead of me," Ron ordered. He pointed to a sandy dune. "That way. This has been long overdue. You fuckers ain't got no respect."

They looked over their shoulders at him. "What the hell's coming down, man?"

"Like I said, you got no respect. You don't want to be buried with them shovels you're carrying, just keep walking and no more talking and do exactly as you're told."

They walked. People were coming out of buildings and tents and watching. Someone ran frantically to get to a radio, but no one approached them.

Ron stopped in soft sand. He looked around and then at Gary. "This is it?"

Gary had it now. He was smiling. "It's it."

Ron pointed with the machine gun. "Right there. Start digging."

They dug, sweating, sand flies hovering in a nasty swarm

about them. Then a shovel struck something. "Hey, I hit something down here," one man said.

"Keep digging. That's George. You dig and I'll explain." The machine gun moved slightly to cover them all, and they resumed digging. "You see, they never let us give George a decent burial. We put him down here with our own hands. George wasn't worth burying. We're going to apologize. We dig up George, you people put him in that canvas, and then we carry his body over to those trees and we plant him again in a decent grave, under trees, where he should have been all this time."

The stench gagged them. What was left of George, swarming over and through with worms and maggots, stared up at them.

"Get him in that canvas," Ron ordered.

Sims was on his knees, retching. "I can't," he choked. "I can't do it."

"Then say hello to God, shithead."

Sims turned up a white face. "You wouldn't!"

"He would." Gary grinned.

They dragged the body, pieces falling away from the corpse, onto the canvas and wrapped it around the remains. Ron had them carry the body and the shovels a quarter of a mile into a thickly wooded area. He pointed to a shady patch of ground. "Dig," he ordered.

It was done, the four men gasping for air. Ron turned to Gary. "I feel better."

"So do I."

"I think George does, too."

Gary looked at the mound of fresh earth. "So long, old buddy."

Sims straightened up. "You won't get away with this."

"Oh? We just did." He smiled coldly at Sims. "I'll tell you something, moneyman. You can carry my piece back for me."

He tossed the machine gun to the startled Sims and started walking back to the camp.

They stared, dumbfounded; then they followed him back. No one ever spoke again about what had happened.

17

The meeting room was obscured from the outside world by thirty feet of steel-reinforced concrete, reached only by heavily guarded sewer conduits from another building four blocks distant. The conduit system was riddled with false passages, traps, alarm systems, and a dozen ways of instantly killing anyone venturing into it. There were several distinct and separate methods of releasing into the conduit a heavy concentration of Green Ring III, a poison gas similar in effect to the German *sarin* nerve gas. Against Green Ring III, a gas mask was as effective as a screen door. It took effect within ten seconds and was irreversible. It was an excellent deterrent to unauthorized approach and passage through the conduit, which was, incidentally, three stories beneath the surface of the heart of Saigon. At the end of the conduit lay the meeting room where four Americans in unobtrusive civilian attire studied computer printouts, photographs, file sheets, and other data relevant to certain men who had earned their attention and scrutiny.

A redheaded CIA field chief tapped a folder. "This one. Previn. According to his reports he's the equal of any ten men."

A man with a shining pate, thick-necked and bullish, who was a former leader of a U.S. Marine assassination team, smiled at his friend. "What's even better is that he's got no military background. He's never worn a uniform."

"Is this file correct, then?" The CIA man passed the

121

folder to the other two men at the table. "His background is a *welder*? They say he's unbelievably cool under fire. He never gets rattled, and he seems to have a covenant with death. It's almost as if he and the grim reaper were close friends."

The ex-marine nodded. "All that and more. Some men have a natural talent for music. Einstein was his own genius. There's da Vinci and the Wright brothers and—"

"Never mind, Bill. I understand. And he has 'it' for his new work?"

"He's the most natural killer I've ever seen. Bees to flowers, bears to honey, Previn to the trigger. It doesn't matter what he uses—autoweapons, gelpacks, plastics, knives. Most of all, he has a natural affinity for always predicting what his opposition will do. And for being able to stick to whatever he plans." The CIA man looked at the others. "I'll repeat that. When he starts an operation, it's with a plan, of course. So far, no matter what else happens, he always keeps to that basic plan, modifying it as he goes, but never veering far from it."

A tall black man nodded sagely. "He could be one of them."

"Let me add something else. Whatever 'it' is, everyone who knows, who understands this business, recognizes him. It's almost as if he were a prophet, a high priest, a guru—he projects a mental message. He's *untouchable*. Did you hear what he did with Sims?" The CIA man chuckled. "You all know Sims. He's killed over a hundred men with his bare hands." He went on to relate the scene with the shovels and the reburying of George. "And when it was all over, he tosses his machine gun to Sims, *turns his back to him*, and walks away."

The black man angled his head slightly. "And what does Sims think now?"

"Think? He thinks Previn is the messiah. At the camp they were giving ten to one that Sims would kill Previn that same night. Someone made a joke about it. Sims broke both *his* legs."

"And what did he do about Previn?"

"I told you. He acts like the man is the messiah."

"I don't think there's any question, then. We tag him. He becomes one of the chosen."

"Hell, yes. I'd almost bet on him."

"I'll have none of that. No frivolity in this matter. It's too big, too serious."

"Yes, sir."

The tall black man had an aura of authority. "Keep me informed about Previn. What's the estimate on his next phase?"

"He won't go six missions more before the break comes."

The black face remained inscrutable. "Will he break?"

The man from the CIA shook his head. "No. Death is only a bother to him, no matter how momentarily serious."

"Very good. I think we have a winner here. Isn't it nice when things work?"

Ron surprised himself. They'd handed him a problem that would have confounded Napoleon or even Alexander. Or Patton, or Rommel. "There's a town with a heavy concentration of specially trained men and women that just came down from Hanoi," they explained. "At least five hundred of them. Their leader is Vo Dong Giang."

That was his first tickle of warning. Never before had they named anyone. The people he nailed weren't warm human individuals, they were objects within a target. When they did give him names, the names didn't mean a damn thing. So, he wondered, why tell him this name? He put the question aside for later consideration.

"They're trained to build up guerrilla concentrations in South Vietnam. Every one of them is skilled in weapons, organization, communications—the works. Every one of them is a leader. They meet tomorrow night in this small valley for their final orders, and then they fan out. We want to get them while they're all together. It'll be our only chance."

Ron rolled a cigarette from one side of his mouth to the other, leaning forward, studying the detailed maps on the table. He didn't respond for a while, and the silence lingered. Finally, Ron stubbed out the cigarette. "None of this makes sense," he said.

The stranger in the group, who'd come into the camp with the information on the mission, looked at him without expression. "Why not?" he asked.

"No one's ever asked my opinion before on any hit," Ron told him. "That's been our way. You people figure what you want and Gary and I go out and do it. For a while now we haven't worked with anyone else."

"Right. The two-man team."

Ron studied him. Why the hell were they pushing the patently obvious? "I don't know your name," Ron said finally.

"Jim."

"Jim what?"

"Whatever you'd like. Smith, Jones, Johnson."

Ron laughed. "Honest, anyway."

"Will you do it?"

"Do *what?*"

"Take out that village with Giang and his people."

"You're asking me to set up a complete strike? Against five hundred freshly trained, heavily armed, and skilled fighters? Who'll be ready for anything? That's all?"

Jim leaned back in his chair and his eyes remained unblinking. "You summed it up well. Yes, we're asking you to do that."

"How many men?"

"Same conditions as before."

"Just the two of us?"

"You're the one who said he wanted no part of large operations, Previn. Jesus Christ, are you changing that now?" The man's eyes were dark and foreboding. "If you're going to crap out of it, just say so. We can't send in a large team. We'd need a whole goddamned strike force."

"You bet your sweet ass," Ron snarled. "And you want just the two of us to do it tomorrow night?"

"You got it."

"Not yet I don't." Ron was thinking furiously. Nothing fit in all this, but something kept him from the only sensible thing to do: tell them to shove it. It was madness, suicide. But he couldn't back away. Something kept pushing him forward. "Tomorrow night," he mused aloud. His eyes went back again and again to the maps. The village lay in a deep valley, surrounded on three sides, with the only road leading to the south. North, east, and west were sharp ridges. A few trails were marked—the only escape routes. Suicide lanes, all of them. He tapped the maps.

"Is this group in there yet?"

"No. Giang and his people arrive tomorrow afternoon."

"I'll need some people to carry stuff there ahead of time."

Gary's hand gripped his arm. "Cut the shit, Ron. We're not going in there against a whole army!"

Ron turned to smile at his friend. "Sure we are," he said softly. "There's a way."

Jim's voice came softly across the table between them. "I'd like to hear about it."

Ron passed the smile on to the other man, but there was no warmth in his expression. "You don't hear anything but what I need. And the manpower to do what I need. And I want that manpower tonight." He glanced at his watch. "I'll need two hours to get everything ready. Then you take it where I say by chopper, you drop us off, and you sit back and wait."

"What will you need?"

"*I'll* take care of that. I'll have it ready in two hours if you agree to the rest of it." Ron was smiling; he knew something the other man did not know. New equipment. A new weapon. In the quantities he'd need, it would weigh a lot, and there wasn't a chance in the world that he and Gary could carry it themselves. Besides, the little valley was too far off, and the terrain too treacherous, to reach in any reasonable time, except by chopper.

Ron lit another cigarette. "Time's wasting, friend. It's got to be now or never."

"You have it."

Gary cursed; Ron ignored it.

"Who's the honcho here who signs no-questions-asked weapons authorizations?" Ron laughed. "Don't be modest, Jim what's-your-name. Just sign the chit. Absolute and open authority. And you can relax. I don't want any atomic bombs."

Jim glanced at the other men. "One chopper load, right?"

"Right. One more thing. No interference from any of you here, or the deal's off. And I mean that. The first fucker who steps in can eat this whole deal."

Ron didn't need telepathy to know that this man had been told to give Ron Previn anything he wanted—short of a nuke. That meant freewheeling. And Ron had that little secret in his head. He had his entire plan formulated; he just needed verification of certain points. He watched "Jim" sign the authorization paper.

Ron and Gary walked across the open base compound. Gary was ready to explode until Ron turned to him and spoke quietly and earnestly. "Before you start, friend, just listen. I've never let you down, have I? Okay. We've done jobs together that fifty men couldn't have pulled off, and we've always come back. Now trust me. I know what I'm doing."

"Ron, there's *five hundred men*—"

"It wouldn't matter if they had five thousand in that village."

Gary stared blankly at him. "Okay, okay. I'm with you."

"Good. Let's get with it. I'm going to the weapons storage bunker. You wait outside for me with a truck. Quarter ton will do it. When I come out with the stuff, you make absolutely sure no one looks at it or questions anything. Then we take it to the chopper, and we're gone."

"Aren't you going to tell me what we're going to do?"

Ron slapped Gary on the arm. "What? And have you run screaming off into the boonies? Like I said. Just trust me."

In the ordnance storage bunker he had a small argument until the grim-faced sergeant who ran the place made a phone call, listened silently, said, "Yes, sir," and hung up with a look of utter disbelief. "The man said—"

"The man said," Ron broke in smoothly, "to stop jacking off, to give me exactly what I want, to tell *nobody* about it, and to mind your own business. Right?"

The answer came slowly. "Yeah, that's right, but you don't rank me, and I don't have to—"

"Shut up. Get the stuff. Do it now. And don't, not now, not ever, talk to me like that, dogshit." The death's-head smile showed. "Or I will blow your head off."

Ten minutes later the sergeant was helping Gary load the truck. Ron watched for a few minutes. "Get it loaded aboard the chopper," he ordered Gary. "Then sit on it with that popgun of yours loaded and the safety off. Anybody opens up what we got, tell them the deal is off."

Gary was noncommittal. "Got it."

They watched Ron walk toward the weather office. The sergeant seemed to shake off a coldness. "Your friend really thinks he's hot shit. I got half a mind to teach him some manners."

"Yeah?"

"Yeah," the sergeant snarled.

"How come you didn't do it? You outweigh him by fifty pounds," Gary said pleasantly.

"He had this paper—"

"Oh, shut up and load, willya?" Gary picked up the first

package. "Jesus," he said with surprise. "What the hell's in here?"

The sergeant shrugged. He was grateful for the change in subject. "Beats me. It's a pressurized tank. It says tear gas or something like that on it."

"*Tear gas?*"

"He's your buddy, not mine," came the grumble.

Ron came out of the weather shack with his maps. He climbed aboard the helicopter and gave the pilot the coordinates. "See this small clearing? The north side of the ridge? You come in low from a long ways off, let us down, unload the stuff, and vamoose. And you go twenty miles due west before you climb. Take her as high as you can on the way out and detour this whole area on your way back here."

"Whatever you say, sir."

The world, Ron mused, is full of surprises. *Sir?* He napped during the flight out.

It was simple—if you had the new chemical aerosols and knew how to use them. Short of an atomic explosion, Ron knew of no weapon deadlier than these chemicals the helicopter had airlifted to the ridge. For the rest of the night, he and Gary dug in. They concealed their equipment under trees and heavy growth. Ron kept testing the winds, studying the skies and the clouds and the pattern of weather. By now he knew the signs. Late in the afternoon he nodded to the sky.

"It's going to be a clear night," he said to Gary.

"That pleases you? A good night so we can be seen that much easier when we start down—," he hated even to say it, "into that village? Goddamn, Ron, we got away with it last night, but the place was just about empty." Gary thought of the lines working their way through the forests and the hundreds of heavily armed enemy down below. "Come to think of it," Gary added, "why'd we drag that wire all the way down this slope, anyway?"

Ron looked at Gary and a slow smile showed. "It's a surprise for our friends down there."

"What kind? A telegram?"

Ron appreciated the remark. "That's good, sweetheart. Very good. You don't know how right you are."

"That's all you tell me?"

"Get some sleep."

Night came and they saw lights flickering in the village. A great assembly gathered, and a man in dark clothing stood on a platform to address the armed multitude. Ron and Gary moved stealthily through the thick growth at the top of the ridge. Ron judged the wind. Perfect. The village lay a thousand feet away from them, and the wind carried naturally across the crest they walked, drifting in a gentle flow downslope.

Toward the village.

Ron went from one cylindrical tank to another until all were open. The hissing of released gas was audible from only a few feet away.

Gary watched it with alarm. "Jesus, Ron, if that stuff is poison gas, we're taking a hell of a chance up here without any protection—"

"Shut the hell up," Ron hissed. Gary went silent. Ron checked his watch. The gas was a lot heavier than air and was released from the tanks through aerosol action. It was invisible and odorless, but he knew what was happening. It rolled and flowed in eddies and currents and sheets down the mountain slope.

It mixed in with the hundreds of heavily armed soldiers, men and women, and villagers. None detected anything unusual. Ron checked his watch again. Just about time. He studied the detonator and battery system from which three long lines of wire snaked down to the edge of the village. He connected the final wires, checked the gauges indicating available electrical power, and placed his hand on the detonator control. By now Gary was more curious than frightened.

"Don't look at me. Look at the village," Ron ordered. "Look good because I'm going to make it disappear."

"No one seems bothered by the gas. I thought it was poison gas." He was almost complaining.

"Nope. It's an aerosol. An electrically conducting gas with unstable molecules. It's inert while it's in the cylinders. It needs at least one hour of exposure to open air before it soaks up oxygen. Then it's on the edge of unstable. But it's like primer cord. Fire won't set it off and neither will impact or chemicals. It needs an electrical charge of a certain voltage, which will happen the moment I close this detonator. Then it all goes up."

"You mean that whole village is a b——"

Instant, fiery, eye-gouging.

Napalm; a hundred times worse than napalm, exploding for a full mile across the length and breadth of the valley.

An act of creation; a vast sheet of fire that exploded into being.

In that instant, the shock wave crushed bodies, skulls, skin, bones, eyeballs, noses, ears; it ruptured internal organs and emptied lungs. It set aflame all 724 human souls in the village—in a split second. It burned the huts and the trees and the dogs and the animals and the people and the dust on the ground and the air within its reach. The sheet of flame was an instantly created river.

By the time the shock wave reached up the hill to Ron and Gary, one full second had passed. First they saw the eye-tearing flame, and there came a moment, only a single moment, one second of silence, as the shock wave ripped outward.

It took one second for the blast to reach the crest of the ridge and slam Ron and Gary to the earth with a terrible blow. By the time they struck the ground, not one living thing, from the smallest insect to the largest animal, was alive down there. The explosion echoed in the distance with an enormous *CRRRAACK!* and boomed back several times. By then the fireball had soared a thousand feet, changed from fiery red to deep purple, and was transformed into a thick upward-spewing cloud of smoke and dust trailing flames from the burning bodies and buildings.

"Let's move," Ron said to Gary as they crawled painfully to their feet. "We got to do this right or we're dead men."

They ran down the north side of the ridge, crashing and banging their way through the heavy brush. When they reached a patch of level ground, Ron went directly for a stream. They stood in the water for a moment, then began backtracking, returning up the ridge. Their tracks mixed with their blundering passage down the slope. In a thick grove, they moved carefully at a right angle to their foliage-crushing passage. Ron covered every sign of his passing. A hundred feet off their "trail," they reached the cave they had widened earlier. Sleeping bags awaited them inside. Ron made sure they had enough air to keep them alive, then he sealed off the entryway with branches and bushes. A man standing right in front of the cave would never have known of its existence.

Ron knew the area would be swarming with natives from nearby villages—including the guerrillas—who would fan out, cover every trail, and send word on ahead to bushwhack them. That's why he'd set his trail, backed up along it, and vanished into the cave. He and Gary would have to stay there for two, maybe three, days. The slightest sound of their voices could give them away. He'd planned for that, too. Both men got into their sleeping bags and covered their faces with nets against the creatures that would be attracted to their warm bodies.

Ron nodded to Gary. "Take the pill." Gary hesitated only a moment, then swallowed. Ron nodded, did the same. He lay back, waiting for the darkness to swallow his mind. The pills would keep him and Gary unconscious for at least forty-eight hours. They wouldn't even be able to make a sound. Absolute stillness. As good as dead—until the search was given up. Then they would wait another twenty-four hours and start back. It would take a week, but no one would be looking for them.

It worked.

18

Their next hit was a small village with only fifteen huts—a center for dissident leaders. Ron couldn't have cared less. A lousy fifteen huts didn't much matter. They'd give it the standard gelpack treatment, spray everything that moved with their withering machine-gun fire, and get the hell out. Gary went in first with the gelpacks, using darkness to spread nine of them before he scampered back to their cover position.

The charges went off expertly, and Ron and Gary waited stoically through the great whooshing sound, the explosive *BLAM* muted by the spearing flame. The center hut went off with a deafening roar. That confirmed munitions storage there. Ron crouched by the usual village food-storage well, using its excellent cover for whatever might happen. Then came the familiar screams of agony and the rushing stench of burning flesh. He tensed, ready for anything with the spaghetti gun and its wicked hollow-point magnums.

This would be the turning point in Ron's life as a killer.

The burning explosives in the center hut cascaded into a wild mushroom of flame. Thin screams sirened into the night, and suddenly, from Ron's right, a small figure darted within his peripheral vision, screaming or maybe shouting, rushing him. No time to determine who or what it was. Instinct and confidence, as well as that deep inner breath of fear, took him over, as it always did. Ron spun around into a crouch, one knee down, leaning just the proper angle into his weapon, and the spaghetti gun shrieked its savage punch at the onrushing enemy. Flame spat from the gun, smoke chittered away in puffs before the wind, acrid and stinking.

Ron stared. Frozen, locked in stone flesh.

Cut in half, literally torn in two by the savage power of his weapon, a small form poised only a moment above the ground.

Blood spurted. The torso fell forward, the trunk and legs askew and spinning away from him, and in the reflection of fire and explosion, Ron stared into the shocked, wide, still-alive eyes of a seven-year-old American boy.

Slow motion, two halves of gore, intestines spilling sloppily, blood gushing, but the face wounded only in the shock of the eyes. Life went slowly, shock taking its own sweet time to encompass death, and at that last moment before the child's face thudded into the earth, Ron had a deep glimpse of the last star-twinkles of life.

Fading. Gone.

He was numb. He was horror, disbelief, shock, pain, a silent scream. He was mad. That was an American child. A kid. One kid—*why didn't anyone tell him an American family was living here in this fucking village!*

He walked slowly from the burning gush of fire that now enveloped the village. The spaghetti gun hung loosely in his hand, and Gary dashed after him. "Ron! Damn it, man, move it! We're—" His voice trailed away. Ron never changed pace. He was ice; zombie. Gary ran before him, stared into his eyes.

Look deeply into the Arctic . . .

Ron stumbled like the walking dead, drowning in horror. When he stumbled, Gary helped him up. When he walked toward a tree, Gary grasped his arm, led him around.

Ron saw only within his mind, the vision repeating itself again and again and again: the tiny body chopped in half, toppling an entire lifetime to thud against the ground with a roar that rocked the world.

In that instant, Ron Previn blanked out the memory of that little girl he had once found lying in the night mud. At that split second, as the face of the boy banged against dirt, Ron lost all memory of saving the life of the girl. It was gone. Wiped. Blotted out.

The girl was gone. And the "new" Ron Previn—the

natural killer—was gone, too. Now the boy took dead-center stage in his mind's eye.

Ultimate sin.

"I've been *trying*, goddamn it!" Gary was red-faced from exasperation and his own plagued nerves. Two days since they'd come back from the village, and in those two days Ron hadn't spoken a word. He didn't eat and he didn't drink. Gary explained what had happened. Harry and Jim came around, and a doctor showed up. He stuck a needle in Ron's arm and they laid him down on a cot, where he slept twice around the clock without stirring. Gary watched over him, ate in the tent, used a bucket to relieve himself, refused to leave sight of the unconscious form.

When he awoke, Harry was there. "I can tell you what happened," Harry said to the figure seated on the edge of the cot, staring. "I can tell you about the boy. It was an accident. We screwed up, not telling you that the boy and his parents—they're missionaries—were in that village. It's not your fault. It's ours. The kid's parents are here in the camp, right now. We know them. We've been trying to explain to them how it happened—"

First words. Eyes spinning back into focus. "They're here? Now?"

Harry nodded. "Yes. In the command tent."

"They know it was me who did it?"

Harry shook his head. "No. All they know is that there was a mission, that we didn't know they were there, because if we had known we'd never have scheduled it. They don't know any names."

"Missionaries, you said?"

"Yes."

"How much money do I have in the box?"

Harry looked briefly at Gary, then back to Ron. "What?"

"Get it for me. Now, please."

"What for? I mean—"

"I'm not going to ask you again, mister. Get it or I'll take it my own way." Ron's voice was much too quiet. Harry noticed that Gary had never relinquished his machine gun, that he watched everything anyone did with Ron.

Harry stood up slowly. "I'll be right back."

He returned several minutes later with a canvas handbag. "It's all there," he said to Ron, placing the bag at his feet. "One hundred and fifteen thousand dollars."

Ron went to the command tent, the two men trailing immediately behind. Several times Harry began to speak, each time biting his tongue. Ron went into the tent, stopped just inside. He saw a middle-aged couple, the man tall and white-haired, his face sorrowful. His wife gripped her husband's hand. No question. Ron walked up to them.

"I can't do anything to undo what happened," he said.

They stared at him in shock.

"I'm the one. I don't want anyone else blamed. I still don't know how it happened, but I'm the one who did it. You're missionaries, they told me. Maybe you can do some good with this." He laid down the bag before them.

"It's everything I have. Over a hundred thousand dollars."

The white-haired man studied him. He forced his throat clear before he spoke to Ron. "I'm sure it's blood money, isn't it."

Statement. No question. It was like ice water in his face and it snapped Ron back to the moment. "Yes, sir. It is. And it's got your kid's blood on it, too." Ron flicked his eyes from the man to the woman and back again to the man. "Nothing can be undone. All you can do is use this to—to—I don't know what the hell for."

The woman came at him with a demon's cry, her hand raking across his face, going for the eyes. Her husband snatched back her arm as five welts oozed blood on Ron's cheek. He hadn't moved a muscle. He stood rock-still, crossed a mental river in his mind. He shrugged and turned to Harry.

"That's it. Get me the hell out of here."

"Okay."

They didn't waste any time. One hour later he climbed into the back seat of a jet fighter. No markings of any kind. All gray. They put a brain bucket on his head, secured his belts and oxygen hoses and intercom connections, and Harry personally removed the arming device for the ejection seat. A precaution. He didn't bother saying anything. Ron looked straight ahead. Not a glimpse to the left or the right of him.

The big fighter boomed out and clawed effortlessly to fifty-four thousand feet. Ron sat in silence, uncaring about the golden reflections off the ocean far below or the swept-wing jet tankers they descended to meet for new loads of fuel. He knew little of the short night created by their own speed, and he didn't know if he slept or was simply in a trance, but he came alert when he saw the earth tilted far over to one side and clouds rushing upward at them. They were going down. They landed at dusk on a concrete strip in the middle of nowhere. Cars drove up, and men helped Ron climb down from the big fighter. They drove off to the side as the pilot started his engines. Moments later, twin spears of fire and a thunder that cracked the heavens beat down on them and the winged machine was gone, a hollow echoing hoarse cry at the last moment of its existence.

Ron didn't know where the hell he was and he didn't give a damn. The men stood outside the car. Ron looked around him. A sea of concrete. Trees and hills bulking in the darkness about him. Then he noticed it. *The smell. It's gone— no rot, no haze or stink, no mobs of goddamned bugs—oh Jesus but it smells sweet! I'm—my God, I'm home* . . .

A figure in the darkness extended a cigarette. Ron took it and accepted a light. He sucked deeply and greedily, taking the smoke into his lungs, savoring the taste. He felt a great shudder go through his body as if an evil wind had passed through him. Of a rush he was full-bodied again, wrapped in his human shell, wearing the mantle of the animal creature.

"Coffee? You look like you could use some. That was a hell of a trip home."

He blew smoke out slowly and nodded. "Thanks. Straight black."

He'd never known coffee to taste so good. He drank two cups and went through one cigarette after another, not nervous or sweaty or feeling a tic, not even sundered by imagination and memory, but immersed in the moment. He went around to the back of the car by a patch of grass, and even the act of urinating in the darkness seemed to him another desperately needed move in shifting from the reality of one world to another. As he walked back to the group of men, he heard a hollow torch thunder in the sky, its volume increasing with every second.

"That's your friend," a voice said, and Ron nodded to himself. Lights appeared in the sky and rushed past like glowing angels and the thunder maw of a volcano. Suddenly, different-colored lights glowed into being on the ground, showing a long strip, and the dark winged beast snarled down from the sky, squealed tires on concrete, and taxied up to them. Ron rested against the car as he watched Gary coming down, stiff and sore, from the fighter.

Seeing Gary plunged him back into the world he had just escaped. He cursed silently. A man approached him, saying, "We go in separate cars. Would you get in, please?"

"You say that nicely."

"No reason not to, sir."

Ron strained to make out details of the face before him. No way. "Why the kid gloves?"

"Mr. Previn, all we know is that you had a rough time and that higher authority saw fit to bring you here. Our orders are to take the best care of you that we can. We're going to a private place in nearby mountain country. Isolated, excellent quarters; the works."

"You spell confinement with pretty words, baby."

"I'm sorry you see it that way, sir."

"You just do your job, right?"

"Yes, sir."

"And if I decide not to go with you?"

"Please, Mr. Previn. We mean it. We don't even know who you are. Our orders are to take the best possible care of you."

Ron shrugged. "Shit, you're just a dogface doing his job like anybody else. No hard feelings. You've got a nice touch. Okay."

The door opened. Ron started in, hesitated, stepped back to look at the other car. In the dim night lights he saw Gary, shoulders slumped, walking with a dragging foot to the other car. "I should have killed him, you know," he said to his shadow.

Pause. Then the careful words. "Why is that, sir?"

"Because he still sucks his thumb, he doesn't know enough to pour piss out of a boot, and your friends where we came from have brainwashed him to a fare-thee-well. The only kind thing you do for vegetables, mister, if they're human vegetables and rotting inside their heads, is to kill them. That's kind. It's merciful. I didn't kill Gary. I should have. He's my friend and I let him down. Now the poor bastard has a lifetime of nightmares ahead of him."

He got into the car and thought about throwing up on the driver. Shit, it wasn't worth the effort.

The driver was nothing, and Gary was the living dead. Ron made a supreme effort to raise a wall around his mind, to make a choice about what to forget and what to remember.

His mind was no longer his own—but he had no way of knowing that.

19

Ron looked out through an enormous window that was framed in stone and timber. They knew how to do it right. He guessed they were somewhere in the Tennessee or Kentucky hills, maybe even West Virginia, on a government preserve that guaranteed absolute isolation. No cars or planes or hikers. The fields shone with splendid growth and the hills rounded off warmly and invitingly. Birds, rabbits, chipmunks, even some raccoons and a fox or two often came within his view. His first sight of several deer had a calming effect on him. Something bright in the skies caught his attention—a shiny winged shape trailing a white swath in the heavens. Probably a Jet Liner whose passengers looked down on a distant pattern of verdant fields and streams and clouds and hills. From up there you couldn't even tell if the earth below were inhabited.

Ron liked that. He looked at a wall clock as a bell chimed. Dinner. They did that well, too. Provided him with a comfortable apartment done in pleasing wood and stone and soothing autumn browns. Luxuriant couches, a well-stocked bar, and a king-sized bed with the sheets changed every day by someone he'd never seen. Someone cleaned, kept his clothes fresh, and . . .

He didn't know how they'd done it, but he'd had a full wardrobe waiting for him. Comfortable sports stuff; jeans and sweaters and T-shirts and sneakers and hiking boots. All he had to do was throw his dirty clothes into a giant hamper, and

138

they came back clean within twenty-four hours. They did it all; magazines and television and radio and all kinds of stereo. But no telephone.

Well, he didn't give a shit about that. There wasn't anyone he wanted to talk to anyway.

He started from the room. Turn right on the carpeted hallway to the far end and right again into the private dining room. He wondered if Gary would be there, and then he remembered it had been two months since he'd seen Gary. Oh, well. He walked slowly down the hallway, a cigarette dangling from his lips, his body comfortable in jeans and a sweat shirt and moccasins. Gary. He recalled the last time they'd seen each other. Gary had come into his room.

"I'm leaving," he announced.

Ron was sprawled on a couch, and he used the remote control to flick off the TV. "Again," he said.

"I said I'm leaving."

Ron nodded. "Okay."

Gary's cheek muscle twitched. "That's all? Just okay?"

"They forcing you to leave?"

"No, of course not."

"Then you're leaving because you want to."

"Well, uh, yes." He always felt so goddamned uncomfortable when Ron did this to him. It was like trying to play a game without knowing the rules.

"And if you want to, you'll let me know where you are and if you ever want to see me. If you don't want to—" Ron shrugged.

"We went through a hell of a lot to end it with a shrug," Gary said blackly.

"A kiss wouldn't make it. You're not my type."

"You son of a bitch, I came in here to offer you half of all the bread I brought home with me!" Gary was nearly wild by now. "I know you left everything you owned back there. Goddamn you, I'm trying to be decent and—"

Ron shifted position, still sprawled, and laughed at the other man. "You're as full of shit as a Christmas turkey. You really think fifty thousand is going to buy off your conscience? Man, you're a walking bundle of nerves. You're living with ghosts. I bet you haven't had a hardon since you got back here." He gestured diffidently. "Good luck. I mean that."

If looks could kill, Ron would have been planted six feet

under, then and there. Gary stalked from the room, and he never saw him again. Ironic—it was the first time he'd ever seen Gary make a decisive move, all on his own. Their last moment together.

But something he'd said nagged at him and had kept on nagging at him. Right now, walking down the hallway to the dining room, it was starting to joggle about in his mind. Two months ago he'd told Gary he bet he'd hadn't had a hardon since arriving in this forest palace. He stopped short. Holy shit, he was the same way. He hadn't gotten it up for three months now, and he'd never had even the slightest desire to do so. For a man who loved rolling in the hay, that stank.

He quickened his pace. Jerry Feldman would be at his dinner table tonight. *Doctor* Jerry Feldman. All of a sudden, Ron wanted a whole bunch of questions answered. He entered the dining room, looked around, and recognized Feldman in the far corner. The doctor waved to him, and Ron saw a woman seated at the table.

It hit him like a bomb. That was the first woman he had seen in the three months since he'd come to this padded cell. Coincidence?

He walked briskly to Feldman's table.

"By my clock," Dr. Feldman said with a smile, "you have asked one question after the other, without interruption and without waiting for any answers, these past three minutes and fifty-two seconds." He tapped his watch. "That is significant, and furthermore, it's what we've been waiting for."

The three had returned to Ron's apartment after dinner; the woman, red-haired and quietly attractive, had played a spectator role, with smiles and pithy comments and some unexpected knee-to-knee contact beneath the table. Now Ron listened to Feldman, poured himself another stiff Cognac, and gestured with his glass. "Why is it so significant?"

"Because for months you haven't asked us any questions. You haven't even thought in that frame of mind. You haven't cared."

"That's ridiculous," Ron retorted. Then he thought about it—the gray areas of time, the blank spaces, the torpor—and he went hungrily for his drink. "Maybe it's not so ridiculous," he mused aloud.

"Think about something," Feldman said. "How much do you remember of the last ninety days? Aside from your relationship with Gary, that is. He was immediate, and he was frontal lobe, so to speak. Aside from him, what do you recall? Trees, nice furniture, the dining room, television?"

Ron strained, and he was dissatisfied with the few pitiful drops that squeezed into his mind. "Goddamned little," he said softly. He felt something he hadn't felt for a long time— the steel in his physical backbone, and in his mind. *We're coming back!* It was a joyous whisper, barely audible, from somewhere deep within his skull. A tiny chorus of voices, flooding his memory cells with gasps of relief; a dot in his cerebral cosmos, but growing larger all the time and taking so long to do it because it had so bloody far to go.

He felt an enormous loneliness blowing away from him, like sand collected in dead wind now subjected to a fresh and fierce breeze, clearing off the outer surfaces and letting in light. He turned back to Feldman, but the doctor got in his words a hair's trigger before Ron spoke.

"You've been talking with your friends again, I assume," Feldman said, his smile stolen from the Cheshire cat.

Ron's eyes narrowed. "Now you tell me how you knew that."

"You admit to it? It's very important that you do." Feldman leaned forward on the couch, fingers clasped, studying Ron with fervent intensity. "A lie now could do great damage."

"Nothing personal, doctor, but fuck you," Ron told him. "Why the hell should I lie to you?"

The intended rebuke didn't bother Feldman at all. He smiled, and his eyes bored into Ron's. "To which one of you am I talking?" he demanded in a suddenly harsh voice.

Ron felt a multiple facial grin within his head. He laughed. "The gang."

"All of them?"

"All," Ron said with a wide grin. "And Jesus, but it feels good."

"We drugged you, you know."

The smile vanished and Ron stared without expression.

"Oh, come on, Ron; if you hadn't already figured it out by now, you would at any moment. We drugged you with tranquilizing agents. A sort of waking stupor. Shut down the active brain cells. Depress imagination. Increase the alpha-wave pattern. In fact, we used the alpha sleep system to keep you out for ten days. It's a remarkable machine. We place electrodes about the head, they emphasize alpha-wave patterns in the brain, and you sleep like a babe for ten days. No drugs were used for that."

The man who'd stalked the jungle trails was alive and well in that room. "Only tranquilizers?"

"Those and no more. You see, we had to bring you down. Severe shock. You know all the details." Feldman flicked a side-glance at the woman, who was quiet and attentive, her smile indicating that she knew something Ron didn't and was amused to watch him floundering. "So why repeat them here and now? Suffice to say you had to be kept on a noncerebral level as much as possible. Turn off the high-powered mental jets until that subconscious of yours could grope with reality. Your, ah, gang, as you call them."

Ron was stalking. "I need to know if anything else was used."

"You already know it wasn't," Feldman said smoothly. "You have a type of mind we can't simply drug. You have a multiple personality, Previn, but in your case it's a blessing instead of a problem, a grasp at survival no matter what, because all of you—the gang—work together. They sometimes work in different ways, but always for the same purpose. So what I say doesn't matter. Don't ask me. I might lie to you. Ask them. They can't lie to you, and we couldn't drug them within your subconscious. You want to know something very important? You're a lousy hypnotic subject. One of you goes out, maybe two, but the rest of the gang plays watchdog. Go on, Previn, ask the watchdogs."

Ron heard no argument from within himself. *He's a slick fucker but he's honest.* Ron didn't know who said that, but it was from some member of himself—the best he could phrase it, anyway—and he nodded his head. "Okay," he said to Feldman. An afterthought hit him. "When did you stop?"

Feldman clapped his hands in delight. "Excellent! Self-prognosis, and with accuracy. Eight days ago. The body finally rejects the last traces, and presto, here you are. I'd like to talk to you some more about—"

Ron held up a hand. "Enough." He turned to the woman. "Marcia, isn't it?"

She smiled. "Marcia Pollak."

"Doctor?"

"Psychiatrist."

"Mine?"

"Yours," she confirmed.

"We have things to talk about?"

"We have been for over a month. You don't remember them because you didn't want to. I gave you permission to push them to the back of your mind. They'll all come forward in the next several weeks."

Doubt trickled from somewhere in Ron's mind, a kind of slow warning. Were they leaving something out? Ron pushed the doubt aside—this was a big day in his life, and he wanted to enjoy it.

"Crawled into my head, huh?"

She nodded.

"How deep?"

"You had a lot to get rid of. Deep enough. I stopped when I felt I'd gone as far as was necessary."

"When was that?"

"The first time you masturbated. It made a deep impression in your mind."

He felt the grin inside him, another rush of doubt, then a blush. He stood silently for a while and then turned to Feldman. "Good night, doc."

Feldman was startled. "I beg your pardon?"

"I said, good night. You're not needed anymore."

"I don't understand—"

"Then let's try; get your ass out of here or I'll throw it out," Ron said quietly. *Quiet cheering in that long corridor in his mind.*

Feldman's face was dark. "I had the impression we had become good friends, Previn."

"Well, doc, it just goes to show you. Next time you pick someone for a friend, you'd better give them a choice in the matter. *Move it.*"

He locked the door behind the doctor. Then he turned and leaned against the door. "What's with us?" he asked finally.

"If I didn't want to be here, I'd be on the other side of the door," came the reply. She kicked off her shoes and tucked her legs beneath her on the sofa. "I would appreciate a drink."

He went to the bar and brought back drinks for both of them. They clinked glasses. "Welcome back to yourself," she said.

"Still here as a headshrink?"

"Uh uh. Off duty."

He took a long pull. "How long does that last?"

"You've forgotten your bedroom manners, Ron. Aren't you tired of questions?" The doubts that had been snagging Ron's mind fled at the sound of her voice; it had been a long time. Ron's guard was down and his gang was on vacation.

She was incredible. She made love like a wanton tigress. All the expertise of a young whore and the rashness of a hot teen-ager. When he awoke in the morning she was gone; there were deep scratches along his back and his thighs. He showered and dressed and went to the dining room for breakfast, a vague discontent walking with him, a new and nagging sense of not being in control. A stranger joined him at his table, and it didn't take so much as a second look to recognize one of the old company pros.

"The name is Jake," Ron heard. "I'm your present and future contact in the world. Enjoy your coffee. You're leaving here within the next two hours. We go from here to my office, and we talk. Don't bother going back to your apartment. Everything you own is packed and in my office. You done? Good. Let's go."

He studied this one. Deceptively big, broad shoulders. He'd been one of the combat people somewhere along the line. Paratrooper, commando, special forces—the works. Smarter than the next man in line, an affinity for killing and for his own survival, and leadership squeezing through it all until "they" tapped him on the shoulder and made him a man who programs other men. Ron winced. Jake had dark hair and hairy arms and a heavy moustache, and his loose sweater didn't hide his muscles. He also had muscles between his ears, as Ron suspected and Jake proved.

In his office, Ron relaxed in a deep soft chair. He felt keenly at rest with himself physically and razor-alert mentally. "First question. Your name really Jake?"

The other man laughed. "I'll bet I'm the first one to use his own name."

"Last name?"

"Why bother? It would be a lie."

"Okay. What now?"

Jake opened an attaché case and spread papers on his desk. "You go from here to Lima, Ohio. Where it all began," he said, "a thousand years ago."

"You're good. Go on."

"We let you off there. Here's your driver's license, draft registration card, Sinclair Oil union card for working the Singapore area, canceled stubs for your employment checks while you were in Singapore, rent receipts, sales receipt for a small boat you sold before leaving the area, the ownership of a used car along with the keys—we'll expect you to handle your own insurance on that, by the way. There's also your character reference from Sinclair as a welder and machinist, records of your immunizations and other shots, and a copy of your income tax paid in full and based on your Sinclair employment. Let's see. Oh yes, here's a list of places where you may be interested in getting a job, some gasoline credit cards, another for Diners' Club, stuff like that. We take you to Lima, there's a hotel room—you're already registered and here's the key—paid for a month in advance. And there's one thousand dollars in expense money in this envelope. Any questions?"

"You forgot my birth certificate."

"That document, along with school records and everything before you left for, ah, Singapore, is undisturbed, and in the family bank vault."

"Why the thousand bucks?"

Jake shrugged. "The rule is we know very little about the specific background of our, well, I'll call you a client."

"And what are you to me?"

"Your contact."

"For what?"

"For *anything*."

"That's a big word."

"And that's a big world out there, Previn. You may not like it. You may not like welding hunks of iron for a living. That's why I'm your contact. You have this telephone number; I want you to memorize it. You can reach me through that number, day or night, seven days a week."

"Why the hell would I call you?"

"You may want to work for us again."

"You mean—"

"It's never the same. But the same line."

"Go fuck yourself. And pass it on."

"All right," Jake said good-naturedly. "I will. Any other messages?"

Ron studied him. "Yeah. How do I reach Marcia Pollak?"

"Who?"

"*Doctor* Marcia Pollak. Headshrink. You know, resident psychiatrist? Dr. Feldman introduced me to her last night."

"I know Feldman. But I never heard of Marcia Pollak, and I've been here two years."

For a long time Ron looked at the man across the desk. He remembered the trickle of doubt, swore at himself for not heeding it, and then thought, what the hell, it was a great night anyway. Finally, he sighed. "That's the way it goes, then."

"Memorize that number. It's your guaranteed action line for a friend, *for anything*."

"If I need any cobra venom, I'll call."

He went out the door without a backward look. Out the door and into what people like to call the real world.

20

Seven years.

It had been seven long, full, eventful, tiring, up-against-the-wall years since he'd walked away from that lovely forested retreat in the hills of a state whose name he didn't even know. It had taken all those seven years for him to begin to believe he might really make it.

He screwed around for the first few months. He never used that hotel room. He took the car and drove the hell out of Ohio and back to the hills and mountains and trees of a small town thirty miles outside Albany, New York. The thousand bucks wouldn't last forever, and there was a machine shop in town that did piddling work. Ron told the boss he could weld better than any thirty men and once word got around business would be pouring in from everybody in Hickory and from Albany and anywhere else the word would reach. The old man snorted his disdain, and Ron looked at him quietly. "No pay for two weeks. You buy my food, that's all. You don't want to hire me two weeks from today, we shake hands and I disappear."

The old farmers went for that sort of put-up-or-shut-up routine. Two weeks later old man Novick offered him $165 a week.

"Two twenty five," Ron countered.

"That's too rich for my blood," Novick said.

Ron grinned at him. "Been nice knowing you, old man."

"You're not leaving, are you?"

147

"Bye-bye." Ron was on his way out the door.

"Goddamn it, I got work orders backed up for two months already!" Novick shouted after him.

Ron didn't turn around but waved airily.

"Okay, okay! You got it! Just get your ass to work!" Novick shouted again.

Ron went back, smiling. "Glad you decided to make it two fifty a week."

Novick spluttered and reddened.

"Look, old man," Ron said, "we both know I'm worth twice that much. Let's cut the horsecrap, okay? You'll be making more money off me than you ever made in your life."

"All right, boy, I'll cut the horsecrap. You're too good for a small place like this. Big-city companies would snap you up once they saw the way you work." Novick sniffed suspiciously. "You on the lam or something? Not that it matters," he said hastily. "I don't care about a man's past. Mine ain't so clean either."

Ron rested a hand on the old man's shoulder. "I'm not on the lam, Mr. Novick. I got no record, and no one is chasing me."

Old eyes peered into his. "Except yourself, son."

"We never talk about this again."

Jim Novick extended his hand and they clasped. "Get your ass to work. The customers are raising seven kinds of hell already."

Two years later, he met Pat. Beautiful Pat, small and frail and a farmer's daughter. Sweet and innocent, but not naïve. Church all her life, her folks still living two hundred years back in Europe where *their* family tree had once rooted deep. He fell head over heels in love, and he was kind and gentle, as if he'd never been any other way. He and Pat did all the things small-town couples do—movies, church socials, long walks over the hills. They'd sit for hours holding hands, and sometimes they'd talk, but Pat wasn't a questioner; she was a planner. They spoke always of the future, almost never of the past. Pat loved him, Ron knew, for his gentleness and for the way he never tried to rush her into anything, or change her, or make her feel uncomfortable. After a while, it was as if they'd never known a life without each other. Ron felt a sense of belonging, of the rightness of things. He felt good.

They were married only four months after they'd met. Mary Ellen Previn came along a year after that, and in another year there was Esther. By then Ron was making four hundred a week and running the business almost single-handed. Old man Novick was failing fast, and one night, after a particularly muggy and frustrating workday, he collapsed from a torn heart muscle.

Ron talked with him in the hospital. "I'm going to make it," Novick said in a weak and hoarse voice. "But it's Florida for me. Too old and too fragile. Doc says a hard winter up here would kill me, while I got maybe ten to fifteen years down there."

"I'd like to run the business, Mr. Novick. Fifty-fifty. You get your old ass on down to Florida and stay alive, and I'll run the place and split it with you right down the middle. You won't have a thing to worry about."

Novick closed his eyes, and a long shudder went through him. Then he looked hard at Ron. "That's better than I hoped for. I was going to give you first choice. Sell the business, you know."

"It's better this way. You've been real good to me and Pat, old man."

Novick sniffed and wiped his nose with the back of his hand. "Well, shoot, you'uns the only *real* family I got." They shook hands, and Ron went back to the welding shop that now occupied an entire block in the small town of Hickory. He felt good. Novick would make it. The old duffer deserved his last years in the Florida sun, and business had never been better. It was a high point for Ron Previn. He had a good job, a wife and kids he loved, and he was home, in the part of the world he loved best. He didn't ask for anything more. Like Pat, he looked always forward, never back. During that time, Ron was not much used to the puppeteer—far away and unknown to Ron—who kept his mind on an invisible electronic string, knowing and even planning his every move. Ron was—he thought—in charge, at home, fulfilled.

And then the god-awful blood disease struck Pat and held her on the edge of death. Ron nearly went mad as he clung to her pale hands at her bedside. A friend looked after the two children, and there was surgery, and Ron wasn't working the welding shop because he didn't dare leave Pat's side. Somehow, his young assistant kept the business going, but still the hospital bills and the surgery ripped his finances to shreds.

Old man Novick had a younger brother; the two men had hated one another for years, but he was a blood relative, and Ron hadn't signed any paper with the old man. While Ron mourned and prayed for his wife only to survive, damn it, that son of a bitch burned the welding shop to the ground to claim the insurance money. It was stupid from the beginning, and Ron couldn't figure why he would even try something so crazy, until the lawyers told him that old man Novick had dropped dead exactly eleven days after he reached Florida. No one had known to tell Ron. The police couldn't prove arson, and the insurance was paid off—to Novick's brother.

Ron was broke, deeply in debt. He kept on trying to take care of his two children and to buoy Pat's spirits. He worked two jobs and seven days a week. It was brutal, but he was making it because Pat was recovering. Oh Christ, slowly, ever so slowly, but it was happening. Pat crawled her way back from the edge of the abyss, sustained by her own strong will and the love of her man that never for an instant wavered. Ron's gentleness, even in his worry and deep fatugue, sustained her; his strength poured into her. He felt it, and he was proud, even when the worry about money and the hellish tiredness pushed him to a low ebb. He was in trouble, but he was making it, and he had what he wanted—security and love and happiness. He was damned if he'd let it go.

Then the past tapped him on the shoulder.

"The usual, fella?"

Ron slipped wearily onto the barstool. "Yeah, Charlie. Nice and cold, please."

Charlie moved skilled hands, and cold beer flowed down the inside of the frosted mug. It had been their ritual for a long time. Ron finished one job, went to eat supper with the kids, and then dashed off to the hospital to spend his evening hour with Pat. That left him twenty-five minutes between jobs, and he would stop in Charlie's Tavern to close his mind and rest on what little limb of sanity might be extended to him. One beer. That was his only luxury. One beer and twenty minutes on this barstool, and he asked nothing more of life.

"How's the wife?"

Ron tipped the glass to the bartender. "Every day a little better, Charlie. Thanks."

"Anything we can do?"

"You're doing fine."

"You looked beat coming in here."

Ron smiled thinly. "A hazard of working thirty-two hours a day."

"Wrap that one up and have one on me."

"Thanks. I could—"

"Hey, you're the one, all right!" Something started to tick, far away in the back of Ron's tired mind—like a warning signal.

Charlie watched without comment. A big man slid into the seat next to Ron's. A bit too much to drink. Overfriendly, sloppy, flap-jawed, a scene-stealer. Ron went through all these things immediately, and they all spelled trouble. He didn't know why, he didn't understand it yet, but his every hackle stood erect and bristled. Without turning his head, Ron told Charlie it was okay. "I know him from somewhere, Charlie."

Charlie grumbled and went off to attend to customers at the other end of the bar. Ron studied the man. No connections, no memories. Nothing. Ron felt himself shifting gears behind his eyebrows.

"What's your name, friend, and where do I know you from?"

A big hand fell heavily on his shoulder and stale beer wafted to his nostrils. "Hey, shit, man, we don't *know* each other. Not by introduction, you know what I mean?" The voice was loud, and it was getting louder. "But I seen you before, man. You know, over there. I was a merchant seaman. Sinclair tanker—and I was working the coast of—"

"Hold it down," Ron hissed. "The whole place is listening."

His remark was met with open astonishment. "Hey, so what? My name's Drexel. Hans Drexel. Old sailing family. I know who you are, fella. Why, they was telling stories about you all up and down the coast of Nam, and—"

"You son of a bitch, hold it down. Nobody here knows anything about my past, and I don't want them to know."

Drexel's eyes widened. "What's with you, Jack? There's a war going on over there, or haven't you heard? What the hell, everybody's killing and burning now. It's a regular busi-

ness with all them helicopters and planes. They're tearing
towns up like confetti. What the fuck is one kid, anyway? The
way I hear what happened, you sort of liked what you were
doing over—"

It was pure instinct. The German seaman was eighty
pounds heavier than Ron, and Ron hadn't even thought this
way for all these years, hadn't so much as lifted a finger
against anyone, but in an instant, the flick of a diaphragm
snapping open, everything he had known and knew how to
do snapped back into his mind and his hands and his body.
He was moving without conscious thought. Words blinked
into existence in his mind: *Shut this bastard up. Shut him up
fast and good. He can destroy it all.*

Ron's knuckles formed a wedge and leaped into Drexel's
Adam's apple. The big man gagged, beet red, fighting for
breath, staring wide-eyed. In a fluid sweeping motion Ron
jerked a beer bottle from the bar, smashed it below the neck,
and hurled himself at some one he hadn't known for years.

The enemy.

The jagged glass ripped across Drexel's eyes. The thin
scream Ron hadn't heard in seven years sliced into his brain
like a needle; Ron jerked Drexel's head back by one thick
ear, and the bottle plunged into his throat. Blood bubbled
and foamed, and before the men around them could move,
even before Charlie hurled himself across the bar to slam into
Ron, Ron had managed four perfectly aimed kicks against the
side of Drexel's skull.

He stood calmly as the bartender wrestled him away. Charlie looked into his eyes, and Ron's calm eyes looked back.
"It's cool, man. Call the police, Charlie. He needs help."

Charlie stared at him a moment before moving away.
Stared and started to ask questions and then changed his
mind. Ron was thankful for that. He liked Charlie.

They booked Ron for assault with a deadly weapon, and
they fingerprinted him and threw him into the local slammer.
The chief of police was as puzzled as anyone else. Bob Stanford turned the lock slowly. "Shit, Previn, I hate to do this.
You're a friend in this town. Man, in the seven years I know
you, you ain't even spit on the sidewalk. What in tarnation
possessed you tonight? I saw that man. You carved him up

like a Christmas turkey. You know he may not make it, don'tcha?"

Ron wanted to ignore him, but the chief meant well, and he was only trying to help. "Yeah. They told me."

"What happened?"

"Not sure, chief. Something he said."

"Something he *said?* What would have happened if he'd *done* something you didn't like?"

Ron shrugged. *Stay cool*, somebody told him inside his head. "Chief, could you have someone find out how my wife is doing?"

Bob Stanford looked at him for a while. "For someone who did what you just did, you're as calm as a sleeping hound dog. Course I'll ask, Ron. If you need something, holler. Sorry about having to lock you up. I'll have to wait until morning to find out about bail for you."

"Thanks."

They didn't need bail in the morning. Sometime during the night an ambulance pulled up to the emergency entrance of the local hospital and four men in white uniforms went inside and talked for a while. The ambulance drove off.

In the morning the entry records for Hans Drexel were nonexistent. He had never been admitted to the hospital. The room assigned to him was occupied by an elderly woman with a broken hip, and she'd been there a week. The records were all in order.

A man in a dark suit—a man Ron had never seen before—stood outside his jail cell in the morning. Dark suit, dark tie, pale blue shirt, waxed shoes, and the inevitable attaché case. He stood quietly as Chief Stanford fumbled for his keys, as nervous as if he were in company with the devil. Stanford opened the cell and walked away quickly.

The man stood outside the cell. "You're free. Go home. We don't know what happened, but we have a good idea. We don't want to know. Just go on home and forget about it." The stranger turned on his heel and walked away. Ron went into the chief's front office and together they watched a black sedan pull away.

"Who the hell was that?" Ron asked the police chief.

Stanford looked at Ron as if he'd grown his own set of horns. "You know what, Previn? I was just about to ask you the same question."

Ron didn't respond. "What happens to me now?"

"Happens?" Stanford's voice was almost shrill. "There is no injured person. There is no assault victim at the hospital. They say there never was. All a big mistake in the records. There are no charges. You are not under arrest. It never happened."

Stanford opened a desk, pulled out a bottle and uncorked it, and took a long swallow; he wiped the bottle on his sleeve and passed it to Ron. "Take a good drink and then get out of here, and don't, whoever or whatever you are, tell me about it."

Ron walked home slowly to change his clothes—clothes that were matted with the dried blood of a man he'd slashed to ribbons, a man who failed to exist the morning after.

Seven years. And they were right there. Snap your fingers and presto; no attack, no victim, nothing. Just blood-clotted clothes.

Holy Christ. Just how much power did they have? Jake had said to call, but he'd never said they'd be calling on *him*. Wasn't the past dead yet? Ron had all he could do to cope with the present—a sick wife, two little kids he loved more than life itself, and a couple of shitty jobs that didn't pay enough to keep a healthy family going, let alone a sick one.

He didn't need any more hassles. Ron tried to push the whole Drexel thing out of his mind; he didn't have the time or energy to cope with it.

21

There isn't any glory in the day to day. No heroics, no battle flags or stirring marches. Day-to-day heroes are invisible. They get up every morning to the same grind, terrible as it may be, and they fall exhausted and unnoticed into the same bed every night. And all you do, sighed a weary Ron Previn, is tighten the muscles in your ass and your back and just stay with it. That was the key. *Stay with it, man. Get a good grip on life and hang in there.*

Ron did that. He hardly saw the two kids, but they were well taken care of by the old woman who doted on them with grandmotherly affection. Better than he could do. When he did see them, he was reassured by their unquestioning love. They seemed to know, those two little girls, that their father was an unsung hero and that their love was what kept him going. They gave, and they accepted, and a few minutes with them each evening was, for Ron Previn, like a blood transfusion to a man who's bleeding to death.

Pat had come back strongly, suffered a relapse, but her chart line was inching upward again. Slow as hell, but better up than down. In a funny way, though, he was distant from Pat. Not that she knew this distance: the Ron who came to see her, who gave her the local gossip and told her little stories about the kids, was still the same steady, gentle Ron she knew and loved. But he was going through the motions when he described "this new job."

"It's a lifesaver, hon, I really mean it," he insisted.

"Here I've been working these two jobs and—shh, this isn't a complaint, it's just the way it is, but I got this new job in that big auto repair place. They rebuild cars and make up special ones, and what they need more than anything else is the best welder in the world, and that's your husband. That's right, *me*. No more two jobs. Sure, I do a lot of overtime, but I get paid time and a half, and it's all at one place and—"

Pat listened, and he kissed her and hugged her gently because she was so frail. But in the back of his mind there was that ticking, that itching, that told him life was one big fucking monotone. His salvation was those personalities inside his head. Or so he thought. They let the Ron who faced the world manage to cope with this sort of trivial shit. *Hold it. Why the hell would I think that way about my own wife and kids? Who the hell thinks it's so trivial, or that it's shit? Why the hell would I think that way about my own wife and kids? Who the hell thinks it's so trivial, or that it's shit?*

The answer kicked him in the belly. *You do, asshole, only you don't even know it. But you will. How long do you think you can keep hiding from yourself?* He turned the voices off, and their laughter seemed to echo down the halls of his brain. *We'll wait,* they said cheerily. *You're like a timer, baby. Just as soon as someone pulls the wire—*

He turned them off. But he kept thinking about the man in the dark suit, and about the slashed bundle of flesh that had appeared so providentially in the bar and disappeared so magically from that hospital room. He simply had to face reality. After all these years, *they* were still with him. They knew when he needed them, and they knew where to find him if they needed or wanted him. But how? He still did not know for certain what government agency had worked him into and through Vietnam and brought him back here. He had heard and read references in the press and on television about the CIA. It was big stuff about how they'd managed wars and knocked off governments and guided national destinies, but he had never given a rat's ass about it. He had that telephone number burned into his mind though, and he could still summon a perfect mental picture of Jake. *Call us anytime. We're your friends. Call us for anything you need. Friends. We're your friends.* He'd needed them, all right. He could have used a better hospital for Pat and a thousand other things, but the biggest debts of all had been left in a foreign land, and he didn't want that account reopened. Want it or not, they'd kept it active, and he might be in a cold cell now with Pat giving up and dying and the kids off to some foster home except for the fact that they'd stepped in and cleaned it up. He owed them for that. They didn't say it and they didn't need to. He knew the facts of life, and he appreciated the way they'd done it all so slickly. And they still weren't pushing him. Or were they? If Drexler had been a setup . . .

They, *they*, *THEY*.

Just how goddamned far were they into his personal life? And why? They had to be watching him, covering his tracks, knowing everything that was happening, because within hours of his cutting up that loudmouthed merchant seaman they'd moved in and exercised one hell of a lot of legal muscle—and all so *quietly*. Without the man in the dark suit, he would never have known who or what or how or why. He still didn't.

What galled and frustrated him was his blindness on the whole matter. He moved in a fog while all around him events were shaping his life. All he wanted was to get Pat out of that hospital and get the family back together and go one day at a time into the future. And if he managed that, would *they* still hang on? Were they just waiting for him to come back into the fold? By now he knew they had kept their word to him. Was fighting every miserable day of his life like this utterly fucking stupid? *It's your pride that keeps Pat where she is. All you need to do is make that call. You know the number. Just ask for Jake, and just like that Pat's in the best hospital with the best medicine and—SHUT UP!*

Shut up because that kind of reasoning was wrong. Pat was Bible family, and if she'd known, even for an instant, that the past of her kind and loving husband included mass murder, burning people alive, and chopping kids in half with machine guns . . . He buried his head in his hands, dejected. Trapped. If she knew, it would be the end of his marriage, and all the hospitals and medicine in the world couldn't help her, and she'd die because the thought of his entering her and loving her and his seed growing in her womb . . . Shame can kill some people. It could kill Pat. Or, if she survived, sure as hell it would kill his marriage. Her love would wither overnight like a plant struck with a lethal fungus.

No; it was better this way, slogging one day at a time.

Besides, he had that rotten core of himself to deal with. He'd cut up and torn Drexel apart with contemptuous ease. The man dwarfed Ron, yet Ron, who hadn't touched a weapon or another human being in seven long years, had handled Drexel with that same old swift sureness. *And he had enjoyed it*. God help him, but it was true. There had been a thrill, an ejaculatory rush of adrenaline, when he had slashed with the bottle, when he'd jerked back the head, back and to the side at the perfect angle to mangle the jugular, and his booted foot slamming into . . .

He groaned. Oh, Jesus, if there was sin here, let there be some way of blotting it out, of absolving that sin. He looked for people following him or observing him; then he shook off that idea before it became its own kind of paranoia. Of course they had him under observation, and if he hadn't noticed it for seven years he wouldn't find them vulnerable now to his sudden examination. Because all they did was look. No touch. Just look. But how? And how deep?

He went through the motions of the days feeling disembodied, lost, wandering. He went to a church because the hope of absolution was still with him, into a confessional, even though he wasn't Catholic. He felt a presence in the booth next to him and slid out without speaking to the priest, but somehow just being in church made him feel better. Maybe it really helped because Pat strengthened swiftly, and the promise of her leaving the hospital was becoming a reality.

They began to talk about how they'd manage when the kids came home, and Ron was full of plans to help with the heavy work and the bedtime rituals. They found themselves holding hands again, and Ron felt a new surge of hope. Maybe everything would be okay this time. Maybe he'd just been paranoid, and Drexel's appearance was only a nasty coincidence. He pushed it all out of his mind and looked deep into Pat's eyes. She looked back, and she strengthened, day by day.

And then that rotten, stinking bitch, Helen, crawled out from under her rock into his life.

She was incredibly brazen about it. He saw this woman standing in the entrance to his welding shop, studying him. The first thing that caught his eye was her self-assurance. He could tell more from the set of a person's eyes than anything they might say or do. He returned her look and knew immediately that despite the fact that he'd never seen her before, this was no casual visit. She wore a dress. No suit, no slacks; not a professional. Too housewifish for that. Brown hair, about five foot four, and no more than 115 pounds. Not unattractive.

He shut down his torch as she walked slowly to him.

"My name is Helen. We have a great deal in common, and we need to talk."

"I don't know you, lady. I don't want to know you. I don't want to seem unpleasant, but I'm not even going to talk to you."

She didn't blink an eye. "I really do think you should change your mind, Ron."

"Okay, you're cute, and you know my name. What else?"

"When we talk, you'll be grateful I kept the conversation only between us." She glanced about them. "Not here. Privately. And it is important. Please; I'm not playing games."

"You hide it well."

"You don't want to fuck up your whole life, Ron."

That did it. She said the words so matter-of-factly there was no further contest. The hook was in and they both knew it. "Where and when?" he said, keeping it as short as possible.

"Let's go outside. Tell your boss you're taking the rest of the day off."

"No need. I work my own schedules."

"Even better," she smiled. "Outside, by my car. I'll be waiting for you there."

He watched her walk away. He closed the shop, called the front office, told them he was leaving to get parts and might not be back until late. He went outside and saw her standing by a blue Chevy. "Drive to the Oaks Shopping Mall and park your car outside the big drugstore. I'll pick you up there and we'll go on in my car."

No use asking questions. Not yet, anyway. Her style did have a certain intrigue, but his patience quotient was short as hell. She saw the danger signs in his face and patted his hand. "I'll make it clear very soon. I've preregistered us at the Thunderbird Motel in Ellentown. No one knows this car. It's a rental. I'm not compromising anything with your family. Please, let's get this over with."

Ron felt the familiar warning prickle at the back of his

skull. Was this another setup? Logic and clear thinking weren't going to answer that one; he'd just have to wing it.

He went back to his old self-training: turn off the part of your mind that thinks. Do it all automatically. *Wait, wait; just like we did when we set up those ambushes.* He was so startled with the thought that he said, "What?" aloud, but there was only silence. He drove to the shopping center, parked, and locked his car, and slid into the Chevy when she drove up. Not a word passed between them on the drive out of town.

The Thunderbird was some motel; no desk. She drove around to the back and had the key in her hand when they approached room 202 on the second floor. They went inside, and a glance told him she had the room set up. Drinks, ice, the minimum but necessary works.

He sat down in an easy chair, and she came across the room with a tall glass filled with ice and whiskey. No water. "Drink it," she told him. Of a sudden he needed the drink, and he drank slowly and steadily and held the glass for a refill. Her eyes widened as she refilled it. He felt the heat spreading through his chest and his belly and his arms and legs. Good. He needed some outside feeling.

"Lay it on me," he told her. "Don't play any more games because I don't like this, and if it becomes necessary, I walk out of here and you get carried out a couple of days from now when they find you."

The sound of his voice shocked him. It wasn't his own voice—not a voice he'd used in the last seven years, anyway.

She countered with an honest burst of laughter. "I could have made book on what you'd say, and I would've won."

He kept his silence.

"Everything I have to tell you, and our rendezvous here, is with my best friend in a sealed envelope. So get rid of all those nasty thoughts. I'm not here to blackmail you. Just to get what's mine. I can't change the past and neither can you, but I learned a long time ago to be smart instead of dead in the head."

"Get to the point."

"Do you know why you didn't frighten me with that asinine remark about walking out of here alone?"

"I don't. But I'm interested."

She took the time to light a cigarette and hand it to him. Jesus, she even knew his brand. She lit one for herself.

"I know all about you, Ron. About as much as anyone can know. Vietnam—just about all of it."

He stared at her.

"I know very well you can kill, even, you might say, on a very intimate level."

"You don't make sense."

"Of course I do. My husband, Ron, was a stupid man. An oaf, really. But he fathered four children of mine, and oaf or not, he was a good provider. But he's dead now."

"What the hell has that got to do with me?"

"Let me finish. Except for the money and the companionship, I don't really miss him. Still, I'm one of those women who needs a man to take care of her in bed. Not one-night stands. And with four kids, getting anything more than a one-night stand is tough."

He came slowly to his feet. The fire was burning in him neatly by now, and he didn't give a shit about any letter with any best friend or anything else.

She knew how to put out the fire. "Don't you understand yet? My name is Helen Drexel. You killed my husband in that bar."

22

He came awake the next morning, unable to collect his wits, fighting off a gray cloud that misted his mind. Something was terribly wrong. He blinked again and again at the bright sunlight spearing the curtains of the room. His mouth felt as if a squirrel had built a nest on his tongue during the night. What in the hell was wrong with him? He couldn't focus, couldn't think. He hadn't had that much to drink, and—drink. That was it. Something in the drink. Only two drinks the whole night. Only those two. Goddamn, he'd been drugged! Wiped out. He felt a body beside his own; he went rigid, then turned and saw the smiling face of Helen. A roar, wordless and of raw anger, exploded from him. His hands shot for and found her throat, his thumbs squeezing into her windpipe. She made gagging sounds, her eyes swelled, and she thrashed about wildly and turned purple before he realized what he was doing. His own strength surprised him. He threw her violently to the floor where she coughed and vomited. He didn't move to help her.

"You drugged me," he said at last, the accusation a whisper against her tortured breathing.

"Y—yes—I had to." She choked out the words.

"The next time that happens," he said with solemn quietness, "you are one very dead bitch, letter or no letter." He went to the bathroom, leaving her in her own filth. He showered in scalding water, returned to the room, and dressed. He went into the coffee shop and sat alone, waiting, not wanting to think. He knew she'd be there, and when she showed, her throat bruised purple and her eyes deep red and still half frightened, he pointed to her car. She got in without a word and took the wheel, starting back for the shopping center where he'd left his car. They remained encased in silence until the last few moments.

"Just play it fair, Ron," she said suddenly, not so much as a single word of preamble to open her gambit. "I'm not asking that much. I'll be in touch with you."

She stopped by his car, and he got out to walk around to her side, leaning close to her. He had a speech prepared, but he didn't bother with it. He leveled his gaze at her. "Go fuck yourself."

He drove back to Hickory without even bothering to look in his rearview mirror to see if she was following.

Jesus, the whole damned night, and Pat . . . he drove straight to the hospital, nearly ran to her room. She was beside herself and her trembling arms clasped weakly at his body. "I didn't know what happened to you. Oh, my darling, I was so *frightened*." Her hand caressed his cheek. "You know, the thoughts—"

"Never mind, hon."

"But I thought there could have been an accident, and the children . . ." She sagged back on the pillow, eyes red, her skin white as snow. "Pat, I just got weak, that's all. I went out and I got drunk. I was so damn tired of working day and night, and so frustrated at not being able to help you, I started drinking, and I woke up this morning in my god-damned car fifty miles away from here."

She nodded slowly, but the light didn't come back into her eyes. When he told her he "came to and drove straight here," she knew it was a lie, and he knew she recognized the lie because she smelled the soap on his body from the shower he'd taken that morning to scour the stink of Helen Drexel from his skin. She said nothing, but he knew she didn't believe him for shit. It only frustrated him all the more. There was nothing he could say, so he kissed her hurriedly and mumbled words about having to get to work because he was late. He almost ran from the room.

Four days of routine. Working fourteen hours, seeing the kids, faithful visits to the hospital, snatched sleep and bites to eat, and the deadly monotony began anew. On the fifth day she called. "Ron, this is Helen. I've got to talk to you." He slammed down the phone, cursing, all the more enraged because Pat was coming home from the hospital that day. The kids were wild with joy, and the old woman who'd been their "grandmother" was willing to join Ron and continue in her work.

They'd planned a celebration, and Ron wanted to hurry home to help the kids hang crepe paper streamers in the dining room and make sure the house was pretty for Pat's homecoming. He was tired, but the joy of having his family back together gave him energy to keep going.

The homecoming was a success. Pat couldn't seem to stop smiling and holding his hand, and the little girls were quiet and helpful, even put themselves to bed so Ron and Pat could have a peaceful hour together, sitting around the festive table, before Ron took her by the hand and helped her get ready for bed. He sat for a while, alone in the dark, thinking. This could be the turning point, the end of the hassle. The beginning—again—of a good life. Ron came as close to praying as he had in a long time. But even in the midst of those thoughts, something was clicking at the back of his mind. He wasn't really at peace. Who the hell was that woman, anyway, and why would she . . .

Two days and no calls. On the third day, five calls at the welding shop. That night, the first call to his home. Another at four in the morning. Inexorable and guaranteed. He changed the number; Helen found the new one. Within ten days of Pat's return from the hospital, her eyes were dark and withdrawn, and Ron was spending half his time stalking about the house, wanting to tear things to pieces with his bare hands.

He wouldn't tell Pat.

"For God's sake, is it something out of your past?"

Thank God for that kind of thinking. "Yes, yes," he burst out. "It's from a long time ago, and it's driving me mad."

Her eyes warmed to him. "Ron, there's nothing so bad we can't talk it away. God is with us. If we join Him, in our strength we can solve anything. All we need to do—"

He whirled on her like an animal about to strike. "Keep God the hell out of this!" he shouted. "You don't understand! Nobody understands! I've got to work this goddamned thing out by myself!" He stormed from the room, but not before he saw the touch of horror of blasphemy in her face. But he couldn't tell her. He couldn't. How the hell did he tell his wife that he'd chopped in half a boy the same age as their own children! But he had to tell her something.

Ron's dreams were fading faster every day as he saw what this was doing to Pat. Even the little girls were beginning to ask questions; Mary Ellen had had a couple of bad nightmares, and Esther had gone back to wetting the bed. Things were getting out of control, and Ron's feeling of helplessness and frustration was crushing him, beating down his hope.

He left the house and went to a local bar. On his fourth drink, it hit him. *Just call this number if you ever need a friend, anything. Call us day or night. We'll always be here to help.*

He had believed hell would freeze over before he would dial that number, but it had happened: hell was one vast sea of ice. He went into the phone booth and gave the number to the operator, calling collect. A woman's voice spoke to him. "Jake won't be available for a few days. Can I take a message for him, please?"

"It's urgent, lady. I don't give a damn where he is or what he's doing. I've got to reach him *now*. It's a matter of life or death."

"I'm sorry, sir. I'll do everything I can."

He slammed down the phone. Helen Drexel wouldn't let go; there was a rotten wall building between him and Pat, and all that wonderful regaining of health was sliding down a greased chute. Where the fuck was Jake! *Just call us, just call us, we're always here, we're your friends.* The rotten, stinking bastards.

Jake called at the shop two nights later. Ron spoke to the man whose voice he hadn't heard in seven years and told him the whole sordid mess, how it was breaking up his marriage and killing Pat, and—

"Relax. We'll take care of it. Just give us a day or two to fix it."

Ron hung up, relief breaking over and through him like a cool wave before he even paused to wonder why Jake had asked for so little information. He brought flowers home to Pat and he was grinning, and it was a beautiful evening. That night, weak as she was, Pat wanted him and made love to him with her hands and for a thousand reasons his orgasm was violent and wild and wonderful. He clung to her the night through.

The sons of bitches didn't do a goddamn thing for a month.

The bright flower of that one night blackened and withered with the incessant calls. Ron had agreed in his mind that Helen Drexel had to die. Not because of anger or hatred, simply a matter of the survival of one or the other. If the calls ended and the woman vanished, there was a chance for him and Pat. If the calls didn't cease, Pat would lose her will to live. The next call from Helen, and he'd give her the liaison she wanted. He wasn't certain yet how he would kill her, but he knew how to set up an accidental death. He knew a hundred ways to do that. He set his mind at peace.

The phone rang early the next morning. "Ron? Jake here."

"You pig bastard," Ron said and dropped the phone back onto its cradle. It rang again. "You're too late," Ron said as he answered it.

Jake's voice grew loud. "Damn it, don't hang up. There are good reasons why we took this long. Will you let me at least explain?"

"What for? I'm going to kill the bitch, that's all."

"Don't. You just don't need to. Look, give us the one meeting, and we'll spell it out. If that doesn't work, we can't keep you from doing what you want. Can we do at least that?"

He was right, of course. Ron agreed to meet Jake and some other people that same night in a motel in the next town on the south highway.

Jake had some "plumbers" with him. Two men and a woman. The professionals who could fix anything. One was a bearded psychologist and the other, the woman, a marriage counselor. Ron never knew who the third person was or what he did, and it didn't matter.

Ron laid it out. "So why go through all this bullshit? I can get rid of her easily. An accident, that's all. And it will *be* an accident."

"There's a better way," said the woman. Dr. Ursula Mendelov. As big across her bust and butt as her name. As strong as a fullback, too, but Jake seemed to respect her. So Ron listened. "You have a problem common to many marriages. Pat believes there's a liaison between you and this woman, Helen."

"There may be no liaison, but I fucked her, remember?" Ron said with scorn.

Dr. Ursula Mendelov rumbled on. "Your wife is looking for biblical justification. Theological renewal of your repentance." She smiled. "That's more important to her than if you slept with a dozen women. Give your wife what her psychological profile shows she wants most of all, and all this will end overnight."

Ron stared in disbelief. "How the hell do you know what *her* psychological profile is? I'm the dude from Nam, remember?"

"It's not that simple, Ron," Jake interceded. "People like you are few in number, but you're in a very special category with us. We've maintained a profile on you and your family. It's necessary, so that no matter what might happen, we're always on top of things."

"Like this last month when you played invisible?" Ron snarled. "And you still haven't answered me about Pat. What the hell has she got to do with your files?"

"Whatever Pat does affects you."

Then they laid a sledgehammer neatly between his eyes and felled him as effectively as if they'd struck him with a real blow. In the next thirty minutes Ron learned that ever since he'd been in Vietnam, and every moment of the day and night since his return, *his life had never been his own*.

Not one moment.

Talk about your turning points—hell.

On this night, in the near insanity of a motel room, Ron Previn discovered that he had been owned, studied, followed, observed, filmed, recorded, shadowgraphed, patterned, and virtually dissected ever since he had first taken up that deadly little spaghetti gun with its plastic magazine of two hundred rounds of hollow point. He had believed himself to be free, only to discover that his freedom was a farce and his dreams and his struggles were meaningless.

They knew every detail of his life for the last seven years—his wife, his children, his work, his IRS records, the clothes he wore, and the things he did; they had followed every moment of every day for all those years. Now they sat with him, knowing more about him than he knew about himself. He was emotionally naked, exposed as to what made him tick, what motivated him, how he would react when jostled or prodded.

He had been going crazy to get this Helen bitch off his back, and they knew everything, yet they had taken a month to arrange this meeting. "There were other priorities," Jake told him, and Ron knew what he would say, where he would tell them to stuff their great program, the bastards, because he'd never broken his oath, his sworn word never to discuss what had happened in his earlier life, and they'd broken their word to him. But his words stuck in his throat when they darkened the room and showed him slides and pictures and films. He watched himself on an early date with Pat. There he was bowling with the guys. Playing poker. Necking in the seat of his car with Pat and—Jesus Christ, how the hell? Then he recognized infrared film, and it began to sink in just how thorough they really were. He needed only a few moments to recognize the logistics of this sort of coverage, the enormous manpower and the organization . . .

He watched films of his wedding and his honeymoon at Niagara Falls. He saw himself in the maternity ward when his children were born, saw—

"Turn it off, goddamn it!" he said between clenched teeth. The film stopped, and they turned on the room lights. He found himself gasping for breath, disbelief surging through him like a tidal flow gone mad. Good God—one moment you think it's your own life, that the past is dead and gone, and then you—

Then you find out you're a puppet on a string.

Oho. That inside voice again, but this time even *they* were strangely subdued. Somewhere, his subconscious had been dealt a devastating blow. He was jerked back to attention by the woman's voice. The sow with the Ph.D.

"We're sorry to hit you so hard with this, but it's to eliminate all doubts that we know whereof we speak, Mr. Previn. The psych profiles are as perfect as it's possible for them to be. We know you have a fine marriage. We know, and you know as well as we do, that there's no chance your wife or your marriage will survive the truth of your background. You can't change that. So we need this psychological profile to ascertain what Pat will do when she hears what she believes to be the truth from you. If you tell her you were weak, that you gave in to temptation, that it was a one-night stand, you'll be telling her what she already believes, what she wants most to hear, because her theological upbringing is based on fall and redemption. Then she can forgive you, wipe the slate clean. You can start again."

He looked at them for a long time. "It might work," he said finally. "What about this bitch, Drexel?"

We'll make sure she never talks to you again," Jake promised.

Ron gripped the arms of his chair and squeezed his eyes tightly. He opened them with a snap. "Okay."

"And that's the whole story, hon. I don't blame you if you never want to see me again. I won't cause you any trouble, and I'll take good care of you and the kids. I—"

She threw her arms about him, weeping, kissing his face and ears and neck and lips. "Shh. Not another word. You were under pressure, my sweet. Let's never mention it again. I forgive you everything."

Ron could tell she really meant it; Pat was as transparent as window glass. They changed the subject quickly and had a pleasant evening. Ron got pizza for the kids, and it was almost as if the whole nightmare might be behind him. He had followed Dr. Mendelov's instructions to the letter.

It worked. Almost.

The experts were so smart they were stupid. There was one hang-up in their neat little package of admitted sin and redemption. Ron didn't hear from Helen Drexel. They kept that part of the bargain. But they seemed to have forgotten that she lived only a few blocks from where Ron and Pat lived, that she was a freaking psycho, that her mind was twisted, and that she was determined to claim her pound of flesh.

She stood outside their house, across the street, for hours. Just stood and looked at the Previn home. There was no way she could remain unnoticed. And there was no way Ron could breathe freely.

When Pat went out, another car followed her. Pat recognized the face, even if she didn't know the name. When she was in the supermarket, the same face stared at her from a distance. Soon, the face and the car became familiar to Pat—familiar, then bothersome; and finally, menacing.

How the hell could Pat not know who the other woman was? And if Ron were telling the truth about a drunken binge, what was this woman doing? Why was she always there like a shadow, an avenging phantom of guilt?

If Pat stayed home, Helen drove slowly back and forth along the street. At night she parked her car under the streetlight. She was quite mad, but she was also effective.

Ron's marriage disintegrated a little more every day. Doubts, questions, and that look of bitter disappointment whenever or however Ron denied any involvement. And if ever he came home late, or was gone a few minutes too long when he went out for cigarettes, it chewed at Pat's vitals.

She was tense and overtired, had begun snapping at the children, and Esther's bed-wetting was becoming a nightly occurrence. Mary Ellen looked away when Ron tried to talk to her. You could cut the tension with a knife.

He was at work when the phone clamored with a terribly shrill sound. He looked up, startled. Why would he feel this way? The same phone, ringing the same way. Nothing different. But he ran for it, and the old woman's voice on the other end was frantic and shrieking. He dropped the phone where it was and dashed to his car, left the parking lot with tires squealing and smoking, and raced home. He saw the flashing red lights and the blue lights and the police car and the ambulance, and he knew what had happened before he slammed to a stop and ran with pounding heart into the house because *oh SHIT!* the priest was there already and even he was too late.

A complete vial of pills.

She was gone.

God save his soul, Ron couldn't cry. It had been all cried out in the stinking jungle and the seven years far behind him, and he knew he had lost, that Pat had lost, that he was hollowed out. The bile sloshed about in his belly and choked his lungs and crawled up into his brain.

He knew the first, fine touch of madness.

23

The pain was a gnawing agony, an exposed nerve in the direct center of his brain that hurt so intensely it had become exquisite, a living thing symbiotic with him. Then, slowly, his mind and body began to accommodate the agony, so that it remained there but was squeezed down to a tiny burning mote that he could endure. He came to accept it, even felt a perverse fondness for the ache, for he knew it would serve as a reminder, sometimes forgotten but always there, of these past years. He did automatically what needed to be done. The part of him that had loved Pat was stumbling and chaotic and virtually helpless. Then, as smoothly as if it had all been rehearsed and kept in readiness for this moment, "someone" stepped forward and took over. He watched and experienced as if from a distance as his fingers punched numbers on the telephone and he conducted a sensible conversation with Pat's sister, who would be on the next flight to Hickory to take the children. Beyond that he remembered almost nothing about his two little daughters. With Pat's death they had vanished from the emotional and warm side of his psyche, as if they had been severed from him, or . . . *or the psyche has come to recognize itself for what we really are*. Damn, there "they" were again, but the part of him that had ached so terribly with Pat's death could find no argument against that statement. Ron went through the motions, ordered her body to be cremated, sent the children safely off to Oklahoma, and made out papers with his attorney, amazed to find out he'd

171

had a fifty-thousand-dollar life insurance policy on Pat. He sent the money to his sister-in-law for the kids, and from that moment on he never again brought them to mind. It was as if he'd had a blow on the head and a whole segment of his past was blocked by amnesia.

He went to his attorney again. "Sell the house for me," he said. "Sell it immediately."

Gus Harris nodded, toyed with a pencil. "Have you spoken to a broker yet?"

Ron swam upward from his daze. "No. What for? You handle it." He was annoyed and showed it.

Harris judged his client and his travail and ignored Ron's hostility. "I wasn't evading the job, Ron. It's just that the timing of the sale can be beneficial to you."

Narrowed eyes, hostile stare. "How come?"

"I happen to know that the Winn-Dixie chain plans to buy that entire block for a shopping center. You can get much more than—what's the house worth?"

"Maybe thirty-two. The mortgate is nineteen."

Harris pondered for a moment. "Would you be willing to leave it in my hands?"

"I want to sell the fucking thing *now*."

"All right. Suppose I buy the house from you. I'll pay you twenty-five thousand clear right now. I'll hang on to the property for six months or a year and I'll make another ten thousand profit off you. But you can get your money immediately and be free and clear of—"

"Write out the check, Gus. I'll sign any forms you have, and you can fill them in later." Ron closed his eyes for a moment, opened them to look directly at the other man. "Thanks."

"When do you want to leave?"

"I'll be out of that house in two hours. I'm not ever going back in after that."

"It's got all your furniture—"

"Keep it."

"I'll do better than that. I'll rent the place until I sell it. Whatever comes in, I'll put in an account for you. Whenever you want it, just call me. It could be a thousand or even more if—"

"Any way you want." Ron stood up. "Take care of the paper work. Call the bank for me, will you? I'll want five thousand in cash now and the rest in traveler's checks, if that's okay."

"It's okay. Good luck, Ron."

They shook hands. "So long, Gus."

He drove to the bank, went through the mumbles of sympathy from the people he encountered, surprisingly without reaction inside him (*nobody can touch us now . . .*), and strode into the vice-president's office. He didn't bother with preamble as Tom Mitchum looked up in surprise. "Gus call you?" Ron said for openers.

"Why, ah—hello, Ron, I mean, yes, he called, but—"

"Is it ready?"

"What?" Mitchum stared.

"Damn it, Mitchum, the five thousand in cash and the twenty thousand in traveler's checks. Gus Harris called you. Is the stuff ready?"

"Why, no, not yet, I mean, we hadn't expected you so soon and we—"

"Shit. I'll be back in an hour. Is that enough time for you?"

"Why, of course! We'll—"

"See you in one hour." He went out the door without looking left or right. In the parking lot he hit the road with tires squealing and drove directly to the house. He wanted this over with fast. He threw what he considered important papers into a small bag and filled one other suitcase with the clothes he wanted. He didn't waste any emotion on what was or had been in what room. No pictures and—he stopped himself. *Cut the past, brother. Cut it completely.* "Damn right," he said aloud. He opened his wallet, removed all pictures of dead wife and live children, and dropped them on the coffee table. He went downstairs to his den.

The .357 Python went into the bag with the papers. A tightly packaged Kurz .380 automatic slipped into a side pocket. He took several boxes of ammunition. He'd never fired any of these guns. He just collected them. Just had them. On the wall were a bunch of hunting guns, some had been there since he was a kid. One very special beauty, a high-powered .44 magnum with an express load that would kill an elephant at three hundred yards or even give a locomotive a bad headache. Four boxes of .44 ammunition into a heavy canvas carrying case and he was on his way out of the house through the garage exit. He loaded up, locked the trunk, and backed down the driveway.

And saw her standing across the street, watching, just like she'd done for so long.

He had backed into the street and started toward the bank when he heard a cry of "Ron! Wait!" He toyed with the idea of hitting the brakes, backing up, and blowing a big fat hole right in her belly. Then he laughed at himself. Who shoots shit? She was probably just part of *his* psych profile; let her get blown away on her *next* assignment. Ron hit the accelerator and headed for the bank.

He drove by day or by night as the mood hit him. West, always to the west. Sometimes he drove the big interstates, but the antiseptic ribbons of concrete annoyed him, and he would take the secondary roads, driving through towns and villages, looking at people. Always looking at people as if he'd never looked at them before. When he got tired, he slept in his car in a motel parking lot; or he'd take a room, soak in a tub, sleep for a while, get up at four in the morning, and start driving again. Moods washed over him like slow-flashing strobe lights.

At times a dull anger permeated his being. Emptiness echoed hollowly through what should have been his soul. But he never once knew the sickness of feeling sorry for himself. That was all gone, banished, forbidden ever to return. The ache for Pat was gone. The kids belonged to another time, another place, another planet, another life. He knew he'd never see them again, and he didn't want to. He was searching inside of himself and he didn't recognize what came up to stare at him. At times he went into total silence, even within his own head. Then a calculating aggressiveness would stalk through the corridors of his mind, waiting only for the opportunity to spring free. But he kept those reins tight as well. He yielded to only one desire: in one nameless town he left his handguns in the car and went to a sports gun shop where he bought a quick-release FBI-spring type shoulder holster for the .357 and an ankle holster with Velcro fastening for the compact Kurz .380. He didn't know why, but he did it. Sometimes he wore the shoulder holster with the .357, or he would want to feel the weight of the .380 about his ankle.

The strangest part of it was that he never even thought of using the pieces.

California was his goal. Bir Sur, along the Pacific Coast Highway. He wasn't interested in any of those muscled-turd platitudes about where there's life there's hope because he had personally delivered too many decent human beings from life with the weapons in his own hands. The sanctity of life was utter shit; he was one of those apostles of indifferent death who knew only too well the impermanence of body or dream.

Yet he realized a truth he had always known: no matter to what heights a man's imagination can reach, he is trapped in the bloated bag of liquids and tissues that make up the human body. Just that and no more. Reality was the thunder-hammering roar of a machine gun, the savage caress of naked flame. Hope was a fleeting shadow of thought, as were all other emotions. Love was a tangled web, a deep swamp through which most people trudged or swam or splashed, delirious in their momentary belly flop of emotion. He thought of Pat, he thought of the love they shared: where in hell was it now?

No matter. The thoughts came as waves and washed over him, some lingering, others broken into thin spray before they could have any effect. And then the surf was real, and he stood on the California cliffs, looked down on the stunning blue Pacific, and smelled the salty sea. He lifted his eyes to the wheeling gulls and drank it all in. He drove north to Big Sur where he enveloped himself in what he hoped would be a cathedral of living tissue, a cathedral of meaning, its spires the enormous redwoods and their stilling of time. He walked among the living giants and stared at the shafts of sunlight spearing down from the lofty heights; he smelled the smell of flora that had been like this for over a thousand years, and he felt the first tremblings of peace. He took off his shoes and socks, felt the earth and grass and leaves beneath his feet, and stopped speechless in the midst of this beauty. Just then, a discarded beer can sliced his foot nearly to the bone.

So be it, and he heard the words with echoing hilarity.

He limped through San Francisco. If the trees hid sharp and rusting metal (two doctor's visits and a tetanus shot), then perhaps he could lose himself in the harsh reality of the

gutters and the clanging of trolley bells and the steep hills
and the lights and the piers.

Hell, it didn't work. The simpering mindlessness of stu-
dents who protested and shouted and had no more sense than
a mosquito made him sad and disgusted. The bland monotony of the days and nights, the rituals of the bars, the shock
of blatant gays, the screaming of sirens, the winos and rejects,
all merged together, and finally he knew it was time to quit.
The voices in his head had grown stronger, and they spoke
not only with greater volume but with a developing authority
he couldn't ignore. He had struggled to escape the mind of
his past, but there was no struggling when one voice stepped
forward from all the others and, with a shock, Ron came up
against the mirror mind of himself.

*Fuck it, man. This is where it's at, and you might as well
face it. Tomorrow is embedded in the cement of your memory,
and unless you want a frontal lobotomy and a shining future
as a carrot, you've got to admit who you are, what you are,
what you're always going to be.* He couldn't deny the voice
because, no matter what corner he turned, it was always
there, forming his thoughts, rebutting his arguments, asserting.

Wandering among the trees of Big Sur or the gutters of
San Francisco was a stupid kind of cop-out. He knew the
change would come, and soon, but not *how*. Something would
go click in his mind, he would cross a line he had forsaken,
and once he crossed it he would never again be imprisoned
within his own head.

That thought struck him with stunning impact. A prisoner within himself? Could that really be the answer? All
those years with Pat, slaving and loving and working his ass
off, his heart torn when she hurt, the pain given to both of
them when his past came to visit. It had been an emotional
charnel house, utter pain, and even the greatest happiness he
had known with his family never shook off the dread he knew
from yesterday and she knew from biblical ravings and vague
shadows of sin in which her childhood was drowned.

That pain was gone now. Could a man really be free,
then? He had known a strange freedom in Vietnam when he
was a sword of death and destruction. But that couldn't be
the way! That was all killing and burning and savagery—

So what's new? said the other voice in him, and he had
no answer.

The click, the crossing of the line, came without warning. He made the decision to leave the fragile reality of San Francisco and fly east, down to Florida, where he had some crazy friends. They were a gang of outlaws, their grasp on reality a collective insanity. Not one among them bowed his head to the monolithic structure of a society built on numbers and digital emplacement within that society. To them life was a sweet irreverence, or it wasn't worth living. God knew he needed a taste of that mead.

He sold his car for cash, no questions asked. He spent a quiet hour in the motel lounge before taking a cab to the airport. Two or three drinks would let him sleep on the flight to Florida. But the shadowed lounge became an uproar with the arrival of several couples, all large, loud, drunk, and willing to accept trouble from anyone. Ron sat in a corner, his back to the wall, and found himself staring at a bearded giant. The man was big in all ways, girth as well as height, and thick unkempt hair fell well below his shoulders. Ron couldn't help it; he kept staring.

The big man couldn't help noticing it, either. He stared back. Nothing. Yet the little man in the corner ticked him off. He climbed from his chair, rumbled over to Ron, and leaned massive hands on Ron's table.

Inside Ron's head there was a frantic rush to see what the hell was happening; everyone was grinning.

The beard opened and a voice growled. "What the fuck are you staring at, little man?"

God, he was a big bastard.

"You little cocksucker, I'm talking to you."

CLICK.

"I was thinking, that's all," Ron said.

"Yeah? About what, you little shit."

Ron sighed. "A long time ago I was a pervert and I was caught fucking a buffalo, and I was wondering if maybe you were my kid."

A girl shrieked with laughter. The big man's face turned purple, and his thick hands jerked at Ron's shirt and hauled him in a single motion from his chair. One enormous fist drew back and started straight for Ron's face.

The muzzle of the .357 magnum stabbed far into the left nostril of the enraged giant. "Don't drop me, sweetheart," Ron said very softly. "You drop me and this thing goes off, and your pea brain and the whole top of your head goes splitter-splatter all over the ceiling."

Mind-splitting laughter in his head.

The lounge froze; blood trickled from the giant's nose. "Now," Ron said. "Shit."

The other man tried to talk, and the .357 jammed up higher.

"Shit or die," he heard.

The stench filled the lounge.

"Now you put your hands slowly into your pockets, and then if you're *very* good, I take this thing out of your nose, and if you walk out the door and keep on walking, right down the middle of the street, I won't blow you into little pieces. Got it?"

The bloody lips quivered.

"God, you stink," Ron said.

Hands in pockets, the big man turned slowly, trailing foulness behind him, and walked away dead center of the busy street, heedless of screeching brakes and blaring horns.

Ron returned the .357 to the shoulder holster, calmly went to the front lobby, and had his bags taken to a cab for the airport. In the cab he removed the shoulder harness and the revolver and locked it in his suitcase.

He slept like a babe all the way to Orlando.

24

He rented a car at the Orlando airport, drove the Bee-line Expressway eastward, picked up the Bennett Causeway, and as he came over a high-rise bridge at sunset, the landscape lay before him like thousands of glittering gems. To his left and far ahead were the lights of Port Canaveral: the fleets of pleasure cruisers, the shrimp boats, the big radar tracking ships, and the nuclear submarines here to test Poseidon and Trident missiles. Far beyond them, to the north, was the searchlight and floodlight glow of the space center where the giant shuttle roared into space. He went through the last tollbooth and onto A1A, through the town of Cape Canaveral, past the massage parlors and the fast-food restaurants. Then he was driving south in Cocoa Beach, passing the neon motels and the high condominiums crowding the ocean. He couldn't miss his destination, immediately south of the Howard Johnson's Motel on A1A, the high edifice of the 2100 Tower looming over the flat sands of the beach front. He parked in the visitor's lot and took the elevator to the top floor. Four penthouses up there, commanding a breathtaking view, especially the northeast penthouse. Mark Matthew—known as the Parson because of his name—lived there in three thousand square feet of what he called "absolutely ugly splendor." As Mark's houseguest, Ron was welcome to stay as long as he wanted.

Ron congratulated himself on having thought of Mark when the California living had gone sour on him. They'd only met a couple of times in Vietnam, but they had recognized each other as kindred spirits even then, and Mark had told Ron, "Come anytime. You're always welcome. And I don't say that to just anyone."

Mark greeted him with a strong handshake. No words for a few moments. Mark stood six foot three and was the most gentle big man Ron had ever known. Startling platinum hair, a warm smile, and a soft touch, but he had won every damned medal the army had to give in Vietnam. He had led a special squad of destroyers, and he'd been wounded seven times. He had a habit of riding a powerful motorcycle into the midst of enemy camps, a machine gun bucking and roaring in each hand, and getting away with it. Only a miracle had preserved his life. One day he'd had it in Nam, and he arranged to trade a half million dollars in gold for a North Vietnamese official he'd captured. He kept the official buried until the money had been deposited safely in the Bahamas, decapitated his prisoner, blew up the secret camp, and was gone the same night from Nam, a sudden victim of combat fatigue who was given an honorable discharge by his grateful government. Since then, he'd been living high on the hog in his Florida penthouse. Ron didn't know how, and he didn't ask.

"Dinner tonight up here with some friends," Mark said. He laughed at the look on Ron's face. "All very close friends. They all have big skeletons in big closets, and they won't tell you about theirs if you don't tell them about yours. The dinner is catered. Best place in town is setting it up. The Surf. They'll handle it all. Now, let's go get your stuff from your car and you can get squared away in your room. You get the view straight out over the ocean. Every morning God sticks the sun right up your ass." They grinned together.

He knew three of the six men who gathered there that night. The conversation was uproarious and public until the meal was done and the caterers gone. Then they talked of deeds done in the past and those under way at the moment. For a while Ron just listened. Tod Newman was a millionaire in faded jeans, sneakers, and a sweat shirt, the same kind of clothes he'd worn before he became a smashing success flying heavy loads of grass in from South America. He was an electronics genius, and he'd driven customs and the narcs up every kind of wall in their attempts to catch him. He relaxed on the couch with a beer and a cigar and an unfailing grin. Chuck Arthur was the shortest in the crowd but also the widest through the shoulders. He stood five feet seven inches and he had hairy wrists almost as round as Ron's thighs. He was a walking beer keg and a special investigator for the homicide squad of the county sheriff's office.

Icarus Maglione was as much a mystery as his name, taken from a Greek mother and an Italian father, and he looked every inch the mad Turk. His shaven skull, his heavy dark glasses, and absolutely no visible means of support made him all the more mysterious. He spoke with a foghorn voice, dropping cigar ashes everywhere. Icarus owned four airplanes, a boat, and three cars, and his favorite pastimes were flying a powerful World War II Thunderbolt fighter at big air shows and taking the gang up in an ancient German bomber he had resurrected from an airplane graveyard in Portugal. "You got here just in time," he told Ron. "The Parson says you drive airplanes."

"Some," Ron told him. "But you're out of my league. I fly small stuff. Spamcans; you know. Cessna or Beech. Stuff like that." Ron studied the professional madman before him. "What's this about my arriving just in time?"

"Day after tomorrow we're all going up to Robins Air Force Base. That's near Macon. You know, Georgia. Someone else is taking the fighter. We're flying a two-day air show for the air force. It's a license to steal. A contest. Who can break the most regulations and get away with it. We put on a whole goddamned war for the show. You can fly right seat with me."

"In a German bomber?"

"Why not? You like Italian planes better? Fuck them; they break in the air. You'll love it."

And he meant every word. They piled into the old airplane that had a hundred-foot wingspan, and half of them were blotto before they ever got off the ground. They carried sixty cases of Coors in the goddamned plane, and Maglione took off with a howl of engines, smoke generators pouring frightening swaths from each wing engine, and everybody cheering as the wheels skimmed the roof of a cabin cruiser in the river just off the runway. Ron looked down to see people in the water shaking fists at them.

The thing had a gun turret in the back, and there was a

redheaded madman named Upyanks firing mock machine guns. He was an insane Polack who'd rigged a propane pyrotechnic system into the fake guns, so that when he squeezed the triggers flame spat two feet from the gun muzzles and a hammering roar burst forth from the turret. "I think I've scared the shit out of more people than a New York cabdriver." He grinned.

Maglione climbed out to four thousand feet, set the bomber for cruise, and pointed. "See that highway? That's I-75. All you do is follow the yellow brick road." He released his seat belt and climbed out of the pilot seat.

"Where the hell are you going?" Ron grabbed the controls.

"Gotta take a crap. I'll be back in a while." And he was gone.

Another man came into the cockpit, sat sideways in the pilot seat, and offered Ron a cold beer.

Ron grabbed the can and took a long swallow. "Here," he gasped finally, shouting above the engine roar. "*You* fly this son of a bitch."

"Me? I'm a fucking lawyer. I don't know how to fly."

"You're all stupid crazy!" Ron shouted. "What the hell do I do with this monster if something goes wrong!"

"Hope the wop gets back before we crash, I guess."

The whole weekend went that way. They flew the show in Confederate uniforms, and three of them jumped at low altitude during the mock battles, opening their chutes at the last possible moment. They razzle-dazzled the crowd, and people milled around to get their autographs and have pictures taken with them. It was mad, mad, mad and marvelous.

Ron wasn't fooled for a moment. Theirs was a comic-serious, hard-as-steel realism because they truly brushed death every time they flew in their exquisitely skilled but maniacal fashion; there was never an ounce of laxity in what they did with their machinery. They were professionals cloaked in misleading beer belches. They all shared a motto he appreciated. Maglione said it for them all. "The whole trick in life is never to die. You know that? I," he announced, "am never going to die. I have discovered the secret of immortality. It was given to me by a two-hundred-year-old monk I encountered while he was jerking off on this snow-covered mountain in Tibet. The secret he gave me was that a man should never be so stupid as to die. The trick is to get killed."

A week passed. Flying, fishing, drinking, incredible meals and supple young women eager to cross the invisible line that led to this inner sanctum. The week sped by in a blur, and it wasn't until he'd collapsed on his bed one night, still unable to sleep for a while, that Ron discovered they had an invisible companion.

No matter what they did or where they went, Ron couldn't shake the uneasy feeling that he didn't really belong with these people, that he was faking his presence. For he was hiding what he was—a killer. The only people who knew about him and his real past was a group headed by Jake. And that bitch Helen. These people, these men who befriended him so openly, were being cheated. By him. And he couldn't hack that. It gnawed at him inside his skull.

So tell them.

He did that the next day. He asked them to listen to him, and the tone of his voice, the look on his face, quieted the horseplay as effectively as if a switch had been thrown. "I've got to tell you guys something. You may not like it, and I won't blame any of you. But if I don't say it to your faces . . ." He shrugged, took a deep breath, and it all came out—the villages and the spaghetti gun and the gelpacks. He stopped in the midst of the telling because they were all quiet, their eyes locked on him, and several of them were smiling. He couldn't talk and he was torn between an anger trying to well up in him and an instinct to wait. Wait, *wait*.

Mark spoke for them all. "You think we didn't know that about you?" he said softly. "Not the details, but they don't matter. You know why you've been so comfortable with this group?"

Ron shook his head, afraid to speak.

Mark smiled, a beatific expression on his face, his eyes glowing; he held out both arms with his palms up. "Look around you. Look carefully. And I'll tell you what you're seeing."

Ron's eyes went around the room, seeing different faces, different expressions, different mannerisms, different people. He turned to Mark, waiting.

"What you have here are some people who wore uniforms and some who didn't. In this room, there's army and air force and navy and marines, special forces and paratroopers and demolition teams, cops and sheriffs and narcs, and most of them have moved from one to the other, including some of the highest-paid mercenaries in the business. In short," Mark said with that gentle soothing voice of his, "every man in this room is a killer."

"I'll tell you something else, kid," Maglione added. "Your cross ain't that big and it ain't that heavy. You used gelpacks, right? Right. So they're bad. You ever drop six napalm tanks in a string in the middle of a town packed nose to asshole with refugees? I did. Orders: They had troops mixed in with the refugees. The whole fucking town was a dump for ammo and fuel and the whole fucking town exploded. The fireball knocked us ass end over teakettle and we thought we'd never get back. I don't think more than six people and a dog got out of that one. And keep this in mind. I flew 118 napalm missions. So you know what that makes me? A *shtunk*, as the Parson over there would say."

"But I—"

Upyanks broke in. "Don't tell us you're worried about yourself because you found yourself liking what you were doing."

Ron spun about. "And why the hell not?" he demanded.

"Because then," Chuck Arthur broke in, "you gotta get in line. You think you're the only dude ever got his rocks squeezed when he squeezed a trigger? Shit, baby, you're playing God. Life and death, small packages and the big economy size. Where'd you ever get the idea that everybody hates war? We got loony bins full of guys with all kinds of medals who cracked up when the wars ended and they didn't have no one else to kill."

"Or know the trip you're on when someone's trying to kill you," Mark tagged on. "It makes it all the sweeter."

"It's all a big kettle of minestrone," Maglione said. He bit off the end of a cigar and spit the tip onto the sixty-bucks-a-square-yard carpet. "Sometimes you're so hopped up it's like being on an acid trip. Other times you're so scared you use up a month's supply of laundry in a day looking for clean shorts. Sometimes it's a mixture of both. So quit fighting it. Be what you are, whatever it is. It may not stay the same. Tomorrow morning you might even wake up in bed alone and find you're with a complete stranger."

"And then again," said the Polack, "you might not. If you come to really dislike yourself you can always change into someone else. You know, take all kinds of shots and drugs and hormones and shave off your body hair and have a sex-change operation." He chuckled. "A lady, no less."

"But only on one condition," quipped Maglione. "You save your balls for us. Send 'em home in a jar, air-conditioned, special delivery."

The voices came from all sides. "We make ball soup. Pretty rare when it's voluntary."

"Sure. Gets you horny. So when you come back, be sure you're wearing a dress. Nothing like fucking your old buddies and not being queer about it."

"You know what this guy needs most of all?"

"No," came the chorus.

"He needs a fucking beer, that's what."

Six cans of beer came flying at Ron.

"G'wan, kid, have at it."

"If you love us, you'll drink them all."

"If you're stupid, you won't drink 'em and *we* will."

Ron gasped after downing four straight.

"See?" Maglione said. "He's a pussycat. Can't drink six without stopping." He rumbled across the room and stuck a foul object between Ron's teeth. "Have a cigar, kid. It might even make you throw up."

"Over the balcony," the Polack instructed. "We got a fairy lives below us and he gets hysterical when we dump vomit on him. Says it mats the hair of his poodle."

"Jesus Christ," Ron said.

"We didn't invite *his* ass," someone shot back.

"All right, you guys, shut up and give your mouths a chance," Mark broke in. "Ron, we got some news for you. We weren't going to tell you, but after everything we discussed we thought you ought to know." He looked around the room and the others nodded.

"You're being tailed," he said to Ron. He paused to let his words sink in. "I'll save you a lot of questions. "This penthouse is bugged. We're talking openly because for a couple of hours their bug isn't working so well. We'll let it come on again after we're through. But the phones are also tapped, and the new doorman downstairs is a phony. In fact, we're all rather impressed. They're tailing you everywhere you go, and one of those broads you shacked up with is one of them. She's good. So good we haven't put the make on her yet."

"But *who*?" Ron asked. The way he'd traveled, there was no chance in the world Jake's people could have followed him across the country.

"Who? Shit, man, it's the Company, of course." Mark smiled again. "That's the only part that's had us puzzled. I mean, we're all in the business, and we've all worked for the same outfit, and nobody's run off with anybody else's daughter. If they want to know what you're doing here, all the fuckers have to do is ask and we'll let 'em in right through the front door."

"Maybe we should ask," Maglione offered. "You in any trouble with those people, kid? They after you?"

Ron shook his head. "No way. They screwed up, not me."

"All in the eyes of the beholder," the Polack offered.

Maglione gestured with a spray of cigar ashes. "Ron, if you want, we'll bring these people to you."

"You know who they are?"

"You think they're the only ones who know how to play this game, kid? You want 'em, you got 'em."

Ron brooded over the matter, raced through a field of decisions, shook his head. "Thanks, Ike. I'll handle it."

They dropped the issue right there. Ron took a lone walk on the beach; he didn't want to become a depressive element among his friends. The pieces were all coming together. He knew their secret. Knew what Jake and Helen and the others had been doing all this time. It was simple. They had hung onto him since the day he had left Nam. They were still hanging on. Perhaps tighter than ever before. But how? He would have to deal with that question just as surely as he knew the sun would rise in the morning.

25

He slept soundly. A salt-scented breeze cooled the penthouse thirteen stories above the ocean. The forefront of his mind was at peace, but the deeper corridors of his unconscious clicked away like a superhuman computer. When he awoke he found that all the missing pieces were in place: he knew what the pressures were, and he knew the pattern he would now follow.

The key words were *psych profile*. He'd been tagged as neatly as a cadaver with a wire tied around his big toe. They had a fixed pattern on him, a psychological profile reduced to computerized readouts and guaranteed predictions. The other guys were free. He wasn't.

So he needed something no one could predict. Random behavior wasn't even good enough because a heuristics computer could add up all its input, weigh all the possibilities, and produce "hunches" better than the best poker player. It could anticipate any "unpredictable" move he might try to make.

The game is now worth the candle. The voice came to him clearly from inside his head; and he agreed.

He went to a pay phone at the Holiday Inn and called Jake. No delays this time; he'd expected that. "You're with the right people," Jake told him. "They're clearing out the cobwebs better than we could." There it was: tacit admission of everything he'd suspected, and a lot that he hadn't.

"Then why the tail on me, Jake? If everything is going

according to your plans, how come the surveillance? You don't need it. You know everything I'm doing. I've never tried to hide from you."

"One of the people in that crowd is a writer," Jake responded in his businesslike tone. "They're clever. That night you spilled everything to them—we're only surmising this, of course—the bugs in that apartment just happened not to work."

Ron didn't reply. He wanted to push Jake just a bit.

"You did that, didn't you?" Jake asked finally.

Ron sweated; Jesus, they knew everything. "Yeah. I did that."

"Well, the last thing we want to see is your story in print."

"Jake, they couldn't care less."

"We don't know that for certain, so we have to take the necessary precautions. We—"

"Call off your dogs, Jake. I'm not asking you. Do you understand?"

This time Jake paused. "Okay," he said after a short wait.

Ron hung up. He didn't believe Jake for shit. He was just a bit too agreeable. When you got down to it, Ron mused, he had even agreed too quickly to end the surveillance. So it must still be on. Yet they weren't pushing him. What in the devil could there be in his psych profile that would make them so certain he would follow any pattern they might predict? He wanted desperately to know what their next move would be, but he didn't have a clue.

For the next two days he walked the beaches, bumming around, troubled, unable to lock onto a course of action where *he* would be the one to dictate the sequences of events. On the third day, he found their ploy. It was a beauty. Not only did he find it—he met it face-to-face. Early in the morning on the beach. He'd gone down at five in the morning to be with the breaking day and watch the sunrise across the ocean.

One other person was doing the same thing. No, he was mistaken. Helen Drexel wasn't waiting for any damned sunrise.

He stared at her with a mixture of ice water and fire boiling through him. He couldn't believe it. In the name of all that was holy, this next step of theirs had never entered his mind. But now that he thought about it, what could be more obvious, more predictable?

"Hello, Ron."

"How the hell did you know where I was?"

"Believe it or not, it was an anonymous phone call. They told me you were in Cocoa Beach and you liked to be up to watch the sunrise."

"I believe you." Helen was the one link with his past he hoped had been severed, and now they'd offered up the whole chain, unbroken.

"It's not going to be like the last time, Ron. No more running out on me. I know you saw me on the street when you drove away."

"You might have waited until her body was cold."

She shrugged. "The past is past. What counts is now."

"You're carrying the ball."

"I'm not joking about that letter being in the hands of a friend. It has everything about your killing. All of it. More than killing," she emphasized. "Murder."

His shoulders slumped. "All right, all right," he said wearily. There was no getting away.

"Don't look so sad," she said, her smile half sneer. "My kids are away for the next two months. It's just you and me. I haven't let a man touch me. I've been waiting for you. I knew we'd be together again." A touch of uncertainty. "It could be very special, Ron. There's death behind both of us. Why don't we just look into the future?"

He was. "With you threatening me, it's a hell of a start."

"You're not giving me any other choice. Not yet, anyway."

You are so right, bitch. But you're not going to know that. None of his thoughts showed, none of his loathing for the poison she exuded that went through every orifice of his body like a fog.

He stepped forward and took her arm gently, started walking north. The first rays of the sun were gleaming off the distant towers of Cape Canaveral, glowing from the salt haze above the shoreline. It was incredibly beautiful. "Okay. I know when to quit. What is it you want? Back to New York?"

She went easily with him, her voice softening. "No, no. I don't care if I ever see that place again. I want something new in life. Not the old. Let's get the hell out of here.

Mexico, maybe. Or a cruise. Let's take the time to know each other without fighting like two animals."

"In two or three days. We'll go then."

She stopped, her hand tugging at his arm. "Why wait?"

"Because I'm staying with some old friends. If I disappear or take off suddenly they'll know something's wrong."

"Who cares what they think?"

"I do," he said as sincerely as he could. "They helped me through some bad times. I'm playing it straight with them. I don't want them to know we met like this. I'll prove it. I'll set up dinner with them tomorrow night." He pointed to 2100 Tower. "It's up there. The northeast penthouse. I'll tell them I called you and you're flying down to Daytona Beach. I've got a rental car and I can drive there to pick you up and—"

"Look, I don't care what kind of crazy drill you want to go through, but I am not going to Daytona Beach, or anywhere else, by myself. Is that clear? From now on we stick together like glue."

"Jesus, Helen, I'm not asking much—"

"No."

"All right, damn it." He sulked for a few moments. "I'll get us a motel room together here."

"I've already got a motel apartment. At the Wakulla. It's just up the beach."

He nodded slowly. "Okay. Where's your car?"

"By the park over there."

"Let's get some breakfast. Then I got to get some stuff for Mark and take it to him."

"What kind of stuff?"

"He's got a pool on the penthouse deck. We've sort of thrown everything into it. I promised I'd help him clean it out. I need some chlorine, stuff like that. Hell, woman, come along with me if you want to."

"I want to, all right."

They drove her car to Merritt Island for breakfast, spent the time in idle conversation. Afterward, he drove to a shop that sold pool supplies and bought concentrated powdered crystal chlorine. "It's strong stuff," he explained. "It'll do the job in one day." He backed out of the parking lot, banging into a lamppost. "What the hell's the matter with this car? The brakes are lousy."

"I don't know from brakes, Ron. For Christ's sake, it's a rental car."

"I'll check. Take just a moment." He stepped outside, lifted the hood and moved things around, and closed the hood and climbed back in. "It's a leak in the brake system. Half the fluid is gone. I'll put some in before we go back to the beach."

"Is that necessary? Let's just turn in the car."

"And lose the brakes on the way back? It's six miles on the causeway. Relax." He pulled into a service station, bought a can of brake fluid, and poured some into its receptacle. He put the can on the floor of the back seat. "It'll be okay. What do you want to do now? It's still too early to call the guys. They sort of had a wingding last night."

"That's perfect. I like it in the morning."

He looked at her and she smiled, her hand moving inside his thigh. "We have an empty apartment waiting."

"Okay," he said.

"Enthusiastic, aren't you? Well, I'll tell you something. I happen to be very good in bed. You'll see."

Helen was everything she promised. Ron let go inside his skull and let his body take over. No faking it; it had to be real. It was. Helen was an animal as well as sexual artist; she went wild with every orgasm. They lay in bed afterward, the air conditioning cooling them.

He sat up slowly. "I need a shower."

"So do I, lover, so do I. Together?"

"Sure."

"Wait a minute, Helen. You wear a wig, don't you?"

"I'm surprised you noticed. I always have a couple of them with me. Beats fighting with your hair when you're in a hurry."

"I can see that," he said amiably. "Lead on to the shower."

She went before him, leaned over to turn on the water. He stood just the right distance behind her. She turned around, smiling. "The water's perfect." Her eyes widened. "What are you—"

He hit her in the stomach with every ounce of his strength, a wicked looping blow that caught her in the solar plexus and smashed the air from her lungs. Her eyes bulged as she lost consciousness and toppled over like a rag doll. He grabbed her. He didn't want a mark on her body. Not a scratch or a bruise. He carried her to the bed. She'd be out for a long time. He dressed quickly, rolling his trousers up to his knees.

He chose a blonde wig from her carrying case, donned it, then added his own dark glasses. He slipped into her robe, left the apartment, and opened the door of her car. Several people were sitting around the motel pool. They paid no attention to the woman in a housecoat. Ron picked up the powdered crystal chlorine and the brake fluid and went back inside. He examined Helen. She was pale, and her lips were blue from lack of oxygen. Perfect. He lit a cigarette and placed it in the bedside ashtray. Then he spread her legs and pushed down on the mattress to make a depression between them. He poured half the can of brake fluid onto the bed so that it formed its own sticky pool. Then he poured most of the powdery crystals over the brake fluid.

The clock was ticking. A woman left the apartment, locking the door behind her. Again, idle looks but no curiosity. Still wearing the wig, the dark glasses, and the robe, Ron got into the car, stowed the rest of the chlorine and the can of brake fluid, and drove off. At A1A he turned left and drove south. After mixing the crystals and the brake fluid, it had taken him just under one minute to get into the car. Four more minutes.

He was well into the southern part of town when all hell broke loose at the Wakulla. Apartment 118 was torn apart by a devastating explosion. Witnesses reported the blast and a huge ball of fire ripping through the windows, shattering glass and pounding in the walls. The manager ran to the room with a fire extinguisher, but it was a futile gesture. He could barely see into the room and was choking on the noxious fumes. He made out the form of a body, flames curling around the skin, charring the remains. —

Ron drove south on the highway until he passed Patrick Air Force Base; he turned into an apartment complex, parked the car, took off the wig, and wrapped it up, in the robe. Then he mixed what was left of the crystal chlorine and the brake fluid, left the keys in the car, stepped out, locked the door behind him, and walked to the edge of A1A. He waited for a break in traffic and crossed the highway. Three minutes after leaving the car, he was on the beach, walking slowly in the low surf, carrying his shoes in one hand, watching the kids surfing and the gulls wheeling overhead. He didn't look behind him when he heard a faint boom, and he didn't look behind him when a louder explosion sounded. The first boom had been the chlorine and brake fluid mixing to create the fireball; the second had been the fuel tank of the car.

Nice.

A woman had occupied the apartment at the Wakulla, and another woman had been seen leaving the apartment and driving off. There wouldn't be any fingerprints in the charred remains of the apartment. Or in the blazing hulk of the car. And he'd been on the beach the whole time.

Bye, Helen.

He was on the balcony sharing a beer with Maglione when they heard the telephone ringing inside. Mark brought the phone outside and plugged it in. "Long distance for you. Person-to-person."

Ron hesitated. There was only one person who knew where he was and would know the unlisted number. "Thanks," he told Mark.

"This is Previn," he said into the phone.

"That was done very neatly." He recognized Jake's voice. "We're sorry to lose her, but she's been a pain in our side for a long time."

His legs felt like rubber. He stared at the telephone, then placed it quietly back on the cradle. Maglione watched him with knowing eyes. Ron shook his head slightly; Maglione understood. The bugs were still working. Ron held the beer can tightly. So they'd played chess with his mind—and her life. They knew he would try to kill her because he *had* to kill her. They had known just how he would react. Her presence would snap that last check he had kept on himself; now he was free to turn back to what he had been before—the killing machine for hire.

Only he hadn't known he was doing it *for them*. The thought was suddenly so funny to him that he broke into loud, bitter laughter. His laugh grew wilder until tears rolled down his cheeks. God, it was funny! They'd maneuvered him into killing for them, and in so doing they had set him free. He was a killer. Okay, *okay!*

A murderer.

You bet your sweet ass! That's what they wanted and that was what they would by God *get*. He knew they wanted more. Back to the old arrangement. You make a hit and you get paid for it in cash. The day of the thatched huts was over. No more skulking in the jungle. Now the game would be bigger, more powerful, deadlier; the risks would be greater. And so could be the rewards. These bastards did that well, all right. They paid. They bought what you were and they honed your own cutting edge.

The right words were *hired killer*.

Only one thing was different; one thing he was sure they hadn't been able to predict: he no longer gave a damn about what happened to him. Live or die; what the shit? He would bet anything in this world, including his life, that the psyche profile crowd hadn't counted on that. Oh, he was getting their game down pat, all right. They'd wait for him to regain his senses, to get over the shock—not of killing Helen Drexel, but of realizing he had done their bidding; then they would own him again.

All these thoughts flashed through his mind as he sat there laughing, while his friends looked on, perplexed.

He looked around at them, sprawled about the penthouse, and then and there he switched gears: there would be no explanations—just a graceful getaway. He stood up and stretched. He knew the bugs were working, that everything they said was being taped. "Guys, I got the itch. I think I'll go on down to Key West for a week or so. You know—fish, drink, get laid. The important things in life."

Maglione ripped open another beer. "Hard to fight that, man." He belched loudly. "When you going?"

Ron grinned. It was as if they could read his mind and were going along with his crazy laughing fit and all this verbal nonsense for the benefit of the hidden microphones. Talk about getting a special delivery message to those creeps who were listening in. Ron smiled at Maglione. "Day after tomorrow, I guess. I'll get a van, keep all my gear in it, stop and sleep when the mood strikes me. I'll see you guys at dinner."

Mark nodded. "Right on, man. The last supper, you know?"

He studied them. They knew.

He left 2100 Tower and drove off to exchange his car for a van. He felt great. The Company was going to pay a god-awful price to get him back in harness. Because he was going to show them just how good he really was.

His heart floated like a moonbeam.

Live or die. Who cares? *I'm free*.

26

He remembered a story his father had told him when he was a kid—and not until this moment had he understood his father's message. It was a lesson in life; and now it applied particularly to the path he had chosen, the mold he had shaped for himself. He grinned with the memory. It was the story about the scorpion and the frog.

"There was this big old green bullfrog, son, and he lived in the reeds and marsh along a riverbank. He was big and old because he was smart enough to recognize danger when it came and to stay well clear of it. He knew which of the other creatures were bad for him, and he managed to stay just beyond the reach of those birds that were after him and that big pike that sought him out. Well, one day the big old bullfrog was sunning himself on a lily pad, only a gnat's eyeblink away from disappearing into the water or the reeds, when a scorpion he knew came along the riverbank. Now here was this frog safely in the water and this mean old scorpion on the dry ground, and the scorpion says to the frog, 'I need to get across the river. Would you carry me?'

"The old frog just shakes his head. 'Why, Mr. Scorpion,' he says, 'I'm an old frog, but I ain't no crazy old frog. If I carry you on my back across this river you'll sting me, and I'll die.'

"The scorpion sort of sneered at the bullfrog. 'Don't be stupid. If I were to sting you, then surely you would die, but then I would drown, and I have no desire to bring on my own end.' Well, the frog allowed as to how this made good sense, and finally he told the scorpion to hop on, and away they went across the river. They were about halfway across when the scorpion, he arches his back all the way up, and zingo, right into the frog goes that poisoned barb. It didn't take no time at all that the frog began to stiffen and to lose all his strength. He knew he was dying. He was hurting fierce, and in his last moments of life, he turned to look that scorpion in the eye.

" 'Now why in the hell did you do that?' asked the frog. 'I'm dying and you're going to die with me because you're going to drown. Why'd you do such a stupid thing?'

"The scorpion, who knew he faced his own end, told the frog that he couldn't help himself, even if it did mean his own death. 'It's the nature of all creatures,' he said, 'to be true to their own character.' And he drowned and they was both dead.

"Remember that, boy, in your years to come. No matter what people say to you, understand their character and you'll always be able to tell what they're going to do—even if they don't know it themselves."

You don't know the half of it, old man, Ron said to himself. He'd already spotted the car tailing him. He knew they wouldn't interfere. That wasn't their job; they were the watchers. And he was going to give them the ride of their lives. He drove to Merritt Island and went through several department and hardware stores, buying a bewildering variety of tools and equipment, loading everything into the van. He filled several five-gallon cans with gasoline, some more with naphtha, others with benzine. He stopped at a U-Drive rental office, picked up a twenty-four-foot enclosed truck, and drove it to a warehouse at Port Canaveral, where he parked and locked the truck. A coastal tanker was berthed near the warehouse, and some of the crew waved idly as Ron walked along the pier. He went to a fishing supply store and called a cab. Ten minutes later, he was gone.

He smiled when he thought of the tail on him. They were going to have one beaut of a time figuring what was coming down. It was simple to him; he was going to give them a calling card.

He had already accepted the new truism of his life: he

was a man who killed because of some inner need or desire or compulsion. He no longer questioned it. But he did not accept the fact that he must kill under contract or orders from the Company. He laughed aloud as he realized the problem he presented to that organization. *Well, gentlemen, we have a puzzle for you to work out. But be careful . . .*

He would never forget what his old man had told him: "No matter what people say to you, understand their character, and you'll always be able to tell what they're going to do—even if they don't know it themselves."

That carried the key. The triple-shift surveillance team assigned to him would do nothing but watch and report. They couldn't do anything else because their actions stemmed from their orders, and their character wouldn't permit countermanding those orders. They were as predictable as gravity. They'd watch and follow and report and keep shadowing him, but they wouldn't interfere. He, on the other hand, was working for himself—he could do as he pleased. He was beyond predictability.

Before the day was out he'd bought several clocks as well as four large oxygen tanks under high pressure. He'd transferred the gasoline, naphtha, benzine, and other chemicals from the van to the truck. He'd gone to a cleaning supply house for carbon tetrachloride and added that to the truck; he'd filled a large bag with electronic and electrical parts; and he'd bought a tape recorder and several small transceivers. He hummed and whistled the day through because he was doing what he liked best.

Living his role. He recognized that there had been more forces acting on him than he'd ever believed. They'd used him as a trigger finger reflexed by Pavlovian prodding. All he had known was to kill, whom to kill, and when—but rarely, perhaps never (because they lied), why. The *why* no longer mattered. He had to, so do it. Kill. It was like working or breathing or flying or making love. He simply had to do it, and now he lived with it comfortably. The odds, of course, were that he was going to die, most likely rather violently, but that didn't bother him because he had been surrounded by so much death he'd become philosophical about it. What was death but the opening and closing of a door?

He thought about everlasting life after death. A touch of his religious upbringing tweaked at him and he laughed to himself. *That* was true control. In fact, the more he thought of it, the more convinced he was that the success of the Company was derived from strict adherence to the tenets of Catholicism. The old priests had to survive and multiply in a world that was ready to do them in at every chance, and the very fact that they'd made it, and prospered overwhelmingly, meant that they were a force with which to reckon. And their methods were about as perfect a dogma to be followed as anyone could find. But it was their earthly effectiveness that impressed him, not the horseshit about there being no atheists in foxholes. The man who wrote that crap hadn't been in enough foxholes to hear shattered men cursing God with their last agonized breaths.

He glanced in the rearview mirror of the van. They were three cars back. Ah hah. So they had a stinger on the van, a small transmitter that let them keep tabs on it even if they lost it in traffic. Great. The last thing he wanted was for them to lose him. He'd find the stinger, and do a little modifying to that system, and they'd have a surprise in store.

He wanted Jake's attention in a way they would never expect and that they couldn't ignore. He could call Jake, but that wouldn't accomplish anything. In this business, words were like spit in the wind. You had to get in there, man, and grapple.

He was now pure machine. He was taking on as a direct competitor the best and the toughest professionals in the killing business. Late that night he found a perverse delight, almost an adrenal rush, knowing he was being watched as he slipped up to the salvage warehouse in Port Canaveral where he had parked the truck. He had a beautiful .45 Colt modified to a .32 barrel with a silencer. First he sat carefully in the truck and shot out three overhead floodlights along the pier. Now the only light remaining was the reflection from the navy sub base across the port. He moved through the darkness and cut the telephone lines, effectively isolating the warehouse. He'd already checked its contents—a lot of salvage from old ships and the stuff to release the cargo of those sunken ships: dynamite, blasting caps, primer cord, detonating wire and controls. He tapped on the door, and a sleepy guard, hand casually on his holster, peered through a small porthole but didn't open the door.

"Whaddya want?"

"I gotta take a piss. Open up, willya?"

The guard blinked. "You crazy? Go piss in the damn port."

Before the guard closed the viewport, Ron fired three times through the door. No way to miss the man on the other side. Then he shot off the lock. He walked back to the pier, started the big rental truck, and backed it up to the entrance. He opened the warehouse door, stepped over the sprawled body inside, and spent the next fifteen minutes loading the truck with the most complete assortment of blasting equipment he'd seen since Vietnam. Finally, he drove away at a comfortable pace and parked in a stall inside the car lot of the Cocoa Beach Police Department. Nothing like being right out front. He went around to the back of the truck and pressed a wide disc against the bottom metal. The disc was identical to the small radio bug transmitter his pursuers had placed on his van, and it would activate in precisely seven hours.

Now he began to play his cards fast and tight. He walked across the lot to the van, climbed inside, and started the engine. He knew his tail was good, and he'd have to be better. He rolled south from the police station for ten blocks, turned left onto the beach highway, turned left again, and was driving north. By now he had a good look at the pursuing car.

He switched on the portable citizen's band radio, making sure he was on the local police frequency. "Ah, breaker, breaker, hope some of you boys in the black and whites are picking me up. I'm coming up on Minutemen Causeway rolling north, and there's a blue Oldsmobile Ninety-eight I just passed, and I saw some guns in that car. Looks like they was three men in there, and it spells trouble."

Forty-three seconds flat. Three police cruisers with blue lights flashing hit the Olds, two behind and one coming head on the wrong way on the one-way avenue, blocking off the Olds. Bye, fellas.

He drove north and turned left on the 520 Causeway until he got to a sprawling apartment complex on Banana River Drive on Merritt Island. He paused just long enough to remove the transmitter from the van. Then he walked to another building where he'd left a third vehicle: an innocuous tan Pinto. He drove south along State Road 3 through Merritt Island, moving carefully along the narrow winding road. Then across an old bridge at the southern tip of the island, east again to a big motel where he parked behind the buildings. He locked the doors, set his wrist alarm, and fell asleep.

He was awake at 6:45. He went into the motel to have some coffee and use the bathroom, came outside, and stuck the bug transmitter onto the Pinto. Then he drove north along A1A, grinning. They would have picked up the transmitting signal by now, but they'd never pick the Pinto out of the heavy morning traffic rolling toward the Space center. Across the Minutemen Causeway he turned left, parked in the lot of the United National Bank, locked the Pinto, and walked quickly a block south to the police station. Into the truck now, after making sure the transmitter was in place and activated. He rolled south two blocks, made two left turns, and was again driving north on A1A in the thick stream of traffic. There was only one way to drive through Cocoa Beach and that was on this highway. Ahead of him, the intersection of A1A and the 520 Causeway would be jammed with the early morning rush hour. He worked his way to the dead center of the intersection and stopped. He locked the brake, removed the ignition key, and locked the doors of the truck, ignoring the blaring horns and shouts. He walked around to the front of the truck, opened the hood, and jerked free the distributor wires, leaving the hood open. Behind him, to the south, he heard sirens. He grinned. His friendly tail must have gotten frantic and this time they were working *with* the police. By now he figured they'd found the Pinto and realized he'd given them the slip; they'd picked up the signal from the truck and were coming as fast as they could move on the traffic-snarled lone highway running north. His fourth car, rented the day before, was parked in front of the Ranch House Restaurant. He climbed in, moved the car along the 520 beyond a small bridge, and eased off the road onto the grass where fishermen often parked.

He waited. He knew what was happening. His tail, along with one or more police cars, had reached the truck. They'd looked inside the hood and seen the ripped wires. The doors were locked. They knew what was inside. "Get this damn thing open!" one of them shouted to a police officer who opened his trunk and ran to the truck. One hard snap with powerful wire cutters and the lock fell away. One of the men in the dark suits they loved so much jerked open the door at the back of the truck.

As the door came back it jerked a wire. The wire led to six cases of dynamite, all primed for detonation. They went off within the space of a fraction of a second. The blast ripped open the highly pressurized oxygen bottles, providing an added impetus to the terrible explosion already ripping outward. Even as the sheet of flame and the steel-hard concussion tore into everything nearby, the shock blasted open the containers of carbon tetrachloride. A giant fireball boomed outward and upward, smashing cars and killing almost everyone within a hundred yards. The shock smashed windows within two hundred yards more, sent cars plowing and crashing into one another, and ignited more than two dozen vehicles. Screams tore the air. A car was blown out of control and smashed into the fuel pump at the Gulf station at the intersection. Flame fed on raw gasoline, and another mighty blast sundered the area. In the first ten seconds, more than 340 people were killed or maimed. Where the truck had been there was now a gaping crater from which poured a thick cloud of poison gas—flame meeting carbon tetrachloride. The choking, lethal fumes started a screaming panic that would bring on the death of another fifty-eight persons.

Ron was long gone, driving casually along the causeway to Merritt Island, switching from the rented car back to the van. He drove across the Hubert Humphrey Bridge into Cocoa, turned north on U.S. 1, and enjoyed the pleasant trip into Daytona Beach. There he rented another van, different make, different color. He parked at a motel, registered under a false name, and transferred the entire contents of the first van into the second.

One hour later Ron Previn rented a thirty-foot U-Haul truck in Saint Augustine. He parked along a secluded street, opened the back doors, and lowered a double ramp to the street. He walked back to where he'd left the van, drove back to the truck, studied the street carefully, and drove the van up the ramp into the truck. He shifted into park, put on the emergency brake, placed two blocks of wood in front and back of the tire, replaced the ramps, and drove away in the truck. At a roadside stop he parked, went to the men's room, and locked the door to a toilet booth. When he came out he was wearing a wig of red hair, a different jacket, and dark glasses. Chewing on a cigar, he slipped back onto the highway.

Ron Previn vanished. That's what he thought, anyway.

27

He left a gnat's swarm of false clues. He was one person transformed into an elusive army of ghosts and shadows, after whom the best field agents of the Company might chase fruitlessly. He drove nonstop to Dayton, Ohio, and parked in the airport lot. Thirty-five minutes later he was on an airliner south to Atlanta. In Atlanta he left his gate, went directly to a telephone booth, called the Quality Inn on the west side of Albany, New York, and made reservations for three nights later, specifying room 101. Then he dialed the operator to make a collect call to that very special number where he could reach Jake. He glanced at his watch. Eleven minutes: perfect. The call went through at once, and there was enough delay, just enough, to know they were tracing the call. He knew they could trace any call anywhere, including a booth, especially a call that had been handled through the operator.

"What you're doing is stupid, Ron," Jake told him, and that pleased Ron mightily because he knew he'd cut through a lot of thick skin to get that reaction.

"Maybe, but it's effective. I don't think you'll have anybody on my ass anymore, Jake. If you do, they go the same way as the others."

"Where are you calling from?"

"Never mind," Ron answered, playing the game. "Listen to me carefully. I know you won't have to write this down because you always tape everything anyway. Now, I want to meet with you people. Your psych profile group. You know,

204

that fat broad and what's his name. And you, Jake. You got to be there. I've made reservations for room 101 in the Quality Inn West just outside Albany. Three days from today. It's got to be room 101, or I don't play." Room 101 was on the corner; no trees outside, no power lines nearby. Ron had checked all that out.

Jake didn't answer immediately. "I may not be able to make it, Ron. There are things to arrange."

"Bullshit." Ron made certain to sound pissed off *just* enough. "You meet me there with those people when I say, or I don't show, not then and not never. And you know I can disappear." He hung up and walked along a corridor to a Delta gate. Six minutes. He went through the gate and took a seat in the coach section. Four minutes later, the doors sealed shut and the airliner started moving from its loading position. When the searchers made it to that phone booth, Ron—the man in the scroungy blond hair and the plaid jacket—would be in the air on his way back to Ohio.

He waited until dark, opened the U-Hall truck, and backed the van out. He closed the truck. Leaving it there was perfect. They had advanced computers and an army of spooks and they'd track down the truck. In an airport lot. They didn't know about the van, so they had no way to go except to check every airline desk, every car rental agency, every cabdriver who worked the airport. It was a huge haystack, and the needle they sought was far gone by the time they even started sifting.

Ron kept driving east. In Buffalo he scanned the telephone book, found a big model and hobby shop, and bought several hundred dollars worth of goods. Forty-five minutes later he was on the road, working the turnpike eastward. One hundred and five miles west of Albany he registered at a rooming house in a small town, and then he drove to a small grass airfield a couple of miles out of town. He struck up a friendly conversation with the old man who owned the field, looked at a line of used planes, went up for a check ride in a swaybacked Aeronca, and bought the near wreck for five thousand dollars even. "I'd make it less, but it's got a low-time engine and a good radio," the old man said to ease his guilt at taking the "city feller." Ron allowed as to how he was pleased with the airplane and said he'd spend a couple of days practicing to oil up his rusty flying.

He was back that night, working in full view of anyone who cared to stop by the ramshackle hangar. He cut through the fabric beneath the left wing and rigged up a shackle with a holding clamp fore and aft under the wing. Pulling a wire from the cockpit through the sliding window to his left opened the shackles. He tested them several times and was satisfied that they worked. He returned to the rooming house and slept until ten, had breakfast, and drove to the airport. The old man was staring quizzically at the underwing shackle.

"Never saw nothin' like that before," he observed.

"It's a camera mount," Ron explained. "I use the old-type aerial camera. I mount it to the wing, like this," he demonstrated with his hands, "and I use this wire to trip the shutter. This way I can use a big negative and get real clear pictures. Doing a survey job. Do it myself and I save a bundle."

The old man nodded. "Guess you knew what you were doing when you bought this airplane."

One hour and thirty-five minutes later Ron cruised slowly, two thousand feet above the ground. He found the Quality Inn West and circled it from a distance, using binoculars to study the layout. There. Room 101—right at the corner of the motel. He knew Jake and his teams would have gone through that room and the surrounding rooms and the whole damned motel with every sniffer and detector they owned. They wouldn't find a thing. They weren't supposed to. They'd also have every road and every corridor covered with more detection devices than Ron knew he could even imagine.

He was pleased with himself as the Aeronca drifted lazily south. He wouldn't start his turn back to the grass field until he was well out of sight of the motel area. He had it fixed perfectly in reference to the highway and the motel sign. He closed his eyes and saw the image in his mind.

Tomorrow morning.

At 5:30 A.M. the Aeronca climbed away from the grass field in calm air. It was still dark, and no one saw the big gasoline-engine model plane locked securely in its shackles beneath the left wing. Ron headed east. The motel would be just about eighty minutes' flying time from the airfield. That would get him there at 6:50.

At 6:45 the telephone rang in room 101. Jake snatched it from the bedside table. "Go ahead," he said quietly.

A strange voice was on the other end. "I, uh, have a message for someone named Jake. I'm supposed to tell him personally."

"Who is this?"

"Never you mind, mister."

Ron had given the waitress specific instructions. "Call this number exactly at 6:45. It's quiet here and you can take a coffee break for yourself. Use the telephone booth outside. Ask for Jake, and don't give anyone the message until they say they're Jake—okay?"

"I don't know," she said doubtfully. "I don't know if this is right to do."

"What's there to do? Just call this number at the time I gave you, get Jake, and tell him that Ron will be there in five minutes for the meeting. Hell, lady, I'm just trying to save my job, that's all. There's ten bucks in it for you, and if that meeting goes the way I think it will, and I sell them tractors, I'll stop by on the way back and add twenty more to that tenner. Deal?"

Of course it was a deal.

"Is this Jake?" she demanded.

"Yes, damn it. What is it?"

"The message is, uh, that Ron will be there for the meeting in five minutes, and you're supposed to expect him."

"Who is this? Where are you calling from?" Jake signaled frantically to an agent to trace the call, but the phone went dead. He held it in his hand and looked at the agent. "Get the others in here immediately," he ordered. "Alert everyone else. He's only five minutes away."

At 6:49, the little Aeronca was at fourteen hundred feet, in a wide circle less than a mile from the motel. Ron fixed it all clearly. The morning sun was shining brightly on the corner of room 101. He leaned through the open window space, jerked a small handle, and started up the engine of the model plane. Then he pulled the release wire. Taped to the top of the instrument panel was a small black box with a miniature radio-control stick and an antenna attuned to the receiving system in the model.

The small machine fell away, twisted several times in the air, and darted straight for the motel. It came out of the sky with a high waspish snarl and tore through the plate glass window of room 101, knifing inside just before the three pounds of plastic explosives in the fuselage were detonated.

The entire wing of the motel showered outward in flame and smoke and debris. Broken bodies tumbled onto the parking lot. The Aeronca turned lazily and flew north, passing from sight.

Good-bye, Jake.

Good-bye, you assholes.

28

It was everything he wanted. The answer to every subliminal dream that had been growing within him for all these years. Now they'd have to come after him. The pursuit was on, the game was heady and the stakes to their ultimate. Life and death at every turn, around every corner. God, it was marvelous!

No more routine, no more answering to anyone save the sharp-eyed moves deep behind his eyes. No more button-pushing, and to hell forever with the human-canine Pavlovian shudder when they did this or that as their computers and their goddamned psych profile specialists directed. Gone; all gone. He couldn't believe the sense of absolute freedom that filled every fiber of his being. Never had the air smelled so sweet or things looked sharper or sounds come more clearly. He loved it, this affair of the even-up game. Its theme was odds out the window and a fresh set of rules any time you wanted. There weren't any rules except to survive, and the only way to survive was *not* to cut and run.

Killing was now its own marvelous means to its own end. No evil, no compunction, no conscience. *Killing was never having to say you're sorry.* He laughed uproariously with the thought, yet he kept himself from being taken so much with his own glibness that he yielded to indiscriminate killing. That was stupid because it jarred the flow and momentum of society. Each death must have its purpose, he mused. And every additional death created for a reason leaves one less critic for a conscience that might yet stupidly rear its head.

That last one was pretty neat, but it didn't matter because he had dwelt overlong on a comparison of two children. Who had been worse off? The little girl they found ravaged in the sewage canal, who must somewhere in her mind relive her horror and pain and shame as long as she lived? Or the young boy chopped in half by the spaghetti gun, who never uttered a word but delivered a thousand-year sermon in that final dying twinkle of life in his eyes as his torso fell forward. The question colored Ron's every action. He had spent much thought on it, and he always came up with an aching head. There is a chrysalis stage of life, and then all creatures who are to fly must crawl and squirm and drag themselves through the larval stage. To be free of pain, one must understand it, and to understand it one must endure it. The act of endurance is the struggle from the cocoon.

Conscience is a curious human invention. Someone, somewhere deep inside him, told him that. And it was true. But that observation was soon countered with another: this same strange human invention—conscience—formed much of the glue that knit human society together.

Well, who gives a shit? asked the collective voice within his head. The voice was right: if you didn't care, then there was nothing about society worth the candle.

He was in a jungle. Man-made, with psychological trip wires, festoons of concrete, vines of electrical cable, underbrush of roads and highways and fences, and fer-de-lance called magnums and .38s and revolvers. He had to evade the all-seeing god-eyes of lasers and infrared sensors and trip wires and photoelectric cells, to elude the jungle tribes of spooks and FBI and all the rest. Above all, he must stay out of the inner sight of the godhead itself—that omnipotent computer served by so many attendant slaves who kept stuffing raw data into its capacious belly as they might feed human flesh into a gluttonous idol. The Company.

He would beat them at their game. This now was a sporting proposition. They would have to come after him with their best men, anticipate his moves, intercept every possible avenue as dictated by the electronic oracle within whose navel lay the raw data of his psyche.

No! Don't think like that. Because there's the trap. They

won't just come after you with their best men. They'll use their best hunters—men and women and machines and systems and organizations. Anyone and anything. Think, you asshole, he remonstrated himself. *Think audaciously and outrageously. That's their Achilles' heel. You've got to be mad, completely and utterly mad. That's the one element that gives the computer a rotten headache.*

He imagined himself in their shoes. What would Ron Previn do next? If he could work it out that way, he would be well ahead of—

NO! NO! That's the most predictable thing you could do!

Sure. They'd plan for that. It was a matter of switching identity on a rapid staccato and repetitive scale and then he'd never beat them. Any good chess player would have the upper hand in that sort of exchange. *But computers play lousy poker because they can't lie worth a rat's ass.*

But *he* could. And he had to figure out some off-balancing acts, too. He went through his own series of larval changes. He obtained the materials for constant changes of appearance. He wore brace straps and knee clamps to force him into odd postures and grimaces. One day he was a greasy Cuban salesman with small rings flaring out his nostrils and just the right flashy clothes for the role. He did absolutely nothing with that disguise except to research the newspaper files of all the towns within a fifty-mile radius of Washington, D.C. The whole idea gave him an inner chuckle. Even the pros leave gaping holes in their walls of nonidentity. He went to a newspaper research office; who would bother with a man looking for a gravedigger's job? He collected the basic information he needed and did the rest by phone. He sent cash by commercial messenger to a commercial computer output office in the heart of Washington, D.C., for grave and burial information, asking a whole slew of questions. He didn't know Jake's last name and could only hope the guy's first name really *was* Jake.

And he found it: burial services for nine men within a certain period of time after that little episode of room 101. No need for secrecy in family bereavement. No security there.

UPS delivered a parcel to each home address. No one questioned a small parcel. When they were opened, a lightweight but powerful spring, working like a jack-in-the-box, released a vicious cloud of itching powder that clung to the skin and the mucous membranes of the nose and set the eyes on fire. Widows and children are strange targets, but they'd be over it soon—except that the very act was so alien to everything the spooks knew that it would rattle the Company to its highest levels—and keep them off-balance. There's a subtle touch of terror when women and children are targets; unquestionably, if he'd managed with itching powder he could have done the same with explosives. This little act would dilute their manpower, thin out their concentration, and give the computer indigestion.

Would his next move be to kill the families? Would he strike at any element of the Company? Had he slipped beyond control and become a mindless marauder? Ron intended that these and a hundred other pertinent questions should occupy a lot of brainpower and man-hours. The truth was, the moment he'd sent off the packages, he'd dismissed from his thoughts any further plans for his victims' families.

Outrageous and unpredictable.

Those were the keys, those were his rules to his game. There are different ways to strike deeply into the heart of an organization, and sometimes an oblique move has the most devastating effect. He figured he had found what he wanted— the steel fist.

His thinking got sharper, clearer. The last place they'd ever think of looking for him would be in school—so school it was. He loaded two suitcases with electronic equipment bought in lower Manhattan and shipped them to a holding warehouse in Jacksonville, Florida. That was another touch to keep the balance slightly off-center. With all that had happened in Cocoa Beach, he was sure they'd maintain a heavy surveillance of that area, fearful that his master touch with explosives might be directed at the highly vulnerable space shuttle at the Kennedy Space Center. He had considered such a move (and he figured they knew he would do so) but dismissed it immediately. It would gain international attention, but in the long run it would be mindless destruction, and his rule was never to pursue that fruitless course. It was the old crap on their part of the criminal always returning to the scene of the crime. But Jacksonville held nothing of interest and it was nearly a 180 north of where they'd be watching everybody and everything.

He flew to Birmingham, Alabama, took the airport bus to a suburban motel, and rented a car under a false identity. Car rentals at any major airport were too risky at this point. He drove south to Palatka in Florida where there was a large but isolated airport, a pulp mill that stank to high heaven, open scrub country and lakes, and a skydiving club with enthusiasm nigh onto hysteria. He had to coordinate many moves simultaneously, mesh them into a single flow. In Palatka he rented a small apartment under the name of Harold Manners. The landlord figured this man was easy to remember, with his dark hair and moustache, a scar along the side of his neck, and a barely perceptible limp. He noticed a motorcycle helmet and other paraphernalia in the car.

"Hope you ain't one of them people drives a motorsickle," he sniffed warily.

Harold Manners shook his head. "Not me. They ain't safe, mister. The helmet's for skydiving."

"Oh. You're one of them crazy ones that jumps out of airplanes."

Ron grinned. "Yeah. It's the berries, ain't it?"

"That why you limp?"

"Didn't think it showed."

"Pretty hard to put something over on me. Wasn't born yesterday, you know." He turned to leave. "But it's a free country, like they say."

Ron drove to the local airport, looked in disbelief at the ramshackle buildings used by the skydiving club, and signed up for a course of twelve jumps.

"You want five statics and seven free falls, right?" A tall, sallow youth looked him up and down. "You ever jump before?"

"Three," Ron said. "Twisted my ankle the last time, but it's okay now."

"Probably had a lousy school."

"No school. I was doing it on my own."

The bean pole rolled his eyes. "And they call *us* crazy. We do it all by the book. Cut no corners. Safety first in everything. That goes for you, too. You're welcome with us, but you got to abide by our rules. We don't want no one getting killed."

"Include me in," Ron said amiably.

He signed up for the twelve jumps, bought a used set of

chutes and gear. He needed all the information he could get in the shortest possible time and with the least attention. Ten days later he had done twenty-three jumps, had checked out in the club's battered Cessna 180, and was even flying other jumpers to altitude. He was accepted completely by the group, yet he managed to retain an element of anonymity.

His evenings were busy, checking the newspapers, waiting for a certain event to arrive. And then he saw what he wanted, and he shifted mental gears. Time for the next step. The steel fist was curling its fingers into a lethal knot.

He talked to the bean pole over coffee the next morning. "The one-eighty available for a couple days' rental?"

His instructor chewed his lower lip. "Depends on the price. We got other jump ships, but we don't want to lose out, you know?"

"How much?"

"Well, you don't need a pilot—say, twenty-eight bucks an hour."

"Sounds good."

"How long you want it?"

"Three days. Leave here tomorrow morning, that's Tuesday, and be back Thursday night or early Friday morning. That way you can have the bird back for the weekend when you're busy."

"We got to have a guarantee of three hours minimum a day even if you don't fly."

"No sweat there. I'm going to Houma."

"Where the hell's that?"

"Louisiana. Crop duster school there. Got some old friends I want to see and I can take care of some business at the same time."

"You got yourself a deal, friend."

He had to move quickly. The old 180 had a three-axis autopilot, which was his single most compelling reason for choosing the airplane. He could have rented one with similar equipment at any airport within a hundred miles, but this way he had the plane without questions. No fuss and no bother and no attention paid to him; they knew him. He left a two-hundred-dollar deposit for the three days' rental of the Cessna.

That night he was in the T-hangar that housed the 180.

No one paid attention to him beyond a wave and a friendly hello. People working on their birds during the night was common practice. But he made certain to lock the hangar. This was going to have to be done right the first time. Without that autopilot, the job might not have been within his capabilities.

He had already prepared his equipment, a radio-control rig he could hook directly to the autopilot. All you needed to control the airplane was to turn knobs, the electrical power tied in the gyros would operate the controls. He set up his equipment so that a robot system fitted over the autopilot. His remote control unit was simply a duplication of the autopilot controls. But he needed a lot more power than he had used with that small model when he'd demolished the motel room. For this job he needed a twelve-volt battery that would both supply the power and transmit it over a distance of at least ten miles.

He'd already modified the parachute equipment, too. That was the easiest part. He needed to carry the battery, the antenna, and the remote control system with him, directly in front of him, within immediate and easy reach. He fashioned a container the same size as the emergency parachute package that clipped to the front of his harness, and he installed the battery, controls, and antenna in the "parachute." That was exactly what it looked like, right down to the D ring. He wanted to test the equipment before leaving Palatka, but there was a definite risk of it being seen by the locals at the airport.

He took off at dawn with a flight plan filed for Houma. He flew northwest for a hundred miles, canceled the flight plan by radio, and turned to the northeast. He set the autopilot and climbed into the back seat. He switched on the remote unit and turned the first knob. Slowly, carefully . . .

It worked like a dream. He climbed, turned, descended, all from the back seat. The trick, he learned in the next half hour, was to do it slowly, so that he wouldn't overcontrol.

He refueled in West Virginia and flew to a small airport in New Jersey, draped a jacket over the instrument panel, and locked the airplane before tying it down for the night. After he paid the tie-down fee and topped off the tanks, he spent the night at a nearby fleabag motel, watching the eleven o'clock news. Excellent. Everything was on schedule.

The steel fist would reach all the way this time. All the pieces were coming together in space and time, flowing to a single point. Ten o'clock tomorrow morning. Before the clock turned to 10:01, the telephones would be ringing shrilly in the White House.

Ron didn't stop to wonder why he was moving so slickly, like an oiled machine. He didn't lie awake pondering, asking himself questions, the way he used to. He just dropped off to sleep like a tired hound after a long day's hunting.

He lifted off from Pottstown Municipal just after nine o'clock, headed just north of east, climbing steadily. He set his navigation homer for Colt's Neck on a frequency of 115.4, which would bring him just southwest of Sandy Hook, on the southern edge of New York Harbor, at an altitude of 9,500 feet. A good day. Scattered clouds at 4,000, well below him, and the usual thick pale rust of haze pressing against the metropolitan area of New York, extending well out across Long Island and north to Westchester. He tuned in one of his radios to 111.2 for ATIS. Air Terminal Information Service was a repeated tape recording, constantly updated, of operations conditions at JFK International Airport. He listened carefully. The winds were out of the southeast at twelve knots. Perfect. The active runway would bring the heavy airliners on their approach from the northwest, coming over land for the longest runway. He set the dial for approach control to listen to the radar vectoring of approaching airliners. Then he dialed his second radio to the tower frequency on 119.1. An airliner would be worked by radar into its landing slot and then would switch to the tower.

"Aeroflot Niner Two Seven descending through ten."

Right on time. The head of the Soviet delegation to the United Nations. Thirty-five top members of the Russian government landing in New York for a special session of the U.N. They were flying in an Ilyushin IL-62, unmistakable with its long body and four engines packaged in the tail. It was brilliant white with red lettering, and it was coming down through ten thousand feet.

Ron flew northeast, just over the top level of the traffic control zone of the New York Terminal Control area. At this altitude, no one would pay any attention to the Cessna except for safety routing. He hung onto the radio chatter. There it was.

". . . Niner Two Seven now to tower on one one nine point one."

"Roger that. Switching to tower now."

Savoring every word, Ron punched in the second radio. The big Russian jet was flying on a southwest heading over Oyster Bay and would hold that heading for a long base leg before turning left to line up with the runway. He heard the words he had been waiting for.

"Aeroflot Niner Two Seven on final."

"Aeroflot Niner Two Seven cleared to land."

Move it!

He had the white shape—small at this distance—in sight through the haze. Everything was set. Ron had been flying the Cessna from the right seat. He jerked the release and shoved his foot hard against the door. The wind tore it away. He heard a bang and his heart leaped. He looked back; the door had glanced off the horizontal stabilizer, but there was only a superficial tear in the metal. Stupid! He should have let that door go long before now. *Stop fucking around—go!*

He released the seat belt, pointed the nose down slightly, climbed out onto the jump step and the wheel, poised there for a moment, and pushed away. The instant he was clear of the airplane he jerked the rip cord, and the chute blossomed out above him. He yanked on the overhead toggles to turn into the wind.

Damn, but it was in the groove. The chute lowered him gently, pointing directly toward the big airport. He pulled the antenna out to its full length and turned the first knob gingerly. Ahead of him the Cessna banked left, then right, under perfect control. He pushed forward on the next lever, and the Cessna steepened its dive, accelerating steadily. He looked beyond the Cessna. There was the white form of the Ilyushin, seeming to hug the ground, no more than a mile from the edge of the airport.

The Cessna dove steadily toward the far end of the runway. Everything was coming together.

But they'd picked up the small plane, skin-tracking it on radar. Their surprise blossomed into concern and then a full cry of emergency.

"Aeroflot Niner Two Seven, you have traffic twelve o'clock your position and descending. Be ready for a go-around—"

"Two Seven, got it. He's heading straight for us!"

"*Two Seven, break right, break right. Go around, go around!*"

The Russian pilot didn't bother to answer. He went full forward on the controls; his copilot started bringing up the flaps and the gear, and he hauled the big jet into a climbing turn to the right to take him over the water of Long Island Sound.

He didn't make it. Under Ron's calm guidance, floating gently toward the shoreline, the Cessna 180 plunged at over two hundred miles an hour, curving to meet the sudden turn of the Ilyushin, heading straight for the airliner. In a last desperate gesture, the Russian pilot pushed forward on the yoke to bring down the nose and bank steeply left. He was well into the turn and would easily have cleared the smaller airplane.

Except that the Cessna, under Ron's perfect control, smashed directly into the cockpit of the big airliner. Flame erupted as the Cessna tanks exploded. In the same blink of time, the pilot was either thrown back in his seat from the impact or some violent instinct brought the yoke full back into his stomach. It didn't matter. The Cessna ripped on into the cabin, splitting open the big airliner. The violent hard-yoke-back motion of the elevators, with the airplane already in a steep bank, sent the Ilyushin tumbling end over end in a slow arc toward the ground.

It was disintegrating even before it struck the ground between the runways. The Ilyushin's fuel tanks exploded on impact, while the plane was still racing ahead at nearly two hundred miles an hour, and the flaming mass of wreckage spewed along the ground—directly into the side of a DC-10 jumbo jet that was taxiing toward the active runway.

The second explosion was even more devastating as the full tanks of the DC-10 went off with a shattering roar.

In addition to the 54 passengers and crew of the Ilyushin, 241 people died in the DC-10.

Four miles away, Ron guided his parachute over the coastal marsh toward a dirt road. He landed hard, tumbling over on his shoulder as he hit. He came up quickly, releasing his harness. Two boys in a car rushed toward him, eyes wide. They skidded to a stop and ran toward him.

"Holy Jesus, mister, you okay? We saw your parachute. Then there was this big explosion and—"

"Give me a hand with this gear, will you?"

"Sure, sure. Mike, you grab the canopy there. I'll help him out of that stuff. Boy, that was sure something, watching you come down like that. Are you hurt?"

"No. I appreciate your help." Ron looked at the youngster gathering up the big canopy. He handed the second boy the harness. "Can you hold that for a moment?"

"Sure can."

Both boys had their hands full. The timing was right. Ron brought the .357 out of its spring holster. Two quick shots did it. He had to be certain, so he fired one more round into the skull of each boy. Brains and blood splashed onto the dirt road. Ron dragged the bodies into the tall marsh grass, wadded up the parachute, and stuffed it beneath one broken body. He stood up and looked around. No one in sight on the isolated narrow road. No one within distance to hear the shots. Besides, everyone would be looking toward JFK airport where flames and smoke licked at the sky. He heard the thin wail of sirens across the marsh.

He got into the car, backed it around, and drove north to pick up the main street. Twenty minutes later he parked the car near a subway entrance. He left the windows down and the keys in the ignition, started down the stairs into the subway. Within five minutes that car would be stolen. Nice to have someone cooperating with him in getting rid of it.

He boarded the next subway train and vanished in the midst of ten million people.

29

It was nineteen miles from Washington, D.C., on an exact heading of 214 degrees. Rolling countryside, horse farms beautifully manicured, white fences following the contours of the hills. Shade trees. A lovely area. Quiet, isolated from the mainstream.

Silos and barns painted a pale lilac. Rambling houses and stables. Some of the finest horses in the world.

Silo four was the one. If you were known and expected, and if Master Computer Control (MASCOMCON) identified you in no less than nine separate ways—including fingerprints, voiceprint, body mass, chemical readout, and retinal pattern—you were allowed to step through a doorway that opened silently. The outside of the door was roughhewn wood. Between the outer and inner panels was carbide steel two inches thick. When the door closed you entered an elevator and descended, clearing your ears as you went, six hundred feet into the earth beneath a four-hundred-foot layer of solid rock.

Here was Headquarters CISD, Sublevel Three. A series of barriers enclosed the Cerebral Control Command Systems (CBCS). The room was enormous, high ceilinged, with 392 separate television monitor screens, 89 computer printout screens, and a bewildering variety of the most advanced electronic and computer systems known to man. Actually these were known to very few men and women.

Four men and two women sat in thickly padded armchairs,

each chair a complete command-readout control system unto itself. Before them were three rows of TV monitors, seven monitors to each row. Behind the six people, within glassed-in walls, another personnel team watched and listened. Through an exquisitely complex variety of electronics, invisible threads to complement thick cables under the flooring, the monitors were connected to satellites, aircraft, vehicles, and remote control centers.

The four men and two women watched a television replay of the violent events at JFK International Airport. They were fascinated with the sight of the Ilyushin approaching the runway. "Hold on five," a woman said, and the screen froze. "Bring in the Cessna, please." Monitor eight glowed instantly, and they watched a ground-viewpoint long lens shot of the Cessna 180 diving toward the ground. "Um. You can see him in the parachute. That really was clever."

"Back to five, please."

Monitor five showed the head-on collision, the violent wrenching motion of the Ilyushin, the spewing wreckage, and the catastrophic blast of the DC-10.

"How many finally?" a man's voice inquired.

"Just under three hundred. The Russians were keeping four of their agents secreted away in a pressurized compartment of the cargo area. We found the bodies. Nothing on their manifest, of course."

"Of course. Let me have the time frame again, if you would."

"Two hours seventeen minutes, as of right now."

"He should be surfacing again in a few moments, and we can pick up the signal. By the way, bring in that scene with the car and those two boys. That's an aircraft monitor, isn't it?"

"Yes. Holding pattern at sixty-five thousand feet. Satellite camera lens, of course." They watched monitor eighteen. At this distance the magnification was severe and the picture less than sharp. But there was no doubt. It was Ron Previn, shooting down the two boys and leaving in their car.

"Overlay, please, on eighteen."

A series of circles glowed on the monitor eighteen screen. The car in which Previn drove toward the subway station was a blur in the midst of traffic, but a pale green light glowed bright, dim, bright, dim, not quite blinking. The green light moved with the flow of traffic in a generally northward direction. Then it went out. A subdued carrier signal tone could be heard.

"He's underground here. A great deal of rock and steel, of course. The signal isn't strong enough to carry, but the tone shows we're getting a continued transmission even if we can't track specifically."

"How long before he emerges?"

"Thirty-nine minutes."

"Do we have tracking and coverage at that point?"

"Yes."

"Would you pick it up at emergence?"

"Of course." The monitor flickered and glowed, then focused instantly. "Airborne surveillance again."

They looked down on the New Jersey Turnpike. The green blip glowed softly from what they recognized to be a Greyhound bus.

"He has no idea we're tracking him, does he?"

"Absolutely none. That drug they used in the jungle camp is completely effective in erasing all memory during the time it's in use. Previn doesn't even know it ever happened. They gave him the drug in a drink and did the necessary surgery while he was under sedation. The transmitter is sealed within muscle tissue so it couldn't produce any binding or unpleasant effects later. Since it's powered by his own body electricity he can't even feel it. When they cut the skin for the incision, they went in right over a wound he'd gotten on a recent mission; he was already bandaged there. They closed the wound exactly as it had been before and used an identical bandage. He never suspected a thing. Healed right up like an ordinary cut. First time they'd ever done it that way. Luck."

"It's amazing what the body can do." A tall man in a dark gray suit leaned forward, hands cupped beneath his chin. "Body chemicals mix and produce electricity and power the ultrahigh frequency."

"Yeah, but what's more amazing is that we can pick it up with a dozen systems, so we always know where he is and where he's going."

"And that almost tells us what he's thinking. That's the weird part. Jeez, I wouldn't want to be him."

"Speed up the monitoring, please," an urgent voice spoke.

"We haven't much time. I understand he leaves the bus soon."

"Yes. We had a surveillance team headed to each place where he was apt to leave the bus. I'll bring it in now on twelve."

Monitor twelve gleamed to life. They watched the screen. "We had this one nailed down. He's using a sports car. Previn left the bus, as you see, rented this car, and—"

"I don't want the nitty details. The pattern is what's important."

"I'll summarize. After renting the car, he went to a sporting goods store where he purchased ammunition for his handgun, as well as a shotgun and a high-powered rifle. He bought some camping gear as a cover. From what we can deduce as to his actions—"

"No. That's the worst kind of mistake. He's beyond our predictive ability. We've got to start directing his energy now. Sorry. Go on."

"He's definitely committed to the Washington area. We will remain with that anticipation until we see evidence otherwise."

"Of course. You must do that. When does he reach the point of commitment?"

"Forty-one miles outside the Washington limits. We've prepared roadblocks there—I apologize, he's there now, and the conflict is already under way."

"Quickly, quickly."

As screen seven came to life, a computer printout above the monitor read LIVE HELICOPTER SURVEILLANCE. The ground boiled smoke and dust. Several vehicles were overturned, blazing fiercely, and a sports car raced down a road away from the highway.

"He's amazing. Single-handed, he hit the roadblock, killed three men in that first vehicle, took *their* weapons. Before the others knew what was happening, he'd used a machine gun to kill the occupants of four vehicles. Then he threw grenades into them all, and now he's escaped the net. Of course, he's aware that the pursuit is closing in on him."

"Turn them off, please."

The screens darkened and the overhead lights brightened slowly. The four men and two women looked at one another. The man in the dark gray suit leaned forward, elbows on the table. "Then we're all agreed?"

They nodded.

"You understand that only a rogue with an extraordinary talent can do it. No agent trained for the job could ever get through the Capitol defense system. It's far too complex and overlaid. The only way we can succeed is to follow through on what we started. We began with 106 people. Only four have lasted through the years, and Ron Previn is far and away the best for surviving situations that would kill a thousand other men. He's like a messiah, burning to kill. It's an affinity we can't define, and it's beyond the dimmest reach of the computers. We don't really control Previn, you know. He can succeed only if we let his own ingenuity remain dominant." The man glanced up at the control room. "As soon as he reaches the military base, activate the screens. No helicopters. Nothing on the ground, you understand. Are those orders clear? High-altitude surveillance only."

"Yes, sir. We're maintaining a drone at six thousand feet. It will give us sharp detail. It should begin in just a few minutes."

"Very good." The tall man addressed his fellows again. "He'll have to get through the security gate on his own. There are only four armed guards there. That won't slow him down."

"What about the road?"

"Ah." A smile along with the pleased sound. "It leads only to that military field. It's an alert base, really. Three jet fighters on scramble alert. We're providing some assistance, of course. Some men are ill, and the base is greatly understaffed. There's a loading vehicle with three small nuclear warheads that are to be fitted to the air-to-air missiles of the fighters. There's something else that's quite vital. The warheads are only five inches in diameter and about eight inches long. One man can easily carry one."

"Yield?"

"Not much. Three kilotons."

Three thousand tons equivalency of high explosives.

"All that fits. Can he break through to get a warhead?"

A smile met the query. "No one has ever stopped him yet. It's absolutely uncanny. I wouldn't bet against him."

"All right. After that?"

"All we do is prod. No direction other than that. The moment he has the warhead and breaks free—he'll go across some fields and through the woods because it's the only safe way out and none of those military blockheads would think of a man running with an atomic bomb in his hands—he's on his own. With one minor exception, of course."

"Oh? Something we don't know about?"

"Correct. We decided it would be in my hands. I've attended to it. But I can tell you now."

"Please do. We—"

"Sir. Contact," came the voice from the monitoring room.

They watched the camera view from the quiet drone a mile over the scene, the view obscured at times because of trees. What they saw fascinated them. The picture was silent, but there was no way to miss the sports car. It drove slowly up to the security gate at the secluded airstrip. As two guards approached the car, a machine gun spat from inside the Camaro and the men toppled over. The car shot ahead, the gun firing in short bursts, and another two men tumbled lifelessly. The Camaro skidded wildly into the compound. Ron rolled out of his side of the car as bullets smacked into the passenger side. The monitor screen showed him tossing several objects over the car, and flames blossomed slowly outward as the grenades he'd taken from the roadblock went off. Smoke covered the scene, but the glowing green light told them he was still there.

"He's on his way. See?"

They looked intently at the screen. "There! He's clear now and—he's got the bomb with him!"

"Good Lord. He's done it."

They watched Previn running steadily through the woods.

"What now?"

"There's a highway up ahead. He'll reach it and in his own inimitable way he'll get his hands on a car. As soon as that happens and he's clear, we'll send the signal through the drone."

"What signal?"

"The one you left in my hands. When we placed that transmitter in his body, we also emplaced a small chemical container. A coded signal releases a plastic valve and injects two drugs into his system. We've already tested it several times; it works like a dream. One drug overloads his adrenaline output. It provokes him to unreasonable anger."

"The other?"

"It stimulates the posthypnotic command I gave him in that jungle camp nine years ago. Ron Previn will be violently angry. At the same time he'll be completely convinced that it was his idea to set off that bomb in the Capitol during the president's address to the House. He's already embraced death. It's been his constant companion. Cradling that warhead in his hands when he detonates it will be his ultimate vision, his transport to whatever heaven abides in that tortured mind."

Silence for a short while.

"When he completes his final act, we move in and take over. It's all set."

"I don't know. Think of the defenses—"

"They're like paper against him. Look at him move. He runs like the wind. He dodges like a fox fleeing from hounds."

"A fox with very sharp teeth."

"I like that. Our very own living, breathing weapon." A soft chuckle came from the man in the gray suit. "That's it Previn. Don't let anything stop you. Keep going. Go—go—go."

ABOUT THE AUTHOR

MARTIN CAIDIN, a prolific and versatile writer with more than eighty books to his credit, is also a commercial and military pilot, a stunt flyer, parachutist and a recognized authority in the field of aviation and astronautics. From 1950 to 1954 Martin Caidin served as nuclear warfare specialist for the state of New York. He analyzed the effects of nuclear and other weapons on potential targets in the United States. As a comercial multi-engine pilot, Mr. Caidin flies his own plane all over the country. He has flown two-engine and four-engine bombers to Europe. For a time he flew his own World War II Messerschmitt in Europe and the United States. Martin Caidin's first novel, *Marooned,* a thrilling account of a space rescue, became a major motion picture, and *Devil Take All, No Man's World* and *Almost Midnight* were all bought for films. *Cyborg,* published in 1972, is not the highly popular ABC-TV series "The Six Million Dollar Man." Mr. Caidin is the author of an impressive list of authoritative books on military air history. Many of them, including *Samurai!, Zero!* and *The Ragged, Rugged Warriors,* are considered classics in their field. Martin Caidin is a charter member of the Aviation Hall of Fame, a Fellow of the British Interplanetary Society and a founder of the American Astronautical Society. Although he and his wife, Isobel, live within sight of the launching towers at Cape Kennedy, Martin Caidin is giving much of his attention these days to the problems we have fashioned for ourselves with nuclear weapons.

*If you never thought a book could make
you quake with fear, prepare yourself
before reading this preview of*

RED
DRAGON

by Thomas Harris,

author of *BLACK SUNDAY*

Over two months on
The New York Times
bestseller list

"THE BEST POPULAR NOVEL TO BE PUBLISHED
IN AMERICA SINCE *THE GODFATHER*."
—Stephen King

You are about to meet a human monster, a tortured being driven by a force he cannot contain, who pleasures in viciously murdering happy families. When you discover how he chooses his victims, you will never feel safe again.

You are about to be thrust so deeply into the heart of his obsession that you will find no escape.

You are about to hope beyond hope that one man—a man with powers he is horrified to use—can stop this cunning savage before he kills again.

You are about to be swept into the arms of the . . .

RED DRAGON

WILL GRAHAM sat Crawford down at a picnic table between the house and the ocean and gave him a glass of iced tea.

Jack Crawford looked at the pleasant old house, salt-silvered wood in the clear light. "I should have caught you in Marathon when you got off work," he said. "You don't want to talk about it here."

"I don't want to talk about it anywhere, Jack. You've got to talk about it, so let's have it. Just don't get out any pictures. If you brought pictures, leave them in the briefcase— Molly and Willy will be back soon."

"How much do you know?"

"What was in the Miami *Herald* and the *Times*," Graham said. "Two families killed in their houses a month apart. Birmingham and Atlanta. The circumstances were similar."

"Not similar. The same."

"How many confessions so far?"

"Eighty-six when I called in this afternoon," Crawford said. "Cranks. None of them knew details. He smashes the mirrors and uses the pieces. None of them knew that."

"What else did you keep out of the papers?"

"He's blond, right-handed and really strong,. wears a size-eleven shoe. He can tie a bowline. The prints are all smooth gloves."

"You said that in public."

"He's not too comfortable with locks," Crawford said. "Used a glass cutter and a suction cup to get in the house last time. Oh, and his blood's AB positive."

"Somebody hurt him?"

"Not that we know of. We typed him from semen and saliva. He's a secretor." Crawford looked out at the flat sea. "Will, I want to ask you something. You saw this in the papers. The second one was all over the TV. Did you ever think about giving me a call?"

"No."

"Why not?"

"There weren't many details at first on the one in Birmingham. It could have been anything—revenge, a relative."

"But after the second one, you knew what it was."

"Yeah. A psychopath. I didn't call you because I didn't want to. I know who you have already to work on this. You've got the best lab. You'd have Heimlich at Harvard, Bloom at the University of Chicago—"

"And I've got you down here fixing fucking boat motors."

"I don't think I'd be all that useful to you, Jack. I never think about it anymore."

"Really? You caught two. The last two we had, you caught."

"How? By doing the same things you and the rest of them are doing."

"That's not entirely true, Will. It's the way you think."

"I think there's been a lot of bullshit about the way I think."

"You made some jumps you never explained."

"The evidence was there," Graham said.

"Sure. Sure there was. Plenty of it—afterward. Before the collar there was so damn little we couldn't get probable cause to go in."

"You have the people you need, Jack. I don't think I'd be an improvement. I came down here to get away from that."

"I know it. You got hurt last time. Now you look all right."

"I'm all right. It's not getting cut. You've been cut."

"I've been cut, but not like that."

"It's not getting cut. I just decided to stop. I don't think I can explain it."

"If you couldn't look at it anymore, God knows I'd understand that."

"No. You know—having to look. It's always bad, but you get so you can function anyway, as long as they're dead. The hospital, interviews, that's worse. You have to shake it off and keep on thinking. I don't believe I could do it now. I could make myself look, but I'd shut down the thinking."

"These are all dead, Will," Crawford said as kindly as he could.

Jack Crawford heard the rhythm and syntax of his own speech in Graham's voice. He had heard Graham do that before, with other people. Often in intense conversation Graham took on the other person's speech patterns. At first, Crawford had thought he was doing it deliberately, that it was a gimmick to get the back-and-forth rhythm going.

Later Crawford realized that Graham did it involuntarily, that sometimes he tried to stop and couldn't.

Crawford dipped into his jacket pocket with two fingers. He flipped two photographs across the table, face up.

"All dead," he said.

Graham stared at him a moment before picking up the pictures.

They were only snapshots: A woman, followed by three children and a duck, carried picnic items up the bank of a pond. A family stood behind a cake.

After half a minute he put the photographs down again. He pushed them into a stack with his finger and looked far down the beach where the boy hunkered, examining something in the sand. The woman stood watching, hand on her hip, spent waves creaming around her ankles. She leaned inland to swing her wet hair off her shoulders.

Graham, ignoring his guest, watched Molly and the boy for as long as he had looked at the pictures.

Crawford was pleased. He kept the satisfaction out of his face with the same care he had used to choose the site of this conversation. He thought he had Graham. Let it cook.

Three remarkably ugly dogs wandered up and flopped to the ground around the table.

"My God," Crawford said.

"These are probably dogs," Graham explained. "People dump small ones here all the time. I can give away the cute ones. The rest stay around and get to be big ones."

"They're fat enough."

"Molly's a sucker for strays."

"You've got a nice life here, Will. Molly and the boy. How old is he?"

"Eleven."

"Good-looking kid. He's going to be taller than you."

Graham nodded. "His father was. I'm lucky here. I know that."

"I wanted to bring Phyllis down here. Florida. Get a place when I retire, and stop living like a cave fish. She says all her friends are in Arlington."

"I meant to thank her for the books she brought me in the hospital, but I never did. Tell her for me."

"I'll tell her."

Two small bright birds lit on the table, hoping to find jelly. Crawford watched them hop around until they flew away.

"Will, this freak seems to be in phase with the moon. He killed the Jacobis in Birmingham on Saturday night, June 28, full moon. He killed the Leeds family in Atlanta night before last, July 26. That's one day short of a lunar month. So if we're lucky we may have a little over three weeks before he does it again."

"I don't think you want to wait here in the Keys and read about the next one in your Miami *Herald*. Hell, I'm not the pope, I'm not saying what you ought to do, but I want to ask you, do you respect my judgment, Will?"

"Yes."

"I think we have a better chance to get him fast if you help. Hell, Will, saddle up and help us. Go to Atlanta and Birmingham and look, then come on to Washington. Just TDY."

Graham did not reply.

Crawford waited while five waves lapped the beach. Then he got up and slung his suit coat over his shoulder. "Let's talk after dinner."

"Stay and eat."

Crawford shook his head. "I'll come back later. There'll be messages at the Holiday Inn and I'll be a while on the phone. Tell Molly thanks, though."

Crawford's rented car raised thin dust that settled on the bushes beside the shell road.

Graham returned to the table. He was afraid that this was how he would remember the end of Sugarloaf Key—ice melting in two tea glasses and paper napkins fluttering off the redwood table in the breeze and Molly and Willy far down the beach.

Sunset on Sugarloaf, the herons still and the red sun swelling.

Will Graham and Molly Foster Graham sat on a bleached drift log, their faces orange in the sunset, backs in violet shadow. She picked up his hand.

"Crawford stopped by to see me at the shop before he came out here," she said. "He asked directions to the house. I tried to call you. You really ought to answer the phone once in a while. We saw the car when we got home and went around to the beach."

"What else did he ask you?"

"How you are."

"And you said?"

"I said you're fine and he should leave you the hell alone. What does he want you to do?"

"Look at evidence. I'm a forensic specialist, Molly. You've seen my diploma."

"You mended a crack in the ceiling paper with your diploma, I saw that." She straddled the log to face him. "If you missed your other life, what you used to do, I think you'd talk about it. You never do. You're open and calm and easy now . . . I love that."

"We have a good time, don't we?"

Her single styptic blink told him he should have said something better. Before he could fix it, she went on.

"What you did for Crawford was bad for you. He has a lot of other people—the whole damn government I guess—why can't he leave us alone?"

"Didn't Crawford tell you that? He was my supervisor the two times I left the FBI Academy to go back to the field. Those two cases were the only ones like this he ever had, and Jack's been working a long time. Now he's got a new one. This kind of psychopath is very rare. He knows I've had . . . experience."

"Yes, you have," Molly said. His shirt was unbuttoned and she could see the looping scar across his stomach. It was finger width and raised, and it never tanned. It ran down from his left hipbone and turned up to notch his rib cage on the other side.

Dr. Hannibal Lecter did that with a linoleum knife. It happened a year before Molly met Graham, and it very nearly killed him. Dr. Lecter, known in the tabloids as "Hannibal the Cannibal," was the second psychopath Graham had caught.

When he finally got out of the hospital, Graham resigned from the Federal Bureau of Investigation, left Washington and found a job as a diesel mechanic in the boatyard at Marathon in the Florida Keys. It was a trade he grew up with. He slept in a trailer at the boatyard until Molly and her good ramshackle house on Sugarloaf Key.

Now he straddled the drift log and held both her hands. Her feet burrowed under his.

"All right, Molly. Crawford thinks I have a knack for the monsters. It's like a superstition with him."

"Do you believe it?"

Graham watched three pelicans fly in line across the tidal flats. "Molly, an intelligent psychopath—particularly a sadist—is hard to catch for several reasons. First, there's no traceable motive. So you can't go that way. And most of the time you won't have any help from informants. See, there's a lot more stooling than sleuthing behind most arrests, but in a case like this there won't *be* any informants. *He* may not even know that he's doing it. So you have to take whatever evidence you have and extrapolate. You try to reconstruct his thinking. You try to find patterns."

"And follow him and find him," Molly said. "I'm afraid if you go after this maniac, or whatever he is—I'm afraid he'll do you like the last one did. That's it. That's what scares me."

"He'll never see me or know my name, Molly. The police, they'll have to take him down if they can find him, not me. Crawford just wants another point of view."

She watched the red sun spread over the sea. High cirrus glowed above it.

Graham loved the way she turned her head, artlessly giving him her less perfect profile. He could see the pulse in her throat, and remembered suddenly and completely the taste of salt on her skin. He swallowed and said, "What the hell can I do?"

"What you've already decided. If you stay here and there's more killing, maybe it would sour this place for you. *High Noon* and all that crap. If it's that way, you weren't really asking."

"If I *were* asking, what would you say?"

"Stay here with me. Me. Me. Me. And Willy, I'd drag him in if it would do any good. I'm supposed to dry my eyes and wave my hanky. If things don't go so well, I'll have the satisfaction that you did the right thing. That'll last about as long as taps. Then I can go home and switch one side of the blanket on."

"I'd be at the back of the pack."

"Never in your life. I'm selfish, huh?"

"I don't care."

"Neither do I. It's keen and sweet here. All the things that happen to you before make you know it. Value it, I mean."

He nodded.

"Don't want to lose it either way," she said.

"Nope. We won't, either."

Darkness fell quickly and Jupiter appeared, low in the southwest.

They walked back to the house beside the rising gibbous moon. Far out past the tidal flats, bait fish leaped for their lives.

Crawford came back after dinner. He had taken off his coat and tie and rolled up his sleeves for the casual effect. Molly thought Crawford's thick pale forearms were repulsive. To her he looked like a damnably wise ape. She served him coffee under the porch fan and sat with him while Graham and Willy went out to feed dogs. She said nothing. Moths batted softly at the screens.

"He looks good, Molly," Crawford said. "You both do—skinny and brown."

"Whatever I say, you'll take him anyway, won't you?"

"Yeah. I have to. I have to do it. But I swear to God, Molly, I'll make it as easy on him as I can. He's changed. It's great you got married."

"He's better and better. He doesn't dream so often now. He was really obsessed with the dogs for a while. Now he just takes care of them; he doesn't talk about them all the time. You're his friend, Jack. Why can't you leave him alone?"

"Because it's his bad luck to be the best. Because he doesn't think like other people. Somehow he never got in a rut."

"He thinks you want him to look at evidence."

"I do want him to look at evidence. There's nobody better with evidence. But he has the other thing too. Imagination, projection, whatever. He doesn't like that part of it."

"You wouldn't like it either if you had it. Promise me something, Jack. Promise me you'll see to it he doesn't get too close. I think it would kill him to have to fight."

"He won't have to fight. I can promise you that."

When Graham finished with the dogs, Molly helped him pack.

SEVEN HUNDRED MILES to the southwest, in the cafeteria at Gateway Film Laboratory of St. Louis, Francis Dolarhyde was waiting for a hamburger. The entrées offered in the steam table were filmed over. He stood beside the cash register and sipped coffee from a paper cup.

A red-haired young woman wearing a laboratory smock came into the cafeteria and studied the candy machine. She looked at Francis Dolarhyde's back several times and pursed her lips. Finally she walked over to him and said, "Mr. D.?"

Dolarhyde turned. He always wore red goggles outside the darkroom. She kept her eyes on the nosepiece of the goggles.

"Will you sit down with me a minute? I want to tell you something."

"What can you tell me, Eileen?"

"That I'm really sorry. Bob was just really drunk and, you know, clowning around. He didn't mean anything. Please come sit down. Just for a minute. Will you do that?"

"Mmmm-hmmm." Dolarhyde never said "yes," as he had trouble with the sibilant /s/.

They sat. She twisted a napkin in her hands.

"Everybody was having a good time at the party and we were glad you came by," she said. "Real glad, and surprised, too. You know how Bob is, he does voices all the time—he ought to be on the radio. He did two or three accents, telling jokes and all—he can talk just like a Negro. When he did that other voice, he didn't mean to make you feel bad. He was too drunk to know who was there."

"They were all laughing and then they . . . didn't laugh." Dolarhyde never said "stopped" because of the fricative /s/.

"That's when Bob realized what he had done."

"He went on, though."

"I know it," she said, managing to look from her napkin to his goggles without lingering on the way. "I got on his case about it, too. He said he didn't mean anything, he just saw he was into it and tried to keep up the joke. You saw how red his face got."

"He invited me to . . . perform a duet with him."

"He hugged you and tried to put his arm around you. He wanted you to laugh it off, Mr. D."

"I've laughed it off, Eileen."

"Bob feels terrible."

"Well, I don't want him to feel terrible. I don't want that. Tell him for me. And it won't make it any different here at the plant. Golly, if I had talent like Bob I'd make jo . . . a joke all the time." Dolarhyde avoided plurals whenever he could. "We'll all get together before long and he'll know how I feel."

"Good, Mr. D. You know he's really, under all the fun, he's a sensitive guy."

"I'll bet. Tender, I imagine." Dolarhyde's voice was muffled by his hand. When seated, he always pressed the knuckle of his forefinger under his nose.

"Pardon?"

"I think you're good for him, Eileen."

"I think so, I really do. He's not drinking but just on week-ends. He just starts to relax and his wife calls the house. He makes faces while I talk to her, but I can tell he's upset after. A woman knows." She tapped Dolarhyde on the wrist and, despite the goggles, saw the touch register in his eyes. "Take it easy, Mr. D. I'm glad we had this talk."

"I am too, Eileen."

Dolarhyde watched her walk away. She had a suck mark on the back of her knee. He thought, correctly, that Eileen did not appreciate him. No one did, actually.

The great darkroom was cool and smelled of chemicals. Francis Dolarhyde checked the developer in the A tank. Hundreds of feet of home-movie film from all over the country moved through the tank hourly. Temperature and freshness of the chemicals were critical. This was his responsibility, along with all the other operations until the film had passed through the dryer. Many times a day he lifted samples of film from the tank and checked them frame by frame. The darkroom was quiet. Dolarhyde discouraged chatter among his assistants and communicated with them largely in gestures.

When the evening shift ended, he remained alone in the darkroom to develop, dry, and splice some film of his own.

Dolarhyde got home about ten P.M. He lived alone in a big house his grandparents had left him. It stood at the end of a gravel drive that runs through an apple orchard north of St. Charles, Missouri, across the Missouri River from St. Louis. The orchard's absentee owner did not take care of it. Dead and twisted trees stood among the green ones. Now, in late July, the smell of rotting apples hung over the orchard. There were many bees in the daytime. The nearest neighbor was a half-mile away.

Dolarhyde always made an inspection tour of the house as soon as he got home; there had been an abortive burglary attempt some years before. He flicked on the lights in each room and looked around. A visitor would not think he lived alone. His grandparents' clothes still hung in the closets, his grandmother's brushes were on her dresser with combings of hair in them. Her teeth were in a glass on the bedside table. The water had long since evaporated. His grandmother had been dead for ten years.

(The funeral director had asked him, "Mr. Dolarhyde,

wouldn't you like to bring me your grandmother's teeth?" He replied, "Just drop the lid.")

Satisfied that he was alone in the house, Dolarhyde went upstairs, took a long shower, and washed his hair.

He put on a kimono of a synthetic material that felt like silk and lay down on his narrow bed in the room he had occupied since childhood. His grandmother's hair dryer had a plastic cap and hose. He put on the cap and, while he dried, he thumbed through a new high-fashion magazine. The hatred and brutishness in some of the photographs were remarkable.

He began to feel excited. He swiveled the metal shade of his reading lamp to light a print on the wall at the foot of the bed. It was William Blake's *The Great Red Dragon and the Woman Clothed with the Sun.*

The picture had stunned him the first time he saw it. Never before had he seen anything that approached his graphic thought. He felt that Blake must have peeked in his ear and seen the Red Dragon. For weeks Dolarhyde had worried that his thoughts might glow out his ears, might be visible in the darkroom, might fog the film. He put cotton balls in his ears. Then, fearing that cotton was too flammable, he tried steel wool. That made his ears bleed. Finally he cut small pieces of asbestos cloth from an ironing-board cover and rolled them into little pills that would fit in his ears.

The Red Dragon was all he had for a long time. It was not all he had now.

He had wanted to go through this slowly, but now he could not wait.

Dolarhyde closed the heavy draperies over windows in the downstairs parlor. He set up his screen and projector. His grandfather had put a La-Z-Boy recliner in the parlor, over his grandmother's objections. (She had put a doily on the headrest.) Now Dolarhyde was glad. It was very comfortable. He draped a towel over the arm of the chair.

He turned out the lamps. Lying back in the dark room, he might have been anywhere. Over the ceiling fixture he had a good light machine which rotated, making varicolored dots of light crawl over the walls, the floor, his skin. He might have been reclining on the acceleration couch of a space vehicle, in a glass bubble out among the stars. When he closed his eyes he thought he could feel the points of light move over him, and when he opened them, those might be the lights of cities above or beneath him. There was no more down or up. The light machine turned faster as it got warm, and the dots swarmed over him, flowed over furniture in angular streams, fell in meteor showers down the walls. He might have been a comet plunging through the Crab Nebula.

There was one place shielded from the light. He had placed a piece of cardboard near the machine, and it cast a shadow over the movie screen.

Sometimes, in the future, he would smoke first to heighten the effect, but he did not need it now, this time.

He thumbed the drop switch at his side to start the projector. A white rectangle sprang on the screen, grayed and streaked as the leader moved past the lens, and then the gray Scotty perked up his ears and ran to the kitchen door, shivering and wagging his stump of a tail. A cut to the Scotty running beside a curb, turning to snap at his side as he ran.

Now Mrs. Leeds came into the kitchen carrying groceries. She laughed and touched her hair. The children came in behind her.

A cut to a badly lit shot in Dolarhyde's own bedroom upstairs. He is standing nude before the print of *The Great Red Dragon and the Woman Clothed with the Sun*. He is wearing "combat glasses," the close-fitting wraparound plastic glasses favored by hockey players.

The focus blurs as he approaches the camera with stylized movements, hand reaching to change the focus as his face fills the frame. The picture quivers and sharpens suddenly to a close-up of his mouth, his disfigured upper lip rolled back, tongue out through the teeth, one rolling eye still in the frame. The mouth fills the screen, writhing lips pulled back from jagged teeth and darkness as his mouth engulfs the lens.

The difficulty of the next part was evident.

A bouncing blur in a harsh movie light became a bed and Charles Leeds thrashing, Mrs. Leeds sitting up, shielding her eyes, turning to Leeds and putting her hands on him, rolling toward the edge of the bed, legs tangled in the covers, trying to rise. The camera jerked toward the ceiling, molding whipping across the screen like a stave, and then the picture steadied, Mrs. Leeds back down on the mattress, a dark spot on her nightdress spreading and Leeds, hands to his neck and eyes wild rising. The screen went black for five beats, then the tic of a splice.

The camera was steady now, on a tripod. They were all

dead now. Arranged. Two children seated against the wall facing the bed, one seated across the corner from them facing the camera. Mr. and Mrs. Leeds in bed with the covers over them. Mr. Leeds propped up against the headboard, the sheet covering the rope around his chest and his head lolled to the side.

Dolarhyde came into the picture from the left with the stylized movements of a Balinese dancer. Blood-smeared and naked except for his glasses and gloves, he mugged and capered among the dead. He approached the far side of the bed, Mrs. Leeds's side, took the corner of the covers, whipped them off the bed and held the pose as though he had executed a veronica.

Now, watching in the parlor of his grandparents' house, Dolarhyde was covered with a sheen of sweat.

Even at the height of his pleasure he was sorry to see that in the film's ensuing scene he lost all his grace and elegance of motion, rooting piglike with his bottom turned carelessly to the camera. There were no dramatic pauses, no sense of pace or climax, just brutish frenzy.

It was wonderful anyway. Watching the film was wonderful. But not as wonderful as the acts themselves.

Two major flaws, Dolarhyde felt, were that the film did not actually show the deaths of the Leedses and that his own performance was poor toward the end. He seemed to lose all his values. That was not how the Red Dragon would do it.

Well. He had many films to make and, with experience, he hoped he could maintain some aesthetic distance, even in the most intimate moments.

He must bear down. This was his life's work, a magnificent thing. It would live forever.

He must press on soon. He must select his fellow performers. Already he had copied several films of Fourth of July family outings. The end of summer always brought a rush of business at the film-processing plant as vacation movies came in. Thanksgiving would bring another rush.

Families were mailing their applications to him every day.

Read RED DRAGON, on sale October 1, 1982, wherever Bantam paperbacks are sold.

THRILLERS

Gripping suspense . . . explosive action . . . dynamic characters . . . international settings . . . these are the elements that make for great thrillers. And, Bantam has the best writers of thrillers today—Robert Ludlum, Frederick Forsyth, Jack Higgins, Clive Cussler—with books guaranteed to keep you riveted to your seat.

Clive Cussler:

☐	14641	ICEBERG	$3.95
☐	22875	MEDITERRANEAN CAPER	$3.50
☐	22889	RAISE THE TITANIC!	$3.95
☐	23059	VIXEN 03	$3.95
☐	05004	NIGHT PROBE! A Bantam Hardcover	$13.95

Frederick Forsyth:

☐	14765	DAY OF THE JACKAL	$3.50
☐	23159	THE DEVIL'S ALTERNATIVE	$3.95
☐	14758	DOGS OF WAR	$3.50
☐	14759	THE ODESSA FILE	$3.50

Jack Higgins:

☐	20642	DAY OF JUDGMENT	$3.25
☐	20541	THE EAGLE HAS LANDED	$3.50
☐	22787	STORM WARNING	$3.50

Robert Ludlum:

☐	20531	THE ROAD TO GANDOLFO	$3.75
☐	11427	THE SCARLATTI INHERITANCE	$3.95
☐	22986	OSTERMAN WEEKEND	$3.95
☐	22812	THE BOURNE IDENTITY	$3.95
☐	20879	CHANCELLOR MANUSCRIPT	$3.95
☐	20783	HOLCROFT COVENANT	$3.95
☐	20720	THE MATARESE CIRCLE	$3.95

Buy them at your local bookstore or use this handy coupon:

Bantam Books, Inc., Dept. TH, 414 East Golf Road, Des Plaines, Ill. 60016
Please send the books I have checked above. I am enclosing $_____
(please add $1.25 to cover postage and handling). Send check or money order
—no cash or C.O.D.'s please.

Mr/Mrs/Miss _____

Address _____

City _____State/Zip _____

TH—10/82
Please allow four to six weeks for delivery. This offer expires 4/83.

THE CHILDREN

They look so innocent with their angelic faces,
their blue schoolboy blazers.
But behind their shining eyes lurks a plan
for cold, brutal murder.

THE CHILDREN

You might meet them anywhere. In the subway.
On a plane . . . In your bedroom.

THE CHILDREN

They are waiting. For you.

THE CHILDREN

A horrifying novel of the new generation of evil
by Charles Robertson
author of *The Elijah Conspiracy*

RELAX!
SIT DOWN
and Catch Up On Your Reading!